The Wicked Husband

Blackhaven Brides
Book 4

MARY LANCASTER

D1714915

Books from Dragonblade Publishing

Knights of Honor Series by Alexa Aston
Word of Honor
Marked By Honor
Code of Honor
Journey to Honor
Heart of Honor

Legends of Love Series by Avril Borthiry
The Wishing Well
Isolated Hearts
Sentinel

The Lost Lords Series by Chasity Bowlin
The Lost Lord of Castle Black
The Vanishing of Lord Vale

By Elizabeth Ellen Carter
Captive of the Corsairs, *Heart of the Corsairs Series*
Revenge of the Corsairs, *Heart of the Corsairs Series*
Dark Heart

Knight Everlasting Series by Cassidy Cayman
Endearing
Enchanted

Midnight Meetings Series by Gina Conkle
Meet a Rogue at Midnight, book 4

Second Chance Series by Jessica Jefferson
Second Chance Marquess

Imperial Season Series by Mary Lancaster
Vienna Waltz
Vienna Woods
Vienna Dawn

Blackhaven Brides Series by Mary Lancaster
The Wicked Baron
The Wicked Lady

Table of Contents

Chapter One

WILLA HAD ONLY just dropped into bed when Haines, her aunt's maid, barged into her chamber.

"Sir Ralph sent you this," Haines uttered, her lips stiff with disapproval as she dropped the paper onto Willa's narrow cot.

If she'd had the energy, Willa would have groaned. She hadn't even had time to blow out the candle, yet alone snatch a nap. Her aunt and cousin had both retired late, despite their apparently afflicted health. And both had thrown sewing tasks at her at the last minute—literally thrown in her cousin Elvira's case—to be completed by the morning. Since the morning would bring a hundred other duties, Willa had had little choice but to sew on the gown's new trim and mend the bonnet before she went to sleep.

Now, fighting through her exhaustion, Willa unfolded the paper Haines had brought, and held it closer to the candle.

Bring the purse, immediately.

Willa frowned. It was definitely her cousin Ralph's writing, and *the purse* could only mean the one he'd recently given his mother with her allowance for her stay in Blackhaven. He'd been generous, since his plan had been to solve all the family's financial problems by offering for the Duke of Kelburn's plain spinster of a daughter. Unfortunately, instead of being grateful for her good fortune, the duke's daughter had ruined his plan by marrying someone else before he got here. No doubt he now wanted the allowance money back, though why it had to be in the middle of the night was beyond Willa's understanding.

"You're to be quick," Haines instructed, curling her thin lips. "And you're to go yourself. The messenger was most particular." Haines sounded outraged, though not on Willa's behalf. She still suspected Willa of having designs on Sir Ralph—which was both ludicrous and ironic.

"Messenger," Willa repeated in dismay. "Why, where is Sir Ralph?"

"In the hotel. The back-room downstairs. The hotel is hosting some kind of party."

"Party?" Willa stared at her. "I'm supposed to dress for a party? At this hour?"

Haines sneered. "Hardly. You're a messenger, not a guest. Just take him the purse and leave."

Why me? she thought drearily as she hauled herself out of bed and reached for the dull, gray, every-day gown she'd only just taken off. Because, no doubt, she was everyone's punching bag when anything went wrong. Somehow, it would be her fault that Ralph's chosen heiress had had the good sense to marry someone else.

Haines hadn't even stayed to help with her laces, so she flung an old shawl around her shoulders, thrust her feet into shoes, and crammed her unruly hair up at the back of her head with three pins.

Five minutes, she told herself as she located the purse in the desk drawer and left the suite. *Five minutes and then I can be asleep…*

The hotel foyer was still well lit and the reception desk guarded by one sleepy clerk who, when she asked for Sir Ralph Shelby, pointed her to the double doors at the far end of the hall.

Four minutes, perhaps only three and a half if I run all the way back upstairs.

She pushed open one door and felt her insides shrivel.

A wall of noise greeted her—voices that were too loud, laugher that was too vulgar. The air was thick with cigar smoke and the smell of brandy, but through it, she made out the gaming tables, the boldly dressed women and the men taking liberties.

This was not the sort of party any lady should attend, let alone be seen at.

For a moment, Willa felt incensed at the young man who had directed her there, for no one would ever have so much as admitted this party's existence to her aunt or Cousin Elvira. But of course, this was not the clerk's fault. It was Ralph's.

Ralph's own valet should have brought him the money which he was obviously about to throw away at the gaming tables. But then, that would not have humiliated Willa. He would never stop, she realized. His vengeance would be petty but utterly relentless. She could look forward to a lifetime of this.

He saw her at once, as though he'd been watching the door, and she knew she was right when his lip twitched once with satisfaction.

"My stake has arrived," he said clearly into the background buzz, which is when Willa saw the man lounging across the table from her cousin.

Her heart lurched, depriving her of breath.

Charles Dacre, Viscount Daxton.

He hadn't changed much in the eight years or so since she'd last seen him. Perhaps his face had lengthened a little, emphasizing his cheekbones and determined chin. His always lean body had filled out impressively, with muscle, she could only assume, since there still appeared to be no hint of fat on him.

And perhaps the disorder of his golden locks owed more to artifice than the innate carelessness of the youth she recalled. But then again, perhaps not, for his necktie was loose and his coat unfastened, giving an impression of disarray. He looked utterly disreputable. Which he was.

Angelically fair and diabolically handsome, young Lord Daxton was instantly, uniquely recognizable. These days he carried an unsavory reputation for hedonistic and downright dangerous behavior. He was, in fact, an unmitigated rakehell.

Inevitably, a girl sat on his lap while he whispered, no doubt, outrageous blandishments in her ear. A lump rose in Willa's throat, not because she envied the unknown woman his very temporary attentions, but because he would never really see Willa at all.

"Rosa's got her claws well into Daxton," a woman's uncultured voice said somewhere to Willa's left, in what she clearly imagined were low and confiding tones.

"Or the other way around," another voice muttered.

"Don't you like him? He's the most handsome man I've ever seen. Like an angel."

"Until you look into his eyes," the other woman disagreed. "They're hard and wild and cruel."

Not cruel, Willa thought, just a little desperately. *He's never been cruel…*

Perhaps fortunately, Ralph put an end to her helpless eavesdropping.

"Here," he snapped as though Willa were a servant, which she was, in fact if not in name. Poor relation, companion, whatever the title, it translated as unpaid drudge.

Every head now turned toward Willa as she walked into the room. Her cheeks burned as drunken voices speculated as to her relationship with Shelby.

"Not his usual style."

"Somewhat dull feathers for a bird of paradise, what?"

"Does Shelby never tire of wagering his women away to Daxton?"

"Oh, the last one wasn't wagered, whatever Shelby says. Daxton stole her, which is why Shelby hates his guts."

"Well, by tonight's luck, he's certainly going to be losing this one, too. And you know, she probably scrubs up pretty well. Who the devil is she?"

Willa's face flamed with anger. It wasn't so much at the insults for, what else were they meant to think? What other woman, except a servant or a mistress, was Ralph likely to have roused from bed to bring him money at this time of night? That her cousin had deliberately put her in this humiliating position, was unforgivable.

The rumors would undoubtedly be dashed tomorrow, when her position with regard to Lady Shelby would be clear, but in these moments, she had to endure this ignominy. She couldn't even look at

Lord Daxton.

Without glancing to right or left, she walked straight to Ralph and set the purse on the table in front of him. He was drunk, too. His muddy eyes were glazed and very slightly unfocused as he regarded her, and his face was an unbecoming bright red. Although the latter might have been due to his cravat being tied too tightly around his stocky neck. His too-high shirt points were wilting.

"As you requested," she murmured, although the note had been more of a command. She turned immediately to walk back out again. *Two more minutes and I'll be safe in bed...*

"Wait," Ralph ordered. There was peculiar relish in his curt voice. Oh yes, he was enjoying her shame.

Schooling her expression to impassivity, she turned back to him, her hands folded in front of her, her eyes focused only on the purse as he looked through the contents. For some reason, she imagined Lord Daxton's gaze on her face.

Unhurriedly, Ralph finished his perusal and pulled the strings to close the purse.

"Take it to Lord Daxton," he commanded.

Willa wanted the ground to open up and swallow her. She most assuredly did not want to be seen by Daxton like this. And by Ralph's s peculiar instructions—he could easily have pushed the purse across the table without even standing up—he was forcing the viscount to see her.

Of course. Ralph never forgot. Once, when they were all children, Daxton had stood up for her, against the older, larger Ralph, and come off best, too. Now Ralph was showing him his protegee in all her humiliation and helplessness. Ralph's servant, and by implication, his plaything.

She wanted to close her eyes, because foolishly, she didn't want Daxton to think that of her. Instead, keeping her expression carefully still, she picked up the purse and walked around the table. Men and rather daringly dressed women made way for her. She caught the odd snigger and amused, less than complimentary phrases as she passed.

Her one hope now, was that Daxton was too preoccupied with his pretty lap-girl to look at her. He had no reason to recognize Willa, or even remember her.

But the girl no longer sat in his lap. In fact, causing something close to panic in her breast, he rose to his feet and bowed in Willa's direction.

Startled, her gaze flew at last to his.

Dear God, if the boy had been engaging, the man was overwhelming. It wasn't just his height or his undoubted beauty. It was his sheer presence, hitting her in the stomach like a blow that thrilled instead of hurt. Everything about him was male and hard, and not familiar at all.

Now that she was closer, she could see the faint but hectic flush to his cheeks, the glitter to his eyes that betrayed how much he'd been drinking. But there was no hope for her in that. The icily sparkling blue eyes bored into hers, devouring her without obvious recognition, searching, though for what, she couldn't begin to guess. But she discerned the flash of anger and contempt in his face. His upper lip curled.

Lifting her chin, she held his gaze, refusing to give any sign of her humiliation before him of all people. She had done nothing wrong. She was here from no choice of her own. And he had no idea who she was.

He reached out and took the purse, his fingers warm as they brushed hers. He tossed it on the table without looking at it, and quite deliberately clasped her hand. Her fingers jumped in his, but before she could react, he stood aside, handing her into the chair he'd so recently vacated.

The courtesy deprived her of breath all over again. Not that she could stay here, because she couldn't.

"You may go," Ralph snapped.

And abruptly, perversely, Willa had had enough. She sat, merely to disobey her cousin, and was rewarded by Daxton's flashing grin. That, she remembered. One of his eyes even closed, before he hooked another chair leg with his foot and sat beside her, reaching for the purse.

For an instant, warmth flooded her because at last she perceived the mischievous boy she'd known. And because the contempt in his eyes hadn't been for her, but for Ralph. It made disobedience all the sweeter, although she had no doubt she would pay for it.

Nor was she silly enough to be flattered by Daxton's silent invitation. She knew it was all part of this bizarre phase of his long-standing quarrel with Ralph. He'd accorded her a courtesy her cousin most assuredly had not, and people had noticed. Whoever they imagined her to be, Ralph had been shown up as a boor.

"Go?" Daxton drawled, throwing himself into the chair next to her and pulling open the purse. "Is the lady not included in your stake?"

Daxton was being deliberately insulting, provoking a fight if he could.

"Of course not," Ralph said coldly.

Daxton rifled through the coins and pushed them across the table. "Pity. She seems to be all you have of value. Play then."

Willa sat rigidly at Daxton's side, wishing she had never given into her anger against Ralph. She'd only made her intolerable position worse. She waited a few moments until everyone seemed lost in the tension of the game. Then, quietly, she began to stand, meaning to exit unnoticed.

Abruptly, Daxton's left hand shot out and closed over hers on the edge of the table. "Don't go."

Astonishment paralyzed her for an instant. She caught a glimpse of Ralph's dark, furious face as he threw the dice. She'd had enough. "I have no desire to see you bring my family to ruin over a stupid game of chance."

The blue eyes turned on her. "Why not? They're pretty much ruining you."

So, he *had* known her. And he'd noticed. He'd always noticed. "I have a home," she said calmly.

A waiter appeared at her elbow, offering a tray containing a glass of sparkling wine.

"No, thank you," she said.

But with a hint of impatience, Daxton seized it and placed it in front of her. "Stay and drink with me. I'll be good."

"No, you won't. And I won't be a weapon in your quarrel."

His head jerked round, as though he were genuinely startled. Then a rueful smile curled his lips. "I suppose I deserve that. It's all got muddled. I'm a trifle disguised."

"Never," she marveled.

His grin broadened and then his volatile attention returned to the dice.

"What are you even doing here in Blackhaven?" she blurted.

He frowned. It might have been an effort of remembrance. "Going to Scotland. Why are you here?"

"For my aunt's health. And my cousin Elvira's. She is *enceinte*."

"*He* ain't here for anyone's health." Daxton jerked his head at Ralph.

It was tempting to tell him the story of the heiress. She bit her lip instead. Daxton spared her a quizzical glance.

"What's in Scotland?" she asked hastily.

"No idea. Never been." He returned to the dice, but not before she'd glimpsed something grim, almost desperate in his drink-clouded eyes. And although this would have been an opportune moment to slip away, she didn't.

Daxton had always been more than the wild, reckless boy everyone had thought him. And now that he'd grown up into this notorious rakehell, she didn't doubt that the boy she remembered was still in there. That dark look troubled her, and at the same time made sense of this ruinous game he played with Ralph.

She knew without being told that Daxton had baited her cousin into it. He was spoiling for a fight, and Ralph had likely appeared at just the right moment. She'd no idea how much Daxton had won from him, but she was sure it was enough to make life difficult for the Shelby household. At the very least, his rudeness in actually counting Ralph's money was surely grounds for a duel.

And so, in spite of the harm it would do her reputation, and despite the punishment she knew Ralph would heap upon her for disobeying him, let alone for sitting with the enemy, she stayed where she was. She even found herself distractedly sipping from the champagne glass. Perhaps it was the wine that gave her the courage to stay.

The game was over quickly, the contents of the purse soon back in Daxton's possession.

"Your health, Shelby," the viscount said cheerfully, raising his glass. "Very glad I ran into you." As he drained the glass and reached once more for the brandy bottle, his restless gaze fell on Willa. His delighted smile was not altogether free of surprise, which at least kept her from feeling too flattered.

"Willie," he said. "You're still here."

"You only ever called me that to annoy me."

"True. I suppose I should call you Miss Blake, now." He sprang to his feet. "Walk with me."

She cast a quick, indecisive glance at Ralph, who was desperately pretending not to feel either the loss of his money or his defeat by the enemy. He was strolling among the other tables, observing the play which had all but stopped for a while as everyone had watched Daxton annihilate him.

"Dash it, Will, do *something* for yourself," Daxton said with sudden violence.

She glanced at him, brows raised. "I thought I was to do it for you."

He scowled before a sudden grin smoothed his brow. "That's how I remember you. Be kind to me, then. Stroll with me to the door. You shouldn't be here at all, should you?"

The girl glaring at her from the wall—the one who'd been sitting in his lap when Willa first arrived—clearly agreed.

"No." Willa rose to her feet. She took a deep breath and lowered her voice further. "Very well, I'll walk with you on one condition. Give me back the purse I brought. You don't need the money, and Ralph has already been humiliated. It isn't his money. It's my aunt's."

Daxton blinked, then stared at her as if he imagined he'd misheard her. Then a laugh broke from him. "Damn it, I must be drunker than I thought. You strike a mean bargain, but it's a deal."

She let out her breath in a rush, relieved that he could still be reasoned with. "Thank you." She took his proffered arm, wondering what on earth the other guests would make of the gesture. Nothing, presumably, if he merely bowed her out of the door. And in this company, she was glad of the escort.

"Bring your champagne," Daxton advised. "You might as well have what fun you can on the way, and in this state, I suspect I'm just not intoxicating enough."

"I don't recall your being so modest," she said wryly.

"I was expecting to be refuted," he mourned. "But you've let me down. Are you happy with them, Will?"

She didn't pretend to misunderstand him. "I'm as happy as I'd be anywhere else. I have a home."

"So you said."

At least he remembered that much of their conversation. He didn't lurch either, but remained perfectly steady as he walked beside her.

"You can't win, can you?" he said abruptly. "Even if you run away. You'd always be somebody's drudge."

"I've thought about it," she admitted.

"And yet here you still are. Better the devil you know?"

"Something like that."

"You should marry a rich man."

She curled her lip. "A different form of drudgery."

Daxton laughed. "Only you would think so. Isn't it the ambition of every well-born girl to marry a rich man?"

"I think it depends on the girl. And very largely on the *particular* rich man"

He frowned, veering away from the fast-approaching door. "That's it!" he exclaimed, staring at her. "Why didn't I think of this before?"

"Because you weren't foxed before?"

He waved that aside. "I'm always foxed. Which ain't exactly selling the idea to you, but you must see it would answer perfectly."

"What would?" she asked.

"Marriage," he said impatiently.

"*What* marriage?"

"Yours," he replied. "To me."

Chapter Two

T HE PAIN TOOK her breath away.

"Don't look like that," he said ruefully. "I'm not so *very* awful. At least I won't be."

"Sober," she managed, "you have no wish to be married to anyone."

"Sober, I might not have thought about it," he allowed. "In fact, I didn't. But now that I do, and you just happen to be here, it's clearly the perfect solution."

"To what?" she demanded, refusing to take him seriously.

He veered her away from two approaching young men, tugging her into a quieter part of the room. "To my financial woes, and your intolerable position with the Shelbys."

"I fail to see how saddling yourself with the expense of a penniless wife would solve your financial troubles."

"Well, it would. I can't get my hands on my grandfather's money until I'm either thirty years old or married. If I have to wait another six years, I'll be dead."

She blinked. "Then you're proposing widowhood rather than marriage?"

He grinned. "No, I'll be good if you marry me."

Something twisted in her stomach. "No, you won't, Dax,"

"No, I probably won't," he agreed honestly. "But I will be *better*, and with the money, I can do things. Think about it, Will. Wouldn't you rather a life free of Shelbys? And you were never remotely frightened of me like all the insipid misses my mother keeps throwing at me. We could even have a little fun. More than *this* at any rate." One backward wave of his hand encompassed the room and, she suspected, by extension, the rest of his life. Or hers.

Again, she had the notion something other than brandy inspired him, but she couldn't allow the rising excitement, the *joy* trying to break out... For there wouldn't, couldn't, be any joy. It wasn't Willa he wished to marry. It was his inheritance. At best, he believed he could tolerate her. But it would never get that far. For Willa, such a marriage to him would be intolerable.

"They wouldn't allow it," she said, grateful at least that she wouldn't have to explain her personal objections to his plans.

He frowned. "Who wouldn't?"

"Your family and mine."

"There's no denying they can be dashed unpleasant," he agreed without heat. "Which is another beauty of elopement."

Her jaw dropped. "You want to elope?"

His eyebrows flew up. "Didn't I say? Aren't we in Blackhaven?"

"Yes, but—"

"Next to the Scottish border."

She blinked several times. "I believe it's only a few miles."

His eyes gleamed, an invitation to mischief. "We could walk out of here now and be in Gretna Green by daylight."

Her breath vanished, along with any words that might have made sense.

"Of course, there will be a scandal," he continued. "My father will kick up a storm and my mother will cry, which is probably worse, but we won't need to go near 'em until it's blown over."

She regarded him with continued fascination. "And my cousin Ralph will be livid."

Daxton grinned with undisguised delight. "So he will! Do you know, I can see nothing against this scheme at all?" Far from a prime motive, his ongoing quarrel with Ralph didn't seem to have entered his erratic head before Willa brought it up. "So, what do you say? Shall we do it?"

She sighed, with a hint of genuine regret. "Of course not."

His eyes narrowed. He'd never liked to be opposed. "You're turning me down?"

"You'll be very grateful in the morning that I did."

"No," he said dangerously, "I won't. If you won't come willingly, I'll simply abduct you."

With a start, she realized they were almost at the door once more. "You wouldn't," she said breathlessly.

His glittering eyes darkened. If he hadn't been quite so foxed, she'd have been flattered to recognize hot, male desire. "Try me," he said softly.

Her heart dived, thundering hard in her breast. He radiated genuine menace, enough to frighten her. She could still escape. She'd always been nimble.

She cast a quick, desperate glance back into the room. Two debauched young men she'd noticed trying to attract his attention earlier, still held each other up while they waited for Daxton to conclude his business with her. She suspected they were ready to go on with him to some less reputable establishment.

And with blinding clarity, she saw that the world was right, that Daxton truly was going to the devil.

"If I have to wait another six years, I'll be dead."

Daxton opened the door, held it open for her to precede him. Her whole body trembled with the hugeness of the decision she was about to make. And as if everyone in the room felt her tension, the voices suddenly quietened, all except Ralph's which spoke with disastrous clarity.

"...lose, he cheated. The dice were clearly loaded."

Dax turned back to face the room. If the noise had quietened before, now you could have heard a pin drop.

Daxton looked directly at Ralph, who stood only a few yards away, amongst a group of people who suddenly stepped back from him.

"You talking about me, Shelby?" Daxton asked dangerously.

"None of your business," Ralph retorted, although two bright spots in his suddenly pale cheeks, betrayed his anxiety. "It is a private conversation."

"I can't let that one go." Daxton sounded almost apologetic.

"Apologize," someone hissed at Ralph. "Or at least deny it. For God's sake man, in this mood, he'll shoot you where you stand."

Ralph glared at the speaker and then, almost defiantly, at Daxton. Of course. Proving he was not afraid. But Willa had grown up with him; she knew that he was.

"My lord," she said, low.

No one paid her any attention.

Daxton said, "I'm busy tonight and tomorrow, but I can shoot you after that. My friends will call on yours."

Ralph sneered. "If that was your shabby challenge, I refuse to fight a duel over your ill manners in eavesdropping."

"You do?" Daxton said with apparent interest, walking up to him. "Then fight it for this." And before anyone could guess his intentions, he drew back his fist and struck Ralph a staggering blow in the face.

As Ralph stumbled into the arms of those nearby, Daxton simply turned around, walked jauntily back to Willa, and offered her his arm once more.

"Don't you dare!" Ralph screamed at her. "I'll wash my hands of you! We all will!"

It was all Willa needed. Laying her hand on Daxton's arm, she walked out of the room with him. He kicked the door shut behind them and yelled for his horses.

Willa barely had time to leave the controversial purse with the reception clerk, instructing him to give it to Haines first thing in the morning. And then they swept out of the hotel.

Daxton flung his arm around her waist. She jumped at the unfamiliar intimacy, though his only intention appeared to be to hurry her up.

"Are you actually covering for him?" the viscount demanded, rushing her across the foyer. "To keep his mother from knowing what he did?"

"No," she confessed. "To keep them all from knowing what *you* did. Ralph would throw it back in your face."

By some miracle, a curricle and pair of fine, high-spirited black horses arrived in front of the hotel just as they stepped out of the door.

"Down you get," Daxton ordered the groom, and handed her up into the vehicle, while the groom ran to the horses' heads. Daxton leapt up beside her. "Let 'em go!" he commanded.

The groom jumped out of the way and the horses lunged forward. At the last moment, someone flew out of the hotel and threw himself on to the step at the back of the curricle.

Daxton laughed. "Carson," he said by way of introduction. "He's here to save you if I overturn the carriage."

It was, she supposed as they bolted up the Blackhaven High Street, a very real possibility. Their chances of reaching the Scottish border were probably slim, in which case, she'd burned her boats for nothing. Certainly, he drove the horses at break-neck speed through the town. They were lucky not to have the Watch after them. But Willa kept her wary gaze on Daxton's hands, which were surprisingly sure and steady, and by the time they drew out of town, she'd stopped worrying. Especially since the useful Mr. Carson had brought not only the viscount's driving coat but a travelling cloak and a blanket which she was very grateful for in the chill of the night.

What in the world had she been thinking of, leaving the hotel in nothing but the gown she stood up in? She hadn't exactly left discreetly either. After Daxton hit Ralph, the story would be all round Black-haven by morning. Lord knew exactly what figure she would cut in it. And yet, funnily enough, she didn't seem to care. Excitement stirred her blood and she was ready to face the world head-on.

In the open country, Daxton gave the horses their heads and de-spite the darkness, they galloped on at full tilt.

Daxton cast her a grin of approval. "I said you weren't frightened," he observed, transferring the reins to one hand while he reached inside the many-caped coat. His hand emerged with a flask which he politely offered her first.

"What is it?" she asked dubiously, fairly certain it was not water.

"Brandy," he replied. "Keeps the cold out."

Recklessly, she took the flask and sipped. Although the strength of the liquid almost took her breath away, she managed to swallow without choking. When she returned the flask to Daxton, his eyes gleamed with amused approval.

As they thundered along the coast road, Willa was overwhelmed by a strange, exhilarating sense of unreality. It was as if there was no one else in the world except the man beside her, humming softly to himself as he drove his horses on at the same thundering pace. The rippling sea reflecting the soft, yellowish moonlight, was one of the most beautiful sights she'd ever seen.

Daxton varied between quietly singing in a rather fine, musical baritone, and making entertaining conversation. Even foxed as he undoubtedly was—although his speech never slurred once—he conversed with wit and unexpectedly deep knowledge about subjects as diverse as literature, European politics, and modern agriculture. She wondered if he talked to keep himself awake. Certainly, he supplemented it with frequent draughts from the brandy flask, until Carson obligingly swapped the empty for a full one.

"Keeps him level, Miss," Carson explained when she frowned at him. "And awake."

It was dawn, and they'd pulled into a posting inn to change horses. Daxton had got down to see to it and was pouring some fresh brandy into his flask under the admiring gaze of the innkeeper's boy.

"Although," Carson added, presumably in the interest of honesty, "he can't last much longer anyway. That was his third night in a row."

Willa's eyes widened. "Hasn't he slept at all?"

Carson shrugged. "A few hours here and there, between bottles. Don't worry, I'm keeping my eye on him. Have we far to go?"

"Gretna Green."

Carson blanched. Then he laughed. "Very well, Miss, he does seem to like you, and you manage him pretty well. But if you change your mind, just say the word and I'll stop it."

"How exactly will you manage that?" she asked, almost amused, although his words caused her a pang of sudden fear at what she was planning to do.

"Hit him," Carson said amiably. "When he's not looking, of course, otherwise I'd never get near him,"

"Won't you lose your place for that?" she asked.

"Lord, no, it's what he pays me for. Among other things."

Willa regarded him with renewed fascination. "He's done this before?"

"Eloped? Lord, no, that's a first. But he's done just about everything else."

The curricle swayed as Daxton leapt back into it. He threw the brandy bottle to Carson and took the reins from Willa's hold. "Another hour and we're there," he said cheerfully.

Dear God, am I really going to do this?

SHE DID. THE infamous blacksmith's shop was easily located in the center of the village, and a large wad of money—presumably that won from Ralph last night—ensured Daxton and Willa were married before the indignant couple already waiting there for the same purpose.

"There, I knew rank had its advantages," Daxton said with satisfaction.

With only Carson and the blacksmith's apprentice as witnesses, it was a simple, casual service, culminating in the crash of the hammer on the anvil, which pronounced them married.

Daxton's fingers tightened on hers. He seemed to be shaking with laughter. His eyes gleamed as he swooped and pressed a kiss on her stunned lips. He raised his head, a faint frown forming between his brows, even while the smile played around his lips.

"Oh yes," he said softly, dark heat burning in his eyes. "I believe we shall deal very well together, you and I..."

A thrill that was half fear lurched through her, but there was no time to dwell on that. Their names were inscribed in a book, together with those of their witnesses. At Daxton's request, a copy of the entry was made on a sheet of paper, which he folded and tucked into his coat.

"Is this really legal?" Willa asked doubtfully. They hadn't even glimpsed a clergyman.

"Perfectly, under Scots law," Daxton replied.

"Let no man put asunder," the blacksmith intoned. "You're legally married, here, England and anywhere else. Good day to you."

"Good day," Willa said politely. "And thank you."

"Thank *you*, Lady Daxton. Wish you both health and happiness."

And then, somehow, they were in the open air and the sun shone down on her upturned face as she watched the scudding of wispy clouds across the sky.

Lady Daxton...

Laughter surged up in her throat. Catching her expression, the viscount grinned and swung her hand high as if they were a pair of children.

"A damned fine night's work," he pronounced.

"Where do we go now?"

"Daxton," he said with unexpected relish.

Willa, who'd expected him to say London, or perhaps whatever place in Scotland he'd originally been intending to visit, blinked with surprise.

"You won't be dull in the country, will you?" he asked, as if the thought had struck him.

Willa shook her head, rather expecting the boot to be somewhat on the other foot.

"Good," Daxton said briskly. "We'll go via Blackhaven and collect our things."

"Would you like to have breakfast first?" Willa suggested. Now that the ceremony was over and nothing very much seemed to have changed, she was aware of her rumbling stomach. She hadn't had much time to dine last night and she was famished.

"Of course," Daxton said apologetically. "We'll stroll back to the inn, have a spot of breakfast and hire a chaise. It will be more comfortable than the curricle, and I expect you'll want a nap."

"Me? *I* haven't been on a three-day spree," she said without thought.

Daxton let out a shout of laughter and threw his arm around her shoulder. "You're wonderful, do you know that?"

The quick, open hug, like his kiss by the anvil, had a peculiar effect on her. Half discomfort, half-thrill, it made her only too aware of his hard, unfamiliar maleness. And the half-formed feelings she'd always harbored for him. She'd always regarded them as childish before.

Breakfast at the inn consisted of ham, eggs, toast, and coffee, consumed in a comfortable private parlor. Or at least Willa consumed them. Daxton lounged opposite her, one hand in his pocket while he drank a mug of ale. He refused to be tempted by the toast, though he did succumb eventually to her offer of coffee.

His mood seemed to turn quieter. Instead of entertaining or conversing, he watched her in silence, his red-rimmed eyes tired and yet increasingly warm. She felt a little like the prey of a large, unpredictable cat. God help her, she'd just delivered herself into the power of this man, relying only on what she'd once known of the boy's honor and volatile good nature. But she had not laid eyes on him for at least eight years, and those years, even by his own admission, had not been well spent. By any standard, he was a hedonistic rakehell and used to getting his own way. They'd never discussed the nature of this hasty marriage of convenience. Was it in name only?

The thought, arriving from nowhere, unsettled her, for she was about to be alone with him for several hours in a closed carriage. Despite the fact that he'd clearly dunked his entire head in a basin of water, she could smell the brandy on him from across the table.

If ever there was a time to "manage" him, as Carson had put it, it would be on the journey back to Blackhaven. For she could hardly summon Carson to prevent his master exercising his conjugal rights. Whatever they were. Willa was a little hazy on the finer details, though she knew they were associated with that particularly hot, clouded look she'd already glimpsed in Daxton's eye. She'd seen something similar in Ralph's too, before and during "the incident", and in other men's faces when they looked at Lucy, the buxom downstairs maid, and imagined they were unobserved. Those other looks had never affected her like this. In fact, she'd found them positively distasteful. Especially Ralph's.

Nerves began to close up her throat and stomach and she stopped eating. She was afraid he would notice the trembling of her hands so she sat with them crossed in her lap, reluctant either to stay or go.

In the end, he rose abruptly to his feet. "I'll see if the chaise is ready."

She was practiced at schooling her expression, so she was sure she remained outwardly calm as he escorted her out of the inn and into the chaise. He climbed in and sat beside her, while Carson sat up on the box with the driver.

One of the horses whinnied, and on the driver's laconic instruction, the carriage rumbled forward out of the inn yard.

The sense of recklessness with which Willa had so blithely entered into this mad scheme had fled, leaving her churned-up and swamped by the reality of what they'd done. But she refused to stare at her hands for the whole journey and so, feeling as if it was a major step in her life, she turned her head and looked at her husband.

His head had fallen back against the squabs, but his warm, clouded eyes were focused on her face. A predatory smile played around his sculpted lips.

"What is it?" she asked, her voice deliberately light. "Have I a smut on my nose?"

"No. I married you, Willie Blake," he said softly, intensely. "You're mine."

Butterflies leapt in her stomach. This would have been so much easier if only he weren't so ridiculously handsome. He shifted, the hard warmth of his thigh pressing against hers, and the childish crush she'd always harbored for him was no longer nearly enough to explain the strength and confusion of her feelings.

"Willa," she corrected nervously. "It's etiquette not to deliberately annoy your wife during the first two hours of your marriage."

A smile flickered on his lips. "No, it isn't." He cupped her cheek and his breath stirred her lips. She smelled brandy and coffee and something more elusive, but God help her, it wasn't unpleasant. It wasn't unpleasant at all.

The smile died. Behind the lust and the clouds of alcohol in his eyes, she read something very like pain. His thumb moved against her skin, brushing her lips, parting them.

"I'll cause you to regret this," he whispered. "I know I will, in the end. But at this moment, it's sweet. I'll make it sweet for you, Willa."

His mouth closed on hers, and her heart seemed to dive downward into her stomach. This was nothing like the kiss he'd given her at the anvil. That had been quick, sealing a promise. This was like the promise itself, both arousing and fulfilling. His lips were warm and firm, and yet surprisingly soft as they caressed hers, sinking deeper with hunger, and then plundering. His tongue darted over her lips and inside her mouth, tasting, exploring with raw need.

She'd never imagined a kiss like this. It overwhelmed her. She clutched his shoulders, unsure at first whether it was to push him off or draw him closer. It was wonder that held her still, and sheer sensuality that did the rest. She never wanted it to stop.

He pushed against her until she lay on the bench, and she held him to her as though afraid he'd vanish. His weight pressed against her aching breasts as he kissed her mouth again, and dragged his lips down her throat. One hand slipped under her skirts, stroking her ankle, her calf, and knee. She gasped as the other closed over her breast, cupping caressing, his fingers sliding beneath the fabric of her ugly gown.

Fresh heat surged through her trembling body as he bared her breast and closed his lips around her nipple. She sighed with pleasure, with a need she hardly understood. *Daxton* was kissing her, as though he loved her. He didn't, of course, but he felt *something*. She knew the significance of the hard shaft pressing between her thighs, and when he lifted his head, sheer, thrilling desire blazed in his eyes.

His hand slid up her thigh. He sighed as he kissed her mouth once more with aching, sensual tenderness. He shifted position again, taking some of his weight off her, and laying his rough cheek against her naked breast.

Her fingers tangled in his unruly, blond hair. In wonder, she stroked its unexpected softness. She couldn't quite believe this was happening to her. It was a dream. She was asleep in bed, and when she woke, there would be no Daxton…

She didn't know how long they lay there before she realized the truth. A sob shook her. She didn't know if she was laughing or crying.

"Daxton, are you asleep?" she demanded.

Perhaps he heard his name, for he grunted and moved his head against her shoulder, shifting his weight. His eyes were closed, his lips relaxed, almost smiling. But he was quite unconscious.

Willa drew her shaking hand over her face, trying to regain some self-control. Somehow, it wasn't quite funny. With an effort, she heaved herself up into a sitting position. His head slid down into her lap, but still he didn't wake. Hastily, she adjusted the bodice of her gown and brushed down her skirts over her ankles once more. There, no one would know.

She allowed the laughter to come until the tears scalded her cheeks, when she forced it back again and instead, gazed out of the window at the spectacular countryside whizzing past.

Only when she felt calm once more did she drop her gaze to the face of the sleeping man in her lap. Her heart turned over. Like this, he resembled much more closely the boy she once knew.

"Dax," she whispered. "My husband. My love."

AN INTOLERABLE HEADACHE drove Sir Ralph Shelby from his bed-chamber far earlier than he would have wished. His jaw ached where the unspeakable Daxton had hit him, and the effects of the copious alcohol were not helping. He went in search of his mother's medicine cabinet.

In her sitting room, he encountered Haines, her abigail. Her stupid, devoted gaze revolted him at that moment because it made him remember that Willa had left the hotel with Daxton.

Last night had been a disaster on so many levels he felt sick. He'd lost far more than he could afford—including his mother's pin-money—and to Daxton, of all people. And the scandal of his cousin, whom he'd deliberately humiliated in the heat of the moment, running off with Daxton could only cause the family harm. To say nothing of depriving his mother and his entire family of her very useful help.

He tried to push past Haines to his mother's room, but she took something from her apron pocket and waved it in front of his face.

He blinked. It was the purse he'd lost to Daxton in a pitifully few rolls of the dice. And it still looked fat. Snatching it from the maid, he pulled it open.

"It's all there," he said stupidly. "How…where did you get this?"

"From the clerk at the reception desk. She—Miss Willa—left instructions, apparently, to give it to me this morning."

Ralph rubbed his aching head. "She got it back from him… What a clever little thing. Perhaps I misjudged her. Is she in her bed, Haines?" he asked hopefully.

But Haines shook her head with idiotic satisfaction. "No, sir. She left the hotel with Lord Daxton, drove off with him in his curricle and hasn't been seen since. I'm afraid she's ruined."

In fury, Ralph threw the purse on the floor. "Damn it!" Then he stared at the spilling coins, a new idea forming in his fuddled head. He'd examine it later for weaknesses, but for now it seemed worth the trouble. He'd got this much money back at least and he could still cause more damage to the wretched Willa, now she was Daxton's damaged ware. It had been done to spite Ralph, of course. Well, Ralph could bite back and would. With luck he'd see her in prison, or even hanged.

That pleasant image would, no doubt, be shattered by his mother.

But he'd see how it went.

"Do me a favor, Haines. Keep the purse with you for now. Don't tell my mother anything about it. Pretend it's missing if she asks. Better still, tell her the truth, that Miss Willa took it last night."

THEY WERE STILL on the main post road south when Willa heard the suddenly loud, warning voices of the men on the box. The carriage slowed to an abrupt halt amidst the complaining shrieks of the horses who still snorted and pawed the ground, as though anxious to get moving again.

Oh dear, Willa thought, craning her neck to try to see more out of the window. *We're not being held up, are we?*

For some reason, she was reluctant to move Daxton's head from her lap so that she could climb down and find out for herself. Before she could talk herself into it, Carson opened the other door.

"Gone, has he?" he said, sparing his master a glance that was neither judging nor affectionate. "Got a girl here, m'lady. In distress. Nearly ran her over. She wants to go to Blackhaven, but the thing is, she's freezing cold, so I don't want to keep her outside with us." Turning, he ushered a damp, bedraggled and shivering young woman toward the door. From her dress, she could have been a servant or the daughter of a small farmer or laborer.

"Oh goodness, you *are* wet!" Willa exclaimed. "What happened?"

"Fell in the lake, ma'am. Trying to get away."

"Away?" Willa repeated, startled. "From what? Or whom!"

"Both of them," the girl said bitterly. "Fighting over me like a bone or a piece of meat."

"Come in, come inside at once. Do we still have the blanket, Carson?"

"Loads of 'em," the servant said laconically, all but shoving the reluctant girl into the coach. "This here's Lady Daxton, who'll be kind to you. That's his lordship, but he's asleep so you needn't mind him."

Gingerly, the girl edged onto the opposite seat, warily eyeing the unconscious Daxton. "Don't want to disturb you, m'lady," she all but whispered. "Soon as I can get warm, I'll go out and sit with them. It's just if I get sick, I won't be able to work."

"Oh no, let's make sure you stay well," Willa agreed eagerly. "Wrap both those blankets around you and sit just *there* where the sun comes in the window... Perhaps his lordship's brandy, Carson?"

Without demur, Carson delved into the great coat which lay on the seat, half under the sleeping viscount and rummaged until he found the flask which he refilled and passed to the astonished girl. Grinning, he left again and the carriage got back under way.

"So kind of you, m'lady," the girl managed when her teeth stopped chattering.

"What's your name?" Willa asked, a trifle uncomfortable at being addressed as "m'lady" all the time. She supposed she should get used to it.

"Clara, ma'am. Clara James. My father's the tenant of Black Farm over by Blackhaven."

"Then you're a bit away from home," Willa observed.

"Oh yes, m'lady." The girl's eyes filled with tears. "I didn't mean to be. I didn't want to be. I *told* Jem it was over between us, but he must've discovered Dan was courting me, for he ups and bundles me into a gig—God knows where he got it from, but I'm terrified he stole it, probably from the coach house at Haven Hall since the house is empty..." She paused for breath, rubbing her eyes. "He said he won't wait no longer to marry me. And I'm only nineteen years old ma'am and my Da doesn't want me to marry Jem. Or Dan, come to that."

Willa's eyes widened. "You mean you were on your way to the border, too?"

If Clara noticed the *too*, she gave no sign of it, merely nodding miserably. "Dan found out, so my family probably knows by now, and he came after us. They started to fight and when I ran to get away from them both, I got knocked in the lake. They pulled me out, but then immediately start slogging away at each other again. I left them to it and prayed I would find a friendly vehicle on the road to take me home."

"Quite right, too," Willa approved.

"I don't want to get you in no trouble, ma'am. Jem's got no respect for quality and might well come after you and… and his lordship there." Clara's gaze fell to the viscount's handsome face in Willa's lap.

"I think he might get rather more than he bargains for if he does," Willa murmured.

"Sleeps well, doesn't he?"

"He's had a busy few days," Willa said diplomatically.

"He's very handsome," Clara allowed. "You been married a while?"

"Not long," Willa got out.

The girl frowned discontentedly. "I'm not sure I *want* to be married now. I think they both want the farm rather than me. Thing is, my father only rents it. The Muirs could sell it tomorrow or put the rent up so high we'd never afford it, and then none of us would have anything."

"Life is full of uncertainties for all of us," Willa said vaguely.

"Even you, m'lady?"

"Even me." *Especially me.*

IT WASN'T QUITE dark when Jem Brown drove furiously into Blackhaven in the same old gig he'd forced Clara into. They could have been married by now, except for bloody Dan Doone's interference. Dan had no business courting Clara. Jem had had his dibs on her and her father's farm well before the incomer, and Jem was not used to losing to anyone.

Having finally knocked Dan unconscious in their fight, Jem had chased after the girl, only to see her get into some hired post chaise. And so he followed, as fast as he could go with one placid horse and an ancient gig. Fortunately, the post chaise hadn't been in too much of a hurry, and he wasn't so far behind it when he entered Blackhaven and drove to the hotel.

There was no sign of the chaise there, but where else would the nobs go? Unless they were local gentry, of course. Jem got down, leaving the horse standing there—it rarely bothered moving unless pushed—and strolled around the alley to the back of the hotel. No one paid him much attention as he wandered about the busy kitchen and up the stairs.

He wasn't quite sure what he was looking for. Some sign of Clara, or who had helped her. The chances were, she'd have gone home to Black Farm, except he was sure the chaise hadn't turned off the main road into Blackhaven. He wanted to know what she was up to and how to get her back.

On the stairs, he caught up with a well-dressed lady's maid, lumbering upwards with a tray of covered dishes in her hands. Since she clearly wasn't Clara, he'd have gone past her without a word, except his quick eye had glimpsed something peeping out from under her apron. The fabric had been caught up by the tray, revealing a few keys and a fat purse dangling from her belt.

Jem was not one to miss an opportunity. "Let me help you with that tray, Miss. It looks awful heavy for you."

"I can manage," the woman protested, flaring her nostrils as though he were the dirt beneath her feet, with less right to address her. That settled it for Jem. While talking and smiling beguilingly, he wrestled the tray from her with one hand while he unhooked the purse from her belt with the other.

At the top of the stairs, he returned the tray to her, tipped his cap, and sauntered off across the foyer and out of the front door. Clara wasn't forgotten, but he couldn't wait to count his money.

Chapter Three

C HARLES DACRE, VISCOUNT DAXTON, opened one bleary eye. Groaning seemed too much effort, and in any case, it would do no good. A day of hell was assured and it would be intense, with that particular heavy quality he associated with a spree of several days and nights duration. No single night's drinking could make a man feel this bad.

Damn it, why did he do these things? Because he'd been enraged, he remembered, after quarrelling with his father and storming away from Dacre Abbey, determined to drive his horses and himself to the devil. Inevitably, he'd taken pity on the horses at least, though he couldn't quite recall where he'd ended up.

The decoration of the room was unfamiliar, but at least he was in a comfortable bed with its drapes partially opened. Licking his parched lips, he turned carefully over, in search of water or even, if God or whoever owned this bed was kind, coffee.

Sunlight shone through partially opened curtains in a single beam, causing a stab of acute pain through his eyes to his head. But more than that, it illuminated the young woman who sat in the window embrasure, her legs drawn up under her gown, a book open in her lap.

The sun caught burnt golden lights in her simply-pinned, dark red hair and cast a glow almost like a halo around a face of unusual beauty—pale skin, a slightly snub nose, long eyelashes, darker than her hair, fanning out over the soft curve of her cheek. Her lips were shapely, her throat slender and elegant. In all, it was a quiet, refined kind of beauty. Not at all the type he was used to in his inamoratas.

And the gown was hideous. Grey and dull and old. That wasn't normal in his inamoratas either, although he was generally more interested in the delights inside than in the outer casing.

On the other hand, she did look vaguely, naggingly familiar—especially that rare, striking color of hair—so perhaps this was some kind of game.

"I don't suppose," he croaked, and was surprised to see her jump. The book slid from her lap and she sat up straight, her stockinged feet shooting straight to the red-carpeted floor. He blinked and began again more strongly, "I don't suppose you have a pot of coffee—several pots of coffee—stashed about the premises?"

She jumped to her feet. "I'll send for some."

She walked to the door. He liked the way she moved, quick and graceful, without any languid affectations. Natural, almost soothing, despite her obvious nervousness and his own monumental if self-inflicted pain.

She opened the door and spoke to someone in the room beyond.

"I'll see to it, m'lady," came a gruff voice he knew much better. Carson, his valet. At least, he called him his valet, but in truth, he had no more training than Daxton's dogs in the skills of a gentleman's gentleman. Daxton just liked having him around because he was impervious to his lord's tantrums and made decent coffee. And never asked stupid questions, whatever outlandish task was required of him.

"Wait, ma'am, you don't want to go back in there," Carson warned in alarm.

"Of course I do," the girl said calmly. "Why wouldn't I?"

Belatedly, Daxton's wits began to catch up. My lady? Who the devil was she? She certainly spoke and walked like a lady.

"Because he'll be like a bear with a sore tooth," Carson said quite truthfully, "and he'll swear worse than any trooper, or anything you might hear in the worst stews in London. Besides, he'll need to eat and he won't want to. He'll throw it and won't care who it hits."

"He won't throw anything at me," the girl said calmly and walked back into the room before he could yell at Carson.

"Won't I?" Daxton threatened, easing himself gently into a sitting position. He appeared to be naked, which reminded him he couldn't yet remember making love to the lady of the house. He hoped it would come back to him, because something about her was very different and very desirable. Even in this state, his body was reacting without permission. And she was still hauntingly familiar.

She blushed rather adorably and averted her gaze from his naked chest. "No," she said. "Gentlemen don't throw things at their—"

She broke off, and he grinned wolfishly.

"Lovers?" he suggested, and her blush deepened, intriguing him further. He wasn't used to mealy-mouthed women in his bed, whatever their class. Of course, in this case, he appeared to be in hers.

Christ, did I seduce a lady of virtue? Surely I'm not that tempting a proposition? Certainly not in my cups after a three-day spree…

At least she had spirit. She didn't back down before his teasing or her own embarrassment. Instead, she met his gaze, although with a certain conscious courage that he rather admired.

"I was going to say wives."

He blinked. "I beg your pardon?"

"Gentlemen don't throw things at their wives," she repeated patiently.

Whatever horror he might have felt at the implications of this was abruptly mitigated by an elusive memory. No wonder she looked familiar to him.

"Willa Blake," he said with an air of triumph, then scowled. "Damn it. Please tell me I'm not in Shelby's house. And excuse the language," he added hurriedly.

"Oh, I've heard much worse," she said vaguely, causing him to hope uneasily that it hadn't been from him. "And no, you are certainly not in the Shelbys' house. You are in your own rooms at the Blackhaven Hotel."

"Blackhaven!" he repeated, clutching his head as memories started to flash back. A gaming party. Ralph Shelby and the sudden desire to pick a fight with him. With anyone really, but Shelby had been conveniently there. Had he achieved his aim?

He flexed his arms and legs, glanced under the covers for signs of injury. He didn't appear to have been shot, which he supposed to be a good thing, though the knuckles of his right hand were certainly grazed. He'd hit someone or something.

Wickenden had been there at some point, too, hadn't he? Had he hauled Daxton off before he'd stepped over the mark? Or had Daxton shot Shelby? Killed him?

God knew. But yes, *Willa* had been there—why, he couldn't imagine, for it was hardly the sort of party for a lady.

He squeezed his eyes shut. "Oh, the devil, this is bad. It isn't very clear yet, but...please tell me I didn't abduct you."

"Not exactly," she said cautiously. "I decided to go with you."

His eyes flew open of their own accord. "Why?" he asked blankly.

She smiled with what he took to be deliberate vagueness, but annoyingly Carson chose that moment to come in with a tray bearing a pot of coffee, two large cups, a bowl of sugar, and a jug of cream.

"*My lady*," Daxton repeated, glaring at his man. "You called her *my lady*."

"Lady Daxton," Carson said with relish. "You took her to Gretna Green and married her before witnesses, and there ain't no getting out of it."

Daxton grabbed the nearest thing to hand, which unfortunately turned out to be a mere pillow, and took aim. But before he could throw, it was suddenly taken from him and placed back on the bed.

Flabbergasted, Daxton watched Willa Blake smooth the coverlet and walk to the table where Carson had just set down the tray. "Coffee, my lord," she said calmly. "With sugar and cream?"

"Black, m'lady," Carson supplied, when Daxton said nothing. He felt he was still two conversations behind this one and the tightening knots of guilt and marriage seemed to constrict his throat.

He watched her approach him again, the girl whom he remembered as sweet and funny, a part of his more innocent childhood.

"What have I done?" he uttered, dragging his hand through his tangled hair so hard that it hurt.

She pushed the cup into his hand and he drank it down without pause. Obligingly, she brought the coffee pot and refilled the cup before fetching one for herself, and returning to her original position on the window seat.

Another fragment of memory hit him. Driving his horses with the reins in one hand, while passing the brandy flask to his passenger, Willa. He had the impression they were both laughing, though he suspected that was a trick of his befuddled brain.

Something else bothered him rather more. He remembered a sweet, tender mouth under his, smooth skin against his fingers, a soft, perfect breast... Or at least, he thought he did. It might have been a dream or simple fantasy.

A quick glance assured him that Carson had left.

"One question," he blurted, because he had to know. "Willa. Did I...hurt you? Force myself upon you?"

Color rose into her cheeks once more, but still she remained outwardly calm. "No, you fell asleep and only woke ten minutes ago."

She might have been lying, but he couldn't help the twitch of his lip. "At least you have that to be thankful for. Did you drive the curricle back here?"

"No, you ordered a post chaise to bring us back. Carson carried you up to your room."

"And how long have I been here? How long have we been...married?"

"We were married yesterday morning," she replied calmly. "And you've been here in this room since we arrived back yesterday evening."

He pressed his knuckles to his forehead, trying to think. "Then it's as well we're married, for I've ruined you utterly. You had best get as far away from me as possible while I get what's left of my mind back."

She stood at once. "I'll be in the outer room."

"Further," he advised. He wanted to shout and swear and break things.

"I can't," she said without emphasis or self-pity. "As it stands, I have nowhere else to go."

He closed his mouth. Of course. Shelby wouldn't have her back in his household when she'd apparently quite publicly eloped with Daxton. This was a problem of monumental, *gigantic* proportions.

"Ruined you or not, I've rather messed up your life," he said harshly.

"Oh no, my lord," she argued, though with a surprising hint of humor in her eyes as she walked across the room. "You assured me you were *improving* my life."

"I hope you didn't believe me."

"Of course, I did," she said, and went out.

WILLA FELT COLD inside. She'd known from the outset she was taking a risk, and she wasn't yet prepared to give up. But she couldn't help wishing he didn't look quite so horrified by the marriage. Clearly, he remembered very little about it and nothing at all about his amorous interlude in the carriage—which was the least of her worries, she reminded herself severely.

He didn't want her anywhere near him.

However, they would need to talk, and very soon. Until they did, she couldn't even write to her aunt, let alone make any kind of living arrangement.

Leaving his lordship to fight with his thick head and nausea, she left his rooms and made her way to Clara's chamber in the attic. Although Willa had introduced the girl as her maid in order to make sure she had somewhere to lay her drooping, exhausted head, there was clearly no space for her in Lord Daxton's chambers. Willa had slept on the sitting room sofa wrapped in a blanket before, greatly daring, she'd gone through to Daxton's room to see if he was awake. She'd imagined, rather too optimistically, that catching him as soon as he woke, they could reach some kind of immediate understanding.

She sighed, then darted ahead to avoid the aristocratic voices she could hear behind her, and ran up the attic stairs.

She discovered Clara sitting on the edge of her bed, trying to put her dried gown back on. The girl looked dreadful—red-eyed and pale, with her nose running like a tap.

"Back into bed," Willa instructed after feeling her forehead. "You are clearly ill. I'll have them bring you some gruel and a fortifying tonic, and if you're no better this afternoon, I'll send for the doctor."

"I'm just so tired, m'lady," the girl said weakly, "but I've got to go home. My mother and father will be worried sick."

"I shall send a message up to the farm that you are safe and unharmed, but prostrated with a cold."

"Really?" the girl said in amazement. "You would do that for me?"

"Well, I think we have to be each other's respectability for now," Willa said ruefully. "So, remember you are my maid."

"It might wash with your people," Clara said dubiously. "Mine won't believe a word of that."

"It might be best if they pretended to. We'll make up some story, if you can keep your quarrelling suitors quiet. I suspect they won't admit to their infamy."

"Maybe not," Clara murmured. "To be fair, only Jem behaved infamous to me. Dan probably thought he was rescuing me."

"Even after he knocked you into the lake?"

"Men," Clara said bitterly.

Having seen her new "maid" comfortably settled, she sent one of the hotel messengers up to Black Farm. Willa then returned stealthily to the viscount's rooms, where a war seemed to be going on.

Through the open door between the sitting room and the bedchamber, she could see Carson standing in the center of the room, bearing a tray, while his master berated him with an impressive array of oaths and insults.

"Take this bloody mess of ill-cooked pottage away and bring me the damned brandy!" he thundered. "What I need is a hair of the blasted dog!"

When he paused for breath, Carson pleaded, "Just eat it, sir. You know you won't be right until you do."

"Don't presume," Daxton snarled. "Damned impertinent waste of—"

Willa took her courage in both hands, praying the viscount was not marching naked about the room on his way to punch his hapless servant. She hurried across to the door, pushed it fully open with the briefest of knocks and walked in.

He was only half out of bed, one naked leg tangled in the sheet, allowing her a glorious glimpse of his powerful thigh and hip, and of course his broad chest and shoulders that she'd already half seen as he awoke. Why on earth hadn't Carson put him in a night shirt?

Ignoring both her embarrassment and the inexplicable fluttering of her heart, she calmly took the tray from Carson.

"Thank you," she said. "I'll make sure his lordship eats."

Carson regarded her with understandable doubt. "I'll just wait here by the door."

"No, that's fine, you may go," Willa said cheerfully, setting the heavy tray on the bed with some relief. "What would you like to eat first, my lord? A little toast? Or straight to this delicious ham?"

Forcing herself, as Carson abandoned her to her fate, she looked up from the plate, straight into Daxton's turbulent eyes. She tried to ignore the bare flesh between. But even unwashed and unshaven, with his fair hair impossibly tousled, he was still the most impossibly handsome man she had ever seen.

Acute annoyance still lingered on his face, but after a tense moment, his lips twitched.

"You're treating me as if I'm ten years old," he observed.

"Why would I do such a thing?" she wondered.

"Because I'm behaving as if I'm ten years old," he said flatly. "In your opinion."

"And in yours."

His eyes narrowed, "Are you going to feed me like a baby?"

"I believe ten-year-olds normally feed themselves, but if you believe it will help—"

A crack of reluctant laughter interrupted her. "You really aren't afraid of me, are you? Very well, bring the muck here and I'll eat it—on one condition."

"Which is?"

"That you share it with me."

"I broke my fast hours ago. At your lordship's expense, I'm afraid."

Daxton lifted the largest plate on the palm of his hand and appeared to be taking aim at the door.

"I know you'll do it," she added. "You don't need to prove it. However, I have every intention of making sure you eat everything."

At least the challenge glinting in his eyes held a spark of humor. "How are you going to do that?"

"I haven't decided yet," she admitted. "But I need to talk to *you*, not to a crapulous shell."

"Crapulous?" His lips twitched.

"Crapulous."

He dragged his leg back under the covers "Don't go in much for flattery, do you, new wife?"

"No," she agreed, ignoring her heated cheeks as she set the tray on his lap.

He patted the bed next to him. "Sit here. And I'd thank you for a cup of coffee. Have one yourself."

She felt his gaze on her face as she obligingly poured two cups. Almost without noticing, he picked up a piece of toast and began to eat. She said nothing, merely set the coffee cup on his tray and sat on the side of the bed, facing him, her own cup and saucer balanced in her lap.

"What do you want to do?" he asked bluntly. "Do you want me to have the marriage annulled?"

They still had that option. There were grounds in non-consummation, but she didn't quite understand the painful twist of her stomach.

"If you think it's best," she managed.

"It would get you shot of me," he said brutally. "I'd make a terrible husband."

"And you don't want to be married."

"Well, I'm not really fit for it," he said. "Or suited to it in any way."

"I can see that," she managed. "Except in so far as you can now get your hands on the money."

He blinked. "I told you about that?"

"It was the main reason you made your offer."

"Christ, I'm a boor," he said ruefully. "Still, better than the alternative." He didn't elaborate, but took a sizeable gulp of coffee. "So, let's put that amongst the *cons* of annulment. We'd be pretty well off and could live independently, without my father constantly closing the purse strings. Also…" He eyed her thoughtfully. "I'm a rotten bargain, but if the marriage was annulled, I doubt you'd be any better off than you were before. The Shelbys wouldn't have you back, would they?"

"I wouldn't *go* back," she said. "I'd do what I should have done years ago and apply for a post as governess. Or something."

He wrinkled his nose. "I feel you'd have better fun with me."

She regarded him with a mixture of amusement and frustration. "Is there no more to life than how much fun we can extract from it?"

"No. Why should there be?"

She regarded him thoughtfully. "You are quite…liberating," she allowed, and he grinned as he lifted a large forkful of ham and egg toward his mouth. Without thought, she took a piece of toast from his plate.

"It is perfectly true," she allowed, "that I would be much more comfortable as Viscountess Daxton. But it would cut up my comfort to know that you abhorred the situation."

He rubbed his forehead as though trying to dispel the monumental headache he must still be suffering.

"Well, I certainly didn't plan to be leg-shackled just yet. It's one of the reasons I was so angry at my father." He reached for his coffee cup, a lopsided smile curving his lips. "In fact, I told him I'd go out and marry the first woman I saw, who was liable to be one of the house maids. It carried no weight, of course, because we both knew I wouldn't do it."

"And here you did."

"Hardly."

"I've a feeling his lordship won't see much difference between me and the chamber maid," Willa said.

Daxton didn't deny it. "Don't worry. We'll keep out of his way until he's got used to the idea."

Willa's eyes flew to his face. A hint of mischief gleamed in his eyes as he thoughtfully chewed his breakfast.

As neutrally as she could, she said, "Then you think we should stay married?"

"On the whole, yes. If you can stand it. If I have to be married to anyone, I'd as lief it was you. And wastrel as I am, my name and fortune are some protection for you."

There was relief in that. Though hardly a declaration of undying love and fidelity, it was a beginning. She didn't ask for details of the marriage he foresaw. Daxton had always lived very much for the day, without much thought of the future. So, she merely smiled at him and finished her slice of toast.

But the smile seemed to have caught his attention and a trace of unease entered his expression. "I'm not a very good man, Willa," he warned.

"You're not a very wicked one either."

His eyebrow flew up. "Compared with Ralph, you mean?"

"I wouldn't dream of comparing you to Ralph," she retorted.

"Has that bas—" He stopped himself, scowling. "Has he hurt you?"

"No, no," she said hastily, for the last thing they needed on top of this scandal was another quarrel with the Shelbys. She wouldn't even put a duel past Daxton if he ever learned the truth. And in fact, there had been no physical hurt involved. Not to her, at any rate.

Thinking of duels, though, she still had to talk him out of the one he'd challenged Shelby to the night they'd eloped. Daxton hadn't mentioned it, so with any luck, he'd forgotten. In fact, since he'd hit Ralph, perhaps it was up to Ralph to pursue the challenge now? Affairs of so-called honor were a bit of a mystery to her.

Daxton was frowning thoughtfully over his fork. "Hmmm. Why *is* Shelby in Blackhaven? Is he ill? For it's not like him to dance attendance on his family."

Willa hesitated. "I suppose I can tell you, since we're married now."

"As your husband, I insist upon it," he said with mock loftiness.

"Well," she said confidentially. "I suppose you heard the *on-dit* in London that Lady Arabella, the Duke of Kelburn's daughter, refused the offer of marriage everyone expected her to accept?"

Daxton frowned, clearly dredging his erratic memory. She doubted gossip of this kind interested him, so it was probably a matter of chance how much information happened to get through to him. "Beaton," he recalled. "Kelburn—and Monkton, too—spent ages bringing him up to scratch. So, she turned him down?"

"Apparently. Her family banished up here in disgrace. Or because she was ill, depending on who tells the story. Anyway, Ralph thought he was in with a shout."

"Why?"

"Well, she doesn't come to London and is a bit of a recluse. Beaton is over fifty. I suppose Ralph thought there would be no rivals. Besides, he met her once, years ago, and seemed to think she would be grateful for his offer, being quite old and no longer very marriageable. So, nothing would do but that we all must travel post haste to Blackhaven. Where we discovered not only that the Nivens had already gone, but that in the unlikeliest social event of the year, Lady Arabella had married someone else. The famous Captain Alban, in fact."

"Serves him right," Daxton said with satisfaction. "Shelby, I mean, not Alban."

"Why *do* you and Ralph hate each other so much now?"

"That's not a story you want to hear," Daxton said hastily.

"Yes, I do."

"Well, it's not one I can tell," Daxton retorted. "Not to you, especially now you're my wife." He pushed the cleared tray away from him, retaining only his coffee cup, from which he drank in a distracted kind of a way. "We'll need different rooms. This isn't suitable for you. And you'll need a maid, too. Hmmm… I'll write to my father and send an announcement to the Morning Post in London. Then there's your aunt and Ralph. I was going to suggest we hang around here for a few days, just to get used to the idea, only you might be uncomfortable with the Shelbys here, too."

She thought about it. "It's very ill-natured of me, I know, but I find I rather like the idea of greeting my aunt on your arm as Lady Daxton." As a viscountess, she even took precedence over her aunt, the widow of a mere baronet.

Daxton grinned. "Glad to be of service. I expect it will really annoy Ralph as well."

"I expect it will. He knows we left the hotel together last night and must have presumed you set out to ruin a member of his family for spite."

Daxton shifted with sudden discomfort, as if not perfectly sure that hadn't been one of his motives. "I didn't behave well," he muttered. "I'm sorry, Willa. If I could undo it, I would."

She knew that, and knew it shouldn't hurt. They hadn't met for eight years, since they were children. Well, she'd been twelve. He must have been around sixteen, a wild, handsome, and charming boy on the cusp of manhood. Now, they were effective strangers. She blinked away the intrusive, delightful memory of the carriage interlude.

She stood up. "Let us make the best of it, then. I'll go and bespeak a larger set of rooms if any are available—"

"Carson will do that. He's listening at the door anyhow."

"No, I'm not," came Carson's indignant tones.

"Go and do it," Daxton commanded. "And then bring me lots of water, a razor, and fresh clothes. Even my wife shouldn't have to see me like this." He frowned. "Is that the only gown you have?"

"I have a slightly better one for Sundays, and a very faded evening gown for dinner. They're still in my aunt's rooms, though. If she hasn't thrown them away."

"We'll go shopping," he pronounced with a grin. "See and be seen. It might be fun. I know nothing about this town, though the world and his wife appear to be here. I'm sure I saw Wickenden the other night."

"Lady Wickenden was born here," Willa said.

"How do you know these things? Is she a friend of yours?"

"Oh no," she said, making hastily for the door since Daxton appeared to be getting out of bed, stark naked as he so clearly was. "I've never met either of them. I just spent a lot of time listening to conversations I had no part in. I'll wait in the sitting room."

She whisked herself to the other side of the door, and then was sorry. She would have liked to have seen more of that large, powerful body.

Hastily shaking the improper thought away, she discovered writing materials and set about composing an announcement of the marriage for the newspapers. It seemed unreal, as though she were writing about someone else.

Chapter Four

S HOPPING HAD NEVER been pleasurable for Willa before. Most of her experience involved standing to one side while her aunt and cousins picked through items and fabrics, and watching while they pirouetted in gorgeous gowns, shawls, hats, pelisses, riding habits, and travelling cloaks. Her opinion had never been sought. She'd only been there to carry the parcels the footman ran out of hands for.

But, setting to one side the fact that Daxton seemed far too comfortable in a ladies' modiste, he turned out to be the perfect shopping companion. He cheerfully admired or criticized her choices, persuaded her to try things she would never have thought of, and ended by ordering everything they agreed they liked. Willa, who had been expecting to make a choice of maybe two day gowns and an evening dress, was stunned.

"But I'll never wear all of those," she whispered to him as the French-born modiste, Madame Monique, flew into a happy panic of activity.

"Of course you will. And we can get some more in London, for you won't want to wear the same few evening gowns to every party."

"Are we going to London?" she asked, wide-eyed.

"Bound to, eventually. I want to go first to Daxton, though."

"Shouldn't we visit your father?"

"No. He can visit us if he likes. Here, Madame," he addressed the modiste. "Could you manage the alteration on the green day gown immediately?"

"You wish to wear it now?" Madame Monique was delighted.

"But, of course! So much better than the grey, which is not my lady's color! Two minutes, if you please…"

Without consulting Willa, Daxton and Madame quietly consigned the reviled grey dress to the rubbish, and Willa left the shop in the smart new pale green muslin with matching pelisse and a sweet little bonnet trimmed with ribbons of exactly the same shade. Beneath them, even her underwear was new, right down to her chemise and the unfamiliar stays.

"My lord, you didn't need to do all this for me," she said, awed. "I'm overwhelmed."

"Well, you shouldn't be. A few fripperies are nothing, and it's time you had something pretty. Also, I wish you wouldn't call me my lord all the time. My name's Charles, though no one uses it except my mother. Or call me Dax as you used to. As you did the other night, in fact."

Her eyes flew to his face as he tucked her hand in the crook of his arm and strolled along the high street. "Your memory is returning?" she asked as casually as she could.

His lips twisted into a lopsided smile. "In flashes, most of them uncomfortable, and some of them possibly dreams. I hope you'll take all my apologies as read because it'll be deadly dull if you have to listen to them from now until Christmas."

"There's no need," she assured him. "Even in your cups, you were less rude…that is, you have always shown me civility."

Unexpectedly, Daxton scowled, as though he saw and understood everything she was trying to avoid saying. It had never been his pity she wanted. But he only muttered something beneath his breath and veered suddenly across the road to a jeweler's shop.

"You'll have my grandmother's jewels," he told her. "But it's all pretty old-fashioned, and you might as well have something to wear here for now. And you should have a ring…"

Stunned, she emerged from the shop wearing a gold ring studded with tiny pearls and carrying a parcel containing a turquoise set that Daxton said would go marvelously well with one of her new evening gowns.

Although wearing the new gown and pelisse gave her confidence, it wasn't so much the material gifts that made her so unexpectedly happy, but strolling through the town on Daxton's arm, basking in the pleasure of his bantering company. His attention was like a ray of sunshine. She knew the clouds would block it soon, but while it was there, she made the most of it. Vaguely, she was aware of people turning to look at them with varying degrees of blatancy, but Daxton paid no notice. He even took her into the ice parlor they discovered on a corner, and sat watching her as she ate the delicious ice.

"Will your reputation stand such a mundane pastime?" she teased.

"What reputation?"

"You must know you're regarded as the most dangerous company after Lord Byron."

"Byron's not so bad," Daxton said carelessly. "Apart from the God-awful poetry."

Willa swallowed her ice too fast and gasped at the cold. "God-awful? Most people regard his poetry as his saving grace!"

"Well, it isn't," Daxton said, looking revolted. "What's my saving grace?"

"You don't have one."

He really did have a devastating smile. It lit up his already handsome face with fun and wicked joy, and made her toes curl. "Not even my personal charm?" he suggested.

"I believe that's counted as one of your dangers."

"Oh, well, I'll have to take comfort in the knowledge I have some."

"You don't actually care, do you?"

"About what people say of me? I've never thought about it," he said frankly. "Though I suppose it explains why the debutantes all look terrified of me, even when their doting mamas fling them at my feet."

As they left the parlor, Daxton said, "What would you like to do now? I suppose we should try and find you an abigail. Perhaps the hotel could help, there."

"Ah, well that was one of the things I wanted to tell you," she began. "I *sort of* have one already."

"Dax?" a male voice interrupted. It came from a group of people who'd stopped to talk in their path—two gentlemen and a young lady. One of the gentlemen was impeccably dressed and darkly handsome with black, sloping eyebrows, but it was the other man who'd addressed her husband. He was much more carelessly garbed in an ill-fitting and badly worn coat, and his hair was rather too long and tangled for fashionable society.

Daxton halted, glancing at the group with more annoyance than interest. Then his eyes widened.

"*Rags?* What the devil?" He thrust out his hand and enthusiastically shook that of the ill-dressed young man. "I thought you were dead!"

"No, no, just rusticating. Never expected to run into you here of all places."

"I never expected to *be* here above a night, but that's a long story." He half-turned toward Willa, drawing all eyes to her. "I have to present to you my wife."

"Wife?" the young man repeated, startled, his eyes flying from Willa to Daxton.

"Wife," the viscount repeated dangerously. "Willa, this is Lord Tamar, whom I haven't seen since he was kicked out of school."

"I wasn't kicked. I left voluntarily." Lord Tamar smiled disarmingly, bowing over her hand with incongruous grace, considering his ragged appearance. "And I'm delighted to make your ladyship's acquaintance."

He had an unconventionally handsome face and intense, curious eyes. But there was little time to study him, for Daxton was casually introducing the other gentleman and his lady. "And this is Lord and Lady Wickenden."

Everyone had heard of Wickenden. Known as the Wicked Baron, he was the acknowledged leader of one of the wilder fashionable sets in London, and for years had been considered the most eligible and elusive bachelor in society. Both he and his wife shook hands with her in a faintly bemused kind of way, and congratulated Daxton upon his unexpected nuptials.

"It was a sudden decision," Daxton said carelessly. "Which reminds me, Wickenden, do I need to apologize to you for the other night?"

"Not to me, no," Wickenden said, although he cast another glance at Willa as though he'd finally recognized her as the poorly dressed girl who'd brought Ralph his money. "Bit hazy, is it?"

"I was a trifle disguised," Daxton admitted. "But I'm dashed if I expected to find so many people in this town. What are you doing here, Rags? I thought your pile was down in the south."

"It is," Lord Tamar confirmed. "I needed somewhere cheap to stay that was full of rich people. I paint these days. In fact, I'll paint you and Lady Dax if you'll let me."

"Depends," Daxton said bluntly. "Are you any good?"

"Actually, he is," Lady Wickenden said warmly. "We've just come from the gallery where you can see several of his paintings."

"I'm nearly finished with Lady Arabella and Captain Alban," Lord Tamar said. "So, I need more *interesting* faces to carry me through the dull commissions."

"Lady Arabella Niven?" Willa said, intrigued. "The Duke of Kelburn's daughter? What is she like?"

"Beautiful, in a unique kind of way. Funny, perceptive, charming. Why?"

Willa couldn't help her unholy delight. "I heard she was plain," she said with satisfaction. "And aging."

Daxton regarded her with amusement, the others with bafflement. "So, what is there to do in this very odd town? Your pardon, Lady Wickenden!"

"I'm not remotely offended," Lady Wickenden assured him. "I lived all my life here until my marriage, so it seems perfectly normal to me. I suspect you find it dull."

"Not so far," Daxton said, rubbing his forehead.

"Then you should come to the Assembly Room ball tomorrow night," Lady Wickenden told him. "We shall be there—along with all the local gentry and the cream of the town's visitors."

Willa turned eagerly to Daxton, who was looking appalled. A provincial assembly ball would be unutterably dull for him. He met her gaze and blinked.

"Perhaps we will," he said unexpectedly. "If you'd like to go, Willa?" His eyes gleamed. "The Shelbys might be there."

"You're a married man now," Wickenden said with mock severity. "You can't go picking fights with people in public and causing your wife embarrassment."

"Lady Shelby is my aunt," Willa said hastily. "I lived with her until...my marriage."

"Well, the Assembly ball is a very popular event in Blackhaven," Lady Wickenden said. "We have two a month now, and even waltz there."

"That's a point." Daxton swung on Willa. "*Can* you waltz?"

"Sort of," she said dubiously.

"Don't worry, we'll practice," Daxton said, drawing her hand through his arm once more. "Do you want to go to this gallery and see Tamar's daubs?"

"Oh yes, and then if we've time, perhaps we could see the harbor and walk on the beach? It might help clear your head."

"Can't do it any harm," Daxton agreed, with a casual wave of one hand by way of farewell to his friends who gazed after them in some bemusement.

"I'VE NEVER HEARD a wife be quite so understanding about her husband's thick head," Gillie, Lady Wickenden remarked in amusement, as she watched the Daxtons saunter down the road together. "Though I expect it will wear thin. I rather like her. She isn't at all the sort of woman I imagined would elope with Daxton."

"She's a poor relation of the Shelbys," Wickenden said. "And she must have been desperate, judging by the way Shelby treated her. And the suddenness of her departure with Daxton."

"I expect Dax was sorry for her," Gillie said.

Wickenden drew her onward in the direction of her old home. "That's what I like about you, Gillie. No one else would imagine Dax sorry for anyone. And I doubt it was pity."

"What, then?" Gillie asked with a teasing glance. "True love? More like true lust, knowing Daxton, and she *is* very pretty."

"And what exactly do you know about Daxton's lusts, Lady Wickenden?" her husband mocked.

Gillie wrinkled her nose. "Only what the rest of the world sees. Opera dancers and Helena Holt. And poor Serena, though I'm inclined to believe him merely careless in that scandal." She frowned. "No one will cut the new Lady Daxton, will they?"

"I should think his rank protects her from that."

"Still, I don't envy her dealing with all Daxton's baggage! Especially not his women. Plus, did it seem to you, she likes him?"

"It seemed to me *he* likes *her*," Wickenden replied. "And, trust me, that is much more interesting. Now, it's time I took you home to rest."

"Rest?" Gillie said a trifle breathlessly.

"Rest," he said firmly. "Although I have in mind a most enjoyable way to relax you…"

FOR WILLA, THE AFTERNOON was delightful.

At the gallery, Daxton seemed surprised by how good his old friend's paintings were.

"Maybe we *should* let him paint us," he suggested, moving on to the next batch of pictures. "We can send it to my father as a gift. What the devil is *this* meant to be?"

"Hush, it's quite clearly a horse," Willa whispered.

"Well, I've never seen one with a head that size,"

Having agreed that the paintings were of mixed quality, they bought one of Lord Tamar's wilder seascapes and arranged for it to be sent to Daxton House. Then they strolled round to the old harbor, admiring the colorful fishing boats tied up there. Finding their way down to the beach, they walked in the sand. Unselfconsciously, Daxton kicked off his shoes and stockings and walked barefoot, and as soon as they were free of the town from where anyone could see, Willa did the same.

The first shoe was easily removed, especially as Daxton held her arm to balance her. Only then, her fingers faltered on the hem of her new gown. Blushing, she glanced up at Daxton. "Avert your eyes, if you please."

"I don't please." He lifted his gaze with peculiar slowness from her foot to her face. Then he turned his head to the side. Hastily, she reached under her gown, unfastened the garter, and pulled off her stocking before switching to the other foot.

Before Willa could, Daxton swept up her shoes with the stockings and garters stuffed inside. He examined the shoes with disfavor. "You need new everything, don't you? Including dancing slippers."

"Oh dear, I didn't think of that. I seem to be rather more of an expense than you bargained for."

He blinked. "You're not a damned expense. Look, those rocks over there, under the castle. Isn't that the scene in Tamar's painting?"

"Oh, I believe it is! Where did you want to hang it?"

"You can choose, when we're at Daxton. You might want to change everything around anyway. I haven't done much with the place, though it's in a decent enough state of repair."

"I thought you regarded it as your home," she said in surprise. "You seem so eager to go there."

He shrugged. "My father handed it over to me a couple of years ago. As it stands, the revenue isn't enough to do more than keep the place ticking over. It swallows most of my allowance, too, in basic repairs for my tenants."

She frowned. "Then how do you afford to live as you do?"

"Credit, my dear," he said wryly. "Everyone knows my father will cough up in the end. And even if he doesn't, I'll inherit the earldom one day. If I live long enough. But the point is, Daxton could be so much more than it is. Now that I can get my hands on my inheritance, I can make the improvements the land needs. My tenants will be far better off in just a few years, and so will I. More than that, my father will have to take note and be persuaded to do the same on all the estates."

This was a side to Daxton she'd never seen before. "What kind of improvements?" she asked unwarily, and was immediately deluged by detailed agricultural theories and modern practices, only half of which she understood. What impressed her was how much Daxton obviously grasped, and how much he'd noticed of his people's difficulties. Difficulties he was determined to eliminate.

After several minutes, he stopped talking and cast her a rueful glance. "Sorry. Didn't mean to bore you rigid."

"I'm not bored," she assured him. "I'd just like to understand more." She didn't only mean the science either. There was clearly far more to her hedonistic husband than people realized.

"I'll show you when we go there."

"Do you want to leave at once?"

"Not really, now I think about it. We'll need to give the solicitors time to sort out the money. In the meantime, we might as well enjoy our wedding trip. And it's pretty enough here if you're happy to stay."

They walked on in pleasant companionship until the incoming tide drove them closer to the shore. Spying a path that led up to the road, Daxton sat on a rock, dusted off his feet, and replaced his stockings and boots, before he glanced up at Willa, who was hovering uncertainly.

He patted the rock beside him.

"I'm afraid of spoiling my new gown," she confided. "It's so pretty and the muslin is so fine, it might catch and tear on the rock."

His lips twitched. "We can buy another," he pointed out, shocking her. But then he took off his coat and spread it on the rock for her.

She sat gratefully and reached for her shoes. But again, he surprised her, drawing one stocking from the shoe she'd stuffed them in and crouching at her feet.

"Oh no," she said in sudden agitation. "You mustn't."

"Don't be silly," he said impatiently. "Give me your foot."

His manner, much more that of the boy she remembered than that of a rake, soothed her enough to reluctantly proffer her foot.

He rolled the stocking on with a degree of expertise that should have bothered her, smoothing it over her sole and ankle and up over her calf. His fingers were cool and sure, and yet for some reason, their touch heated her skin. She wanted to beat his hands away, and she wanted them to stay, to roam higher. She remembered only too well those wild moments of abandon in the carriage…

Worse, she wondered if *he* were remembering them, too, for his deft fingers slowed, lingering over the last couple of inches as he reached for the garter, wound it around her leg and tied it. Then, almost delicately, he slipped the worn old shoe over her foot and fastened it, too.

She swallowed. "Thank you," she got out. "I can manage the other."

"Be still," he retorted, though he no longer sounded impatient. Instead, his voice was strangely husky, sending pleasurable little shivers up her spine. This reaction took her so much by surprise that she let him take her other foot and roll on the stocking with agonizing slowness. She was afraid to breathe. Tying the garter, his fingertips brushed the inside crease of her knee, and she swallowed back a gasp.

With the same slow deliberation, he eased on her shoe and, the foot still resting on his thigh, he raised his gaze to her face.

She remembered that clouded heat in his eyes, at once so exciting and so weakening. He liked women. By all accounts, he liked them a lot and they reciprocated. She could understand that only too well. But she was his wife. Whatever her vulnerabilities or her desires, she had to be more than those other women. She didn't just want to gain his attention. She wanted to keep it.

With an effort she tore her gaze free, slid her foot off his lap, and jumped up, snatching his coat off the rock and shaking it out, just to give herself something to do, to hide the trembling of her foolish body.

"There. Respectable again," he observed sardonically.

Chapter Five

A S IT HAPPENED, Willa didn't have to wait until the ball to encounter her aunt.

She and Dax had taken possession of their new rooms at the hotel, which provided a bedchamber for each of them, a tiny room for a servant, and a sitting room. Since the first of Willa's new evening gowns had been delivered, Daxton proposed they dine publicly in the hotel, and show the world they were married. Willa rang for a hotel maid to help her dress—a brief visit to Clara's room having found the girl sound asleep, which was probably the best thing for her. Then, duly laced and stayed, Willa dismissed the maid and admired her new gown in the glass from every angle she could. She felt rather strange in the new stays, but they certainly gave her chest more shape. The maid had brushed her hair until it shone like burnished chestnuts, though the girl was not so good with the pins. Willa re-pinned it and examined herself doubtfully.

In the glass, she met Daxton's gaze. He stood at the half open door.

"Will I do?" she asked nervously.

He blinked. "You look beautiful. But then, you always do, you know. Shall we go down?" The carelessly thrown compliment made her blush.

She'd never felt remotely beautiful before—mostly either awkward or invisible, depending on the company. Daxton looked as handsome as ever in fresh black evening clothes with a snowy white cravat. A few tight lines around his eyes were the only visible aftereffects of his recent spree.

"Oh," he said, stopping in the middle of the sitting room and lifting a small box from the table where he must have dropped it earlier. "I found this among my things when Carson unpacked again. I bought it for someone else and never gave it, but you might like it tonight at least."

It was true she had no jewelry apart from the new turquoise set which seemed too elaborate for the occasion, and the red-trimmed cream evening gown did leave her neck and chest somewhat bare. Opening the box, Daxton took out the contents and dangled a gold chain from his careless fingers. On the end of it was a shining round pendant, a small ruby surrounded by a spiral of diamonds.

Her eyes widened, for it was a beautiful and expensive trinket, and could not have been the casual gift he'd made it sound. He'd bought it for a mistress.

"I never gave it," he repeated. "Until now."

She smiled. "It's beautiful, Dax. Since I ran away with you, I seem to be showered with gifts."

"The wages of sin," he said with a quick grin and walked behind her to fasten the fine gold chain around her neck. She shivered at the brush of his fingers on her sensitive skin. Then he stepped around her, examined her critically and nodded approval. "Just the thing." He offered her his arm.

The public areas of the hotel were busy with guests going out for the evening or, like Dax and Willa, heading for the dining room. As they descended the staircase, looking down on the foyer, several heads turned toward them. Willa even saw an elegantly bewhiskered gentleman nudge his companions to draw their attention. Involuntarily, Willa's fingers grasped Daxton's sleeve.

"It's just curiosity," he murmured. "The rumor mill will have been spinning about both of us. Brazen it out and it will pass. And remember, you have nothing to be ashamed of."

It was true, she hadn't. The marriage mart was called so for a reason. All members of the ton bought and sold into matrimony for money, land, political influence, and social ambition. She and Dax were not so very different.

An inconvenient flash of memory popped into her mind—the abandoned interlude in the carriage that had given her a taste of physical pleasure. And absolute clarity. She'd known she would fight for him, for a life with him if she could. And today had shown her that it was possible. At the very least, they could be friends…

"Shelby ahead," Dax murmured in her ear. "He's just entered the front door."

Snapping her attention back to present reality, she saw her cousin Ralph in evening dress, make his way across the foyer to his mother and sister who seemed to be waiting for him impatiently. He looked grumpy and put-upon. But then, he generally did.

"Ready for a little fun?" Dax inquired. "Or shall we give them the cut direct?"

"No," she decided. "I owe my aunt a private explanation at the least. Let us be civil."

Besides, there was an undeniable if reprehensible pleasure in watching her family's faces as they caught sight of her approach. No one could swagger quite like Dax, and he attracted more attention than the Shelbys did. But Ralph saw him first. Emotion flashed across his face. It might have been annoyance, or even fear, for after all, the last time they'd met, Dax had challenged him and knocked him down.

Then Ralph's lip curled in contempt. He said something to his mother as he made to turn his womenfolk toward the dining room door. Only then, finally, he recognized the well-dressed lady on his enemy's arm and his jaw dropped spectacularly.

Her aunt's eyes widened impossibly. She clutched Elvira's arm.

Elvira goggled. "Good lord, it's *Willa*."

The cut-direct, however, seemed likely to come from Willa's aunt, who began to turn furiously aside.

Dax refused to allow it. "Ah, Lady Shelby," he called, when they were still a yard or so away. "Well met. My wife was eager to assure you of her safety and wellbeing."

Since most of the foyer must have heard that, her aunt could do little but turn back and incline her head stiffly to Daxton.

"*Wife?*" Elvira blurted in undisguised dismay. She had, after all, married a mere esquire, although he was the heir to a respectable fortune.

"Were you hoping to be an attendant?" Dax asked her. "We preferred a quieter ceremony."

"I'll bet you did," Ralph said nastily.

Dax regarded him consideringly. Alarmed, Willa opened her mouth to try and smooth over the situation before Dax knocked her cousin down again. Then it struck her that she didn't actually care. On the whole, she rather wished he would. So, she merely dropped his arm so as not to impede him.

The action was not lost on her aunt, who clutched her son's arm instead. "Lady Daxton," she got out between closed teeth.

"Aunt," Willa said pleasantly. "Good evening, Elvira."

"Please, go in," Dax said, reclaiming Willa's hand and placing it back on his arm. "Let's not stand on precedence. It's not as if we're dining together after all,"

Ralph all but stalked inside with his rigid-backed mother on his arm, leaving Elvira to trot behind them.

"Neatly done," Willa approved, swallowing back the laughter.

"I was about to say the same to you. They really thought I was going to punch Ralph on the nose."

"Were you?" she asked with interest.

"Say the word and I still will."

At first, Willa found dinner somewhat nerve-wracking, Very aware that she and Daxton were the center of most diners' attention, she found it hard to think of anything else. Gradually, however, Daxton's charm began to work its magic, and she relaxed in his company, resuming the conversation and banter of earlier in the day.

Dax was clearly on his best behavior. He barely touched his wine and drank only one glass of brandy when the meal was finished. Willa couldn't help the comfortable sense of wellbeing creeping over her. Of course, it was the first time she'd sat down to an undisturbed dinner for years. Her aunt and cousins had sent her on constant, minor errands during most meals, and the result was she'd eaten little and emerged exhausted.

"That was delightful," she said warmly. "Thank you, Dax."

"It's only dinner," he said, in surprise. "And only tolerable at that. Apart from the company."

She laughed. "Well recovered," she mocked.

He grinned, unrepentant. "I meant it. Shall we stay longer or retire?"

Although they had their own bedchambers, her heart immediately lurched in mingled fear and anticipation. But when her gaze flew to his face, she was immediately distracted. His recent dissipation had taken its toll and he was obviously exhausted.

So was she. She'd slept very little last night, and not at all the night before.

"I believe I'm tired," she said, and he rose immediately to hold her chair for her. It was odd, after the rest of her life, to be treated with the ordinary courtesies due to a lady. "My aunt has gone," she observed, as they left the dining room and crossed the foyer.

"Good thing, too. Friday-faced set of dullards. How do you come to be related to such people?"

"Luck," she said wryly. As they climbed the stairs, she remembered another duty. "I'll just run up to Clara's room and make sure she ate the meal I had sent up to her."

"Clara," he repeated. "The girl you and Carson picked up on the road, whom you're pretending is your maid?"

"Well, at least until she straightens things out with her family."

"Hmm," he said noncommittally.

Her errand eliminated the inexplicable awkwardness she felt in reentering their rooms with him. Part of her hoped he would have retired by the time she returned. Another part wanted him to be waiting. And amorous. But somehow, Dax sober was a very different prospect from Dax on the tail end of a drunken spree. And there were so many arguments against intimacy. For one thing, the marriage couldn't then be annulled due to non-consummation. And for another, she didn't want to give into temptation until he felt something for her. If he ever did. She wouldn't hold out for love, but she needed his *care…*

Clara was asleep once more, but it seemed to Willa she slept more easily, and at least the plate beside her bed was almost empty. Content, Willa blew out the candle still burning in the room and left again.

In the wider passage downstairs, she all but ran into her aunt. And this time, Lady Shelby was in no hurry to run away. The passage was empty and she actually waited for Willa to reach her.

"Lady Daxton," she sneered. "Don't think I don't know how you achieved it. You're nothing but a common thief."

Willa blinked in astonishment. "I imagined you gave me food and clothing freely. What have I ever stolen from you?"

"Don't pretend innocence with me, you sly little lightskirt. I know you took it, bought yourself into this marriage with it while Daxton was in his cups. You deserve each other."

"Took what?" Willa demanded again, ignoring the rest from sheer curiosity about this one point.

Her aunt's lips curled back so far, she was almost snarling. "My purse! The one Ralph gave me the day you ran away."

Willa opened her mouth to deny it robustly—until it struck her that technically, she had taken it. It would do her no good to accuse Ralph of ordering her to do so and then losing it all to Daxton at dice. To her aunt, Ralph could do no wrong. Besides which, Willa was fairly sure Ralph had accused her in the first place to cover up his own ill-behavior. And the wretched Haines no doubt backed him up from spite, swearing quite truthfully that she'd seen Willa take if from the room.

She frowned at her aunt. "It should have been returned to you."

"It should never have been taken in the first place!"

Willa was not about to argue that one. "I'll look into it," she said shortly and walked past her aunt.

She headed immediately downstairs to the reception desk, but when she asked for the purse which she'd left for Lady Shelby's maid, the clerk had no idea what she was talking about. Although he looked in all the secure cabinets to please her, there was no purse to be found. Of course, it was not the same clerk she'd given the purse to, but if he couldn't find it and her aunt had never got it back, where on earth was it?

In deep thought, Willa made her way back up to the rooms she now shared with Dax. The viscount sprawled on the sofa, flicking through the book she'd found that morning.

He glanced up at her. "Mrs. Radcliffe?" he teased. "Really?"

"I enjoy her novels immensely," Willa said with dignity. "And you needn't look so superior for I found it in your bedchamber."

"Did you?" He cast it aside. "I should pack my own valise."

"Dax, do you remember giving me back my aunt's purse that you won from Ralph?"

Dax scratched his head. "Sort of. You gave it to the boy on reception duty."

"For my aunt's maid."

"That's what you said."

"I thought so. But the thing is, my aunt doesn't have it. She thinks I stole it. And she won't keep quiet about it. I know her. Your wife will be branded a thief in the eyes of anyone who matters."

"Who is it who matters so damned much?" Dax asked.

"People…Your friends… Your father!"

Dax shrugged. "My friends aren't stupid enough to listen to spiteful gossip from that quarter. And my father has yet to listen to anyone at all, so we're in the clear. Ignore her. Ralph will have stolen it back." He rose to his feet yawning. "I could sleep for a week. Do you need anything before I fall upon my bed and snore?"

It might have been an offer to act as lady's maid. Either way, she turned it down with a smile. "No, I too shall retire. Goodnight, my lord."

His lips quirked and he bowed exaggeratedly. "My lady." He took her hand and kissed it with a flourish. "Sleep well."

His smile, the brief touch of his lips, made her heart race, but he only strolled away to his own bedchamber, where apparently Carson waited for him. She felt rather lonely as she walked to her own room and closed the door.

However, struggling out of her new gown and stays without assistance involved so many contortions that she soon found herself laughing and remembering the fun of the day. And tomorrow, she would still be his wife.

IN THE MORNING, Clara was much improved. Willa found her out of bed and getting dressed. She even obliged Willa by fastening her new day gown for her.

"If you wish, there is a small chamber in our suite of rooms where you can sleep," Willa suggested.

"Oh, I don't know, m'lady. Is there no word from home, yet?"

"None, I'm afraid. The messenger returned from the farm with no reply."

"I should go home," she said drearily. "But Mrs. Frame won't have me help her now I've lost my good name, and I'll be bringing in no money."

"I think you need to talk to your parents in person," Willa said. "I'll come with you if you like and explain that you've been with me nearly all of the time. Really, it's this Jem who should be in trouble over the incident, not you. Won't your new suitor—Dan?—have told them this?"

Clara scowled. "He's angry at me, too."

"Well, you must be my maid for now, and of course you shall be paid for it. Come down when you're ready."

Her sitting room was empty when she returned, with no sign of Carson or Dax. She went to her own bedchamber and began tidying away her night things. A few moments later, a robust knock sounded at the outer door. Thinking it must be Clara already, she went and opened it.

A young man in a floppy wool jacket stood before her—pointing a large, old-fashioned pistol at her heart.

"Where is she?" he demanded.

Willa stared at the pistol. "Where is who?"

"Back inside," he snapped, with a nervous glance up and down the passage.

Willa obeyed, desperately trying to grasp what was happening. "Please put the pistol down and I'll try—"

The pistol jerked menacingly in his hand. "Clara. Clara James." His gaze darted about the room. "Call her. Bring her here, now."

"She isn't here," Willa said, "and if you imagine waving *that* at her is going to get her back—"

"I'm not waving it at her, I'm waving it at you! Who are you anyway? His procuress?"

Willa frowned. "I don't know what that means, precisely, but I expect it's insulting." Worse, she began to suspect the young man was mad. This must be Jem, the rejected suitor who'd abducted Clara. No wonder she'd thrown him over.

"I won't have her with that man another instant!" he said desperately. "Bring her to me now!"

"What man?" Willa demanded, losing patience, despite the alarming way he jerked the pistol around.

"Daxton!" the man said with loathing. "Lord Daxton. I know she's in his clutches, so bring her to me now!"

"Oh, you completely misunderstand," Willa began with premature relief.

"Enough!" the man roared, and actually seized her by the arm, dragging her toward the nearest door, which happened to be Daxton's bedchamber. Willa pulled back instinctively, terrified now for Dax. But the man's grip tightened, and they struggled, sliding one pace forward and another back until, wild-eyed, he brandished the pistol in her face.

Worst of all, Daxton's bedchamber door flew open and the viscount himself strode out in pantaloons and shirt sleeves. "What the deuce is—"

His eyes widened at the violent scene before him. The pistol jerked around to point directly at him. But with a roar, he flew at Willa's assailant, who instinctively released her to deal with the larger threat.

In that instant, Dax looked terrifying. Sheer murder glinted in his hard, furious eyes.

Then the pistol fired.

Chapter Six

DAXTON FELT THE BURNING in his arm and knew he'd been hit, but such was his fear for Willa and his rage against the man who threatened her, he kept going. The gunman could no longer shoot her, but Dax wouldn't let him touch so much as a hair on her head again.

A look of appalled terror crossed the man's face, quickly followed by panic, and then Dax struck him hard in the jaw. The empty pistol clattered to the floor.

"Dax!" Willa cried. "You're bleeding!"

Dax didn't care. He drew back his arm once more, but she caught it and clung on. "Dax, wait," she pleaded. "It's a mix-up. He thinks you abducted Clara and debauched her, or some such—"

The gunman let out a cry of distress.

Dax scowled. "Who the devil's Clara?"

"The girl we met on the road, remember? We're pretending she's my maid?"

"Well, what the devil is it to *him*?" Dax demanded, clenching his fist once more. Willa clasped it in both of hers, distracting him, because even in this fraught situation, her touch was sweet.

"I think he must be Jem," she said, as if he should know who in hell that was. "Clara's original suitor."

"I certainly am not!" the erstwhile gunman exclaimed, affronted. "My name is Daniel Doone."

"Dan!" Willa exclaimed. "Really? Oh well, either way, he seems to believe you are the villain of the piece and are holding poor Clara against her will."

"Holding her against…" Dax stared at Daniel Doone. "Even for me, that's a trifle rum, especially with my wife in the next room!"

"Wife?" Daniel repeated in an appalled kind of voice. "Oh God."

"He thought I was your procuress," Willa explained. "Whatever that is."

Daxton's jaw dropped. "How many procuresses do you know? Be careful," he added dangerously.

"None," Daniel admitted.

"Well, for future reference, none of them look anything like my wife!"

"Dax, sit down," Willa pleaded. "Your arm is bleeding. He shot you!"

"So he did." Dax glanced at his sleeve where a dark red stain was spreading against the pristine white of his shirt. Impatiently, he ripped the beautiful linen with his teeth and exposed the wound. "It's as well he—or his antiquated firearm—shoots like a cow, because he's only winged me. Pretty sure the ball isn't even in there."

Willa took him by the good arm, all but forcing him onto the sofa. She looked rather white and her hand on his shoulder trembled as she held him down. "You," she said severely to Daniel Doone. "Go and fetch a doctor. Now."

Daniel, as white-faced as Willa, muttered, "Yes, m'lady," and fled, abandoning his pistol without apparent thought.

"Last we'll see of him," Dax opined.

"I won't mind that," Willa said shakily, "providing he sends the doctor before he flees to the hills."

Dax scowled. "What do we want with a damned quack? The ball barely grazed me."

"But didn't you *see* he had a pistol?"

Dax opened his mouth to say something flippant, but at the last moment, he caught Willa's gaze and realized the truth. Her fear, her trembling, were for him. Her talk of doctors wasn't mere feminine fussing. She was afraid he would die.

He was her husband, her provider, her protector. He'd brought on himself all those responsibilities he'd never wanted. But it came to him now that it wasn't the provider she was so terrified of losing. It was him. Her friend.

Well, no one would have taken *him* on if they hadn't cared a little. And he liked that she cared. He found himself smiling at her, which at least brought the color back to her cheeks. Without warning, she whisked herself away into her own bedchamber and emerged a moment later with her washing bowl.

He tried to stand. "Good grief, Willa, let Carson do that! Where is the scoundrel?"

"Sit," she commanded. "And I have no idea where Carson is." She set the large bowl down at his feet and knelt beside it, frowning as she concentrated on his arm.

His impatient words died in his throat. His arm stung and throbbed, and as she cleaned the wound he couldn't deny her ministrations hurt more. But the acknowledgement of those things seemed to be only at the back of his mind. The front was focused on her face, on her bottom lip clamped between her teeth as she worked, on the gentle yet sure touch of her hands.

"I should be shot more often," he said stupidly, because he tended to speak—and act—before he thought.

Her eyes flew to his face. But at that moment, the door crashed open and Daniel Doone strode back in with a saturnine, plainly dressed gentleman somewhere between thirty and forty years old.

"Good God," Daxton said. "Never tell me you're the doctor."

"There would be no point since you've guessed it, My name's Lampton."

"Daxton." He was disappointed that Willa made way for the doctor, who examined his arm without shock or disapproval.

"This young man says he shot you."

"He did."

"Hmmmm."

A tentative knock on the half open door heralded the arrival of a young woman in a plain dress and cap. No one but Dax seemed to see her.

"I'm sorry, sir, I didn't even mean to fire it!" Daniel Doone exclaimed. "And I realize I've misunderstood everything, but if you could only tell me where Clara is—"

"I'm right here," the young woman at the door said wrathfully. "And you'd better stay away from me, Daniel Doone."

Far from staying away from her, Doone charged toward her. "Clara! Thank God!"

Clara fended him off with both hands. "Thank her ladyship, rather, but keep your distance!"

Dan, his expression somewhat ludicrously mixed between dismay and relief, stopped dead.

"This him, is it?" Carson said, laconically, wandering into the room. "Want me to knock him down for you."

Daniel bridled. "Who's this?" he demanded.

"I'm his lordship's valet and—" He broke off, his attention distracted by his master's bleeding arm. "What happened to you?"

"I shot him," Doone said, miserably.

Carson strode forward, his arm swinging back with unmistakable intent.

"Carson!" Willa snapped. "It was a mistake. He brought the doctor."

Surprisingly, if grudgingly, Carson dropped his arm. "Suppose it explains why all the hotel staff and several nobby guests are flapping about and calling for the Watch. Should have known the gunshot was in here." Carson came closer, peering at Dax uneasily. "You ain't going to peg it, are you?"

"Of course I'm not," Daxton scoffed.

"Is he?" Carson demanded of Dr. Lampton, who was delving into his bag.

"No. Not if he does as he's told." The doctor emerged from his bag with a large jar of vile looking ointment which he hefted admiringly in one hand. "It's a lucky day for both of us," he told Dax. "You are the first patient I've had the chance to use this on, but I'm told the results are miraculous."

"Told by whom?" Willa demanded.

"Another physician of my acquaintance. Don't look so worried, my lady. I know exactly what's in it. It should prevent corruption and speed the healing."

Willa still looked doubtful, but Dax was already bored with the whole process.

"Slap it on," he invited cheerfully. "Why are you all standing around gawping? Carson, I'll need my coat. You, Clara, is it? If you're going to be my lady's maid, go and find her bonnet."

"What do I want with my bonnet?" Willa asked, bewildered.

"It's customary when one goes out."

"Why am I going out?" she inquired.

"To buy dancing slippers. And whatever other fripperies one needs for a ball."

Alarm crossed her face as she understood. "You can't accompany me! You're shot!"

"Grazed," he corrected. "I've had worse during a night in—" He broke off in the nick of time. "In lots of places," he finished hurriedly.

"Doctor Lampton, please tell him he can't do such a thing," Willa pleaded.

To Daxton's surprise, the doctor shrugged and, having applied the evil ointment, rummaged in his bag for a bandage. "That is between you and his lordship, ma'am. He hasn't lost a lot of blood, so I see no reason to confine him to his bed. On the other hand, sir, use the arm as little as possible to give it the chance to heal. No riding, driving your own carriage, boxing, or other sports. No long, bumpy journeys."

Daxton frowned at the last. "You needn't think I'm going to stay here just to drink the damned waters."

"Between you and I, the waters are immaterial," the doctor said, efficiently binding the wound. "But if you didn't want to stop here, you shouldn't have got shot."

Dax rather liked the doctor, who glanced up from his work with raised eyebrows. "Do you want the magistrate?" he asked bluntly.

Daxton glanced at the pale, anxious young man who'd shot him. "He seems sorry enough already. I believe it was a misunderstanding. My wife's fault," he added provokingly.

His wife narrowed her eyes and he smiled at her until a breath of laughter escaped her lips. Making her smile seemed to be becoming an obsession with him.

THE ACHE IN his arm was less than he'd imagined it would be—thanks, no doubt, to whatever was in the muck Dr. Lampton had slathered over the wound. Coupled with the rare clear-headedness of a morning after a night of very little drinking, Dax felt, on the whole, pretty pleased with his world.

After a light luncheon taken in their own sitting room, Willa asked if he would mind very much practicing some dance steps with her.

"Did you never get to go to parties with the Shelbys, then?" he asked, frowning.

"No, but I didn't mind."

"Not even *their* parties?"

"Occasionally, but not to dance, more to look after Lady Shelby or my cousins."

He grunted and stood up. Everything he heard about her life with the Shelbys reinforced his dislike of the whole family. On the other hand, he'd never imagined practicing dance steps could be quite so much fun.

Since she wouldn't let him move his injured arm, they merely walked through the country dances to the sole accompaniment of his voice. He sang nonsense, some of it in rhyme, until she joined in with her own efforts. The result was often hilarious, although he wasn't sure it improved her dance steps. She seemed to get muddled as to which hand to offer and which way to turn, but she possessed a natural grace that would carry her through.

"You'll do," he pronounced, "Though we haven't waltzed yet."

For a change, he began to whistle a popular waltz tune, and she instinctively lifted her arms like a mirror image of his. She flushed, withdrawing her hand from his waist before she'd quite touched him. Taking her hand, he placed it on his shoulder, swept his good arm around her waist, and took her other hand in his, keeping it lower than usual to avoid opening his wound.

Having whistled the introductory bars, he moved into the main theme with enthusiasm, and suddenly found himself driven backward, sideways, and turned. It was hard to whistle and laugh at the same time, but he did his best for several moments before the laughter took over.

"Oh dear," she said, quite prepared to join in. "Am I as bad as all that?"

"No, no, you're graceful, enthusiastic…decisive! Only it's customary for the man to lead."

"Oh." She flushed, quite adorably. "In the only dancing lessons I've had, I usually took the man's part with Elvira and my younger cousins. I suppose I have to throw off the habit."

"I don't mind following you," he assured her. "Only, I'll forget and we'll end up both leading and either falling into each other or pulling in opposite directions. Besides, your other partners might not quite like it."

"I suspect they wouldn't," she agreed.

"This time," he said, taking her back into his arms. "You follow where I lead. Without looking at your feet."

"Very well. And maybe I should sing this time? Then you can laugh more easily."

He grinned. "We'll both sing and see who laughs first."

It was still funny, as she fought with her natural inclination to go her own way, but she was happy enough to laugh at herself, and after a few minutes, singing in perfect if breathless harmony with him, she relaxed into the dance.

Dax found it unexpectedly sweet to hold her, this only erratically remembered childhood friend who'd grown into such a lovely young woman. Her eyes smiled in between bouts of endearing concentration, and she felt soft and supple in his arms. Moreover, she was his wife. He could hold her improperly close if he wanted to—and he did, only refraining out of respect for her. For he was a very physical man, and his desire was obvious enough to scare her into a hasty divorce.

More than that, though, his memory of the night they'd bolted to Gretna Green was returning in flashes. And the upsurge of inconvenient lust for his new wife inspired another sudden recollection. Her sweet lips yielding to his, kissing him back with a naive, melting eagerness that had inflamed him then and still did. He could remember the soft curve of her breast under his mouth and the warmth of her smooth skin.

He wasn't entirely sure she'd told the truth that he'd only gone to sleep. He might well have ravished her in his drunken stupor. He only hoped he hadn't hurt her. At least she didn't appear to be afraid of him, although from her heightened color and occasional breathlessness, she wasn't quite comfortable being so close to him.

Nevertheless, he was reluctant to let her go, and only did so when the tea tray was brought in—not by Carson or even Clara, but by Daniel Doone, the other two following behind.

Dax supposed he should feel embarrassed at being discovered dancing with his own wife in the middle of the day, while singing with her, too. However, his chief emotion was irritation at being interrupted. As a result of which, dropping his hands from Willa, he scowled at Doone.

"You don't work for me."

"I don't know what else to do to apologize," the man said miserably. "Mr. Carson suggested I carry the tray."

"Carson's an idle opportunist. Put it down on the table and go away."

"What have you got there?" Willa asked Clara, who was clutching a large box.

"It was delivered from Madame Monique," Clara explained. "So I brought it up with me."

"Oh goodness, another gown," Willa said, awed. "Do you suppose it's the turquoise silk?"

"Yes," said Dax, who'd sent word to Monique to that effect.

He found it rather fun to look after Willa, and in a novel kind of way. Of course, he'd been known to dance somewhat erratic attendance on his mistresses, but it had always been in return for favors, whether explicit or understood. With Willa, he had nothing to gain but her happiness. Perhaps it had begun as responsibility, because he'd put her in this impossible situation, but he'd discovered he liked it.

AFTER TEA, DAX left Willa preparing for a bath, with both Carson and Doone vying to carry the hot water for her. Dax suspected it was a ruse on Carson's part, to get Doone to do most of the work. Nevertheless, for someone who'd spent all her life pandering to other people's unreasonable whims, Willa did seem to have the knack of inspiring devotion in those around her.

Dax strolled downstairs to the foyer, which was quiet at this hour and, discovering a young man he recognized at reception, he asked him about Shelby's purse.

"The lady gave it to me for Miss Haines," the boy said nervously. "Lady Shelby's maid."

"Yes, I remember that. And did you give it to Miss Haines?"

"First thing in the morning, sir, just before I went off-duty. Did I do wrong?"

Daxton regarded him. He could have been lying. But he'd have to have been pretty stupid to steal the purse, knowing he'd be the first suspect when it went missing. "No, you did exactly what was asked of you," Dax said carelessly. "Someone else has mislaid it."

Deep in thought, Dax sauntered off to explore the seedier parts of town. Here, he became distracted by an elaborately out-of-place building with Greek columns flanking its vast, pink front door. Curtains of fine black velvet hung in the nearest window.

"Might have known I'd find you here," said a familiar voice, and Dax turned to find Lord Tamar at his side, The down-at-heels artist carried what looked like several canvasses wrapped in cloth under one arm.

"Where is here?" Daxton inquired. "Because if I didn't know better—"

"You do, dear boy, you do. It's precisely what you think, and a rather fine example, too. Unexpected in Blackhaven, but there you are. I'll introduce you, if you like."

It was tempting, particularly given his recent unrequited lusts, but Dax only grinned and shook his head. "How big a cad do you think I am? I've only been married five minutes."

"Five minutes, five years, don't see that it makes any difference," Tamar said, reasonably enough, though he walked on without any further attempts at persuasion. "Your marriage does seem to have taken the world by surprise."

"None of the world's business," Dax said repressively.

"Perfectly true, but you can't blame it for being interested. The newspapers have followed your exploits for years."

"Mostly lies," Dax said, from habit.

"So, what brought the world's wickedest bachelor to marriage at last?"

Daxton scowled. "I like her."

"Suspect you liked lots of others before her, too. Didn't marry any of 'em, did you?"

"They were married already," Dax admitted. "Apart from the opera dancers." It had, generally, been part of the attraction, even with the gorgeously adventurous Helena, his last mistress. "And don't start lecturing me. It would be rich coming from a man so well known in the town's only brothel!"

"That *would* be rich indeed," Tamar agreed. "For anyone in my family. Forgive the nosiness. Are you taking Lady Dax to the ball tonight?"

"I have that honor,"

"Ask her to put me down for a waltz."

"They're all taken," Dax said at once. "Have you been before? What's it like? Horribly provincial?"

Tamar shrugged. "I suppose so. Don't go to London much myself, so I'm no judge. There will be cards and dancing and champagne. Pretty women—even beautiful and interesting women. You'll know some of them. Kate Grant, who used to be Lady Crowmore, and her eccentric vicar husband. Lady Arabella and Captain Alban, if you're lucky. The Wickendens, of course, and their Spanish stepmother."

"You like it here," Dax accused.

"More than I expected, to," Tamar admitted. "I expected to find only sick and spoiled people, just hoped they'd be self-absorbed enough to want their portraits painted! And have fond enough memories of the place to buy my landscapes. But the place sucks you in. You come for a month and stay for three."

Dax, who had no intention of staying even three weeks, said nothing.

"This street leads back up to the harbor," Tamar told him. "And here is the tavern from hell, where one can, nevertheless, buy exquisite brandy. Care to join me?"

Dax considered. "Not now," he said at last. "After the ball."

"Deal," Tamar said, and swerved into the tavern. A miasma of smoke and noise drifted out into the street in the brief moments that the door was opened. It reminded Dax of many a convivial evening, but, curiously, he had no regrets about walking away.

A COUPLE OF HOURS later, Dax emerged from his bedchamber in his best black satin breeches and perfectly fitting coat. For once, he'd paid attention to his cravat and thought optimistically, that even Wickenden might approve of it. Not that he cared overmuch. He was still enjoying the novelty of impressing his wife if he could.

God knew that worked both ways. She spilled out of her own

bedchamber, resplendent in the turquoise silk gown over the paler lace underdress, her hair dressed higher than usual, leaving a long, shining coil to fall to her creamy right shoulder.

"How do I look?" she asked, twirling for his benefit.

"Stunning," he managed. For he'd never seen her look more beautiful. It wasn't the dress, he thought. Or not just that. The new turquoise jewels winked in her ears, at her throat, and around her wrist, emphasizing the fine color of her eyes, but it wasn't those either. They only reflected her beauty.

She was happy.

The realization made him smile. "You are beautiful and will outshine every woman present."

She laughed. "I won't. But I feel almost pretty. And elegant. Thank you, Dax. And I must say, you're looking very smart yourself."

It was almost like approaching a stranger. The lust of the afternoon hadn't gone, it was only enhanced now by something very like awe. It was a heady combination. Perhaps she read something in his eyes, for her cheeks flushed slightly under his gaze, and she began fussing with her bracelet.

"I don't think it's properly fastened," she murmured.

As she bent over her wrist, his gaze fell on the pale curve of her neck. He wanted to press his lips there.

"Let me," he said.

Almost reluctantly, she let one hand fall away and offered him the other. He unfastened the bracelet, adjusted the clip, and refastened it. "There."

Because he couldn't help it, he bent over her wrist and softly kissed the skin by the bracelet. Her pulse galloped under his lips.

Slowly, she raised her eyes to his, and for the first time, he read something very like fear. And yet, she didn't run or even pull away. He straightened, drawing her hand through his arm as though nothing had happened.

But something had. Something huge. He wanted his wife. And not just as he'd wanted various other women throughout his adult life.

This was different, wrapped in care and wonder. He wanted to seduce her very badly, and he didn't doubt that he could. But he wanted it to matter to her. For the first time in his life, he wanted to spend time courting and winning a woman. And he didn't even know why.

Chapter Seven

WILLA WAS UNDENIABLY shaken. Although the delicate caress of his lips on her wrist had caused her skin to tingle, it was the sudden intensity in his eyes that made her heart really race. She didn't even know why, or what that look signified, just that it tuned her inside out.

Over dinner, taken publicly in the hotel dining room, he told her he'd spoken to the clerk to whom she'd delivered the purse.

"He gave it to Lady Shelby's maid as you asked, so either the maid stole it or your aunt is simply being mean. I don't think the clerk's lying."

Willa thought about it. "I don't think my aunt was either. She really thought I'd stolen from her to bribe you into marriage with me."

Daxton blinked. "If I need to be bribed, it would take a lot more than that paltry sum."

"It isn't paltry to her." Willa frowned. "But I can't see Haines stealing from them. She's utterly devoted to my aunt and cousins, especially Ralph—" She broke off, her eyes widening. "She gave it to Ralph! He has engineered this whole thing to hurt us."

"Well, he can't, can he?" Dax said reasonably. "Both he and his mother would look incredibly foolish if they accused you of stealing something half of Blackhaven saw me win from him. Even without the clerk's testimony."

"That is true," she said, only partially relieved. "But he is vindictive, Dax, and he never forgets."

Dax cast her a suddenly perceptive glance, but he didn't ask, merely offered her more wine.

After dinner, they strolled along High Street to the Assembly Rooms. The street was well-swept for the event, so that ladies were in little danger of dragging their skirts through the usual dirt on the road.

The Assembly building was new and ornate, with several doors leading off a gracious foyer. A group of military officers were escorting several dazzlingly bejeweled ladies through double doors at the end of the hall. Music and happy chatter drifted from inside.

"Change your shoes and do any last-minute primping in the cloak-room over there," Dax murmured. He knew she had no experience of attending events like these. "I'll wait for you here."

In the last few days, Willa had attended a disreputable party full of rogues and courtesans, eloped with a drunk stranger, and faced an angry gunman. Yet suddenly, nothing in her life had ever seemed quite so frightening as approaching that cloakroom alone.

Worse, as soon as she stepped inside, she came face to face with Lady Shelby. Magnificent in a lavender silk gown and the last diamonds Ralph had not yet sold, she looked down upon Willa with more contempt than surprise.

A lifetime of submission—with only occasional, well-punished revolts—should have sent Willa scurrying out of her path. But surprise seemed to have rooted her feet to the floor. Several other women stopped talking to watch the encounter.

And it was Lady Shelby's gaze that fell. "Lady Daxton," she murmured in a repeat of the previous night's meeting, and stepped aside.

"Aunt," Willa returned.

"Elvira!" Lady Shelby snapped.

Elvira scurried across the room. She might have been *enceinte*, but there was no obvious sign of it. She too glittered with jewels, some of which even winked in her diaphanous pale lemon ball gown. The gown was cut exquisitely, obviously by some hideously expensive artist of the needle in London.

For the first time, Willa wondered if she looked merely provincial to London eyes, and not the elegant lady she was imagining herself.

But as her cousin looked her up and down, a twinge of envy sparked in Elvira's eyes.

"Very fine, Cousin," she tried to sneer.

"Thank you. You look very well yourself," Willa said generously, and with a slight bow, she passed on to the nearest vacant chair.

As her aunt and cousin left, she hoped no one could see that she was shaking. This was ridiculous, but she'd never felt so uncomfortable in her life. She'd been expecting her aunt to yell "Thief!" at her. But convention and precedence had got in the way. Before she made such an accusation against a peeress of the realm, she would need to see how society welcomed—or did not the new Viscountess Daxton.

When she was with Dax, she simply enjoyed the fun of it. Here, surrounded by strangers avid for gossip, strangers who must have heard by now of Daxton's shocking elopement and mésalliance, she felt suddenly very small and alone. And it was a very different kind of loneliness from that she'd grown used to in the Shelby household.

Almost blindly, she unfastened her shoes and slipped them off. She wished she'd brought Clara for the purpose, since a few other ladies seemed to have maids with them.

"Lady Daxton," someone greeted her as she donned her new dancing slippers.

Jerking her head up, she recognized young Lady Wickenden, whose face was just as kind and friendly as yesterday.

Willa returned the greeting with relief.

"Do you know Mrs. Grant?" Lady Wickenden inquired, drawing forward an astonishingly beautiful young woman with jet-black hair, wearing a gown of dusky pink gauze.

"How do you do?" Willa murmured, hoping she didn't sound awkward.

"I have been hoping to meet you," Mrs. Grant said. "I'm acquainted with your husband."

She was sure Dax would make it his business to be acquainted with anyone as lovely as Mrs. Grant. It was a lowering thought, for she could not compete.

"And your aunt," Mrs. Grant added.

"Oh dear," Willa said before she could help it. She would be ostra-cized utterly by Blackhaven society.

To her surprised, Mrs. Grant's eyes danced. Nor did her amuse-ment appear to be malicious. "Welcome to Blackhaven. Don't be daunted. Everyone likes to know everyone else's business, but they are good people, like Gillie here, who is a native."

"And you are not?" Willa managed.

"Lord, no, I just married the vicar," said the surprising Mrs. Grant.

Although both Lady Wickenden and Mrs. Grant seemed ready to leave the cloakroom, they waited for her to put her dancing slippers on and walked out on either side of her.

Dax waited where he'd left her, although he'd been joined by Lord Wickenden. Just as Willa had expected, her husband broke into smiles as he saw Mrs. Grant.

"Dax, you reprobate," she greeted him, giving him her hand. "Do you have to set society by the ears in every town?"

"Only if society has got nothing better to do that pay me any atten-tion," Dax said, bowing over her hand. "Do you know, you're more beautiful than ever? The sticks must agree with you." He dropped her hand as a modestly dressed but very good-looking man hurried through the front doors and came straight toward them. "Is this your vicar?" he asked outrageously.

"Yes," Mrs. Grant said, quite unoffended as she took her husband's arm with quite natural affection. "This is my vicar, Tristram Grant. Tris, Lord and Lady Daxton."

Mr. Grant might have been expected to look somewhat askance at Daxton for any number of reasons, not least of them the friendliness of the acknowledged rake with his wife, but he merely shook hands with perfect courtesy and congratulated Daxton on his marriage before requesting a dance of Willa.

"Get in line, Grant," Wickenden drawled. And by the time they reached the ballroom door, Willa had promised a dance to each.

"You'll be fine, now," Mrs. Grant murmured. "Wickenden for

cachet and Tristram for respectability. Of a sort! Just enjoy yourself."

And before she could recover from the astonishment of that, her hand was once again on Daxton's arm and they were being formally announced at the door.

Although the music didn't stop, the noise dropped markedly as everyone turned to stare at the runaway couple.

Instinctively, Willa lifted her chin in defiance.

"That's the girl," Dax breathed. "Let 'em look."

For whatever reason, Daxton's friends seemed to have decided to look after her. They all sat together, sipping champagne until Mr. Grant claimed his dance with Willa. At the same time, Dax stood up with Lady Wickenden, although he winked encouragingly at his wife.

"You'll forgive me if I step on your toes?" Willa said earnestly to Mr. Grant. "Oh, and please just drag me back if I go in the wrong direction. I'm not used to dancing."

Mr. Grant looked amused. "I think I'd rather just go with you and see if everyone else follows. You'll be credited with a new dance."

Willa couldn't help laughing, and in fact, the unusual vicar was so entertaining that she forgot to be anxious and simply enjoyed his company.

And from then, it seemed, her social success was assured. Daxton, Lady Wickenden, and Mrs. Grant were all besieged for introductions to her and her dance card was quickly filled, all but the two waltzes of the evening, which she had kept for Dax.

For a time, Dax watched her success with an air of pride. Then, as if reassured she didn't need him, he sauntered off to the card room. He hadn't emerged by the time Lord Tamar strolled into the ballroom and swerved almost immediately in Willa's direction.

At the time, she sat with the amiable Lady Wickenden enjoying a rare moment of rest and trying not to be disappointed that Dax was late for their dance. For the orchestra had just struck up the strains of a waltz, and couples were taking to the floor.

Lord Tamar, who appeared to be wearing the same worn coat as before, without any of the niceties of evening wear, greeted the ladies in his unconventional way, and asked Lady Wickenden if she would mind very much being deprived of her companion during the waltz.

"If Lady Dax will dance with me, that is," he added with his engaging smile.

"You're very kind," Willa said gratefully, "but I have promised the waltz to Dax."

"Oh no," Tamar said in shocked tones. "Even I know you don't dance with your own husband! Tell her, Lady Wickenden. Besides..." He looked around him ostentatiously. "I don't see him."

"Tamar," Lady Wickenden said quietly, but at that moment her husband appeared, distracting her with a glass of lemonade.

Another glance toward the card room door convinced Willa that Dax was not coming. Well, she would not sit there pining stupidly. Dax would be the last man to expect it. In fact, he would quickly find her clinging annoying. Besides which, Tamar was his old friend, and Willa rather liked him.

She stood up. "Very well then."

Grant for respectability and Wickenden for cachet, she remembered. And Tamar for a hint of social recklessness. But then, a woman just married by elopement to Lord Daxton must surely be regarded already as just about as reckless as it was possible to be.

"You must talk Dax into letting me paint you both," Tamar said as they danced, his intense eyes scanning her face. "The portrait will be my wedding gift to you."

"That would be very kind of you, especially considering you haven't seen him for so long. I'm not sure a gift is required."

"Oh, it is," he assured her. "We were very thick together at school."

"I imagine the pair of you got up to all sorts of mischief."

He grinned reminiscently. "Oh, we did. We even managed to escape and play with the town lads at night. Made friends with them after a couple of fights.... Used to row across to Windsor sometimes, too, in secret. Then there were the cows... But there, I won't bore you."

"Oh, I'm not remotely bored," she assured him. "Tell me more." For the rest of the dance, he entertained her with tales of their adventures and troubles at school, how they'd got the better of older boys through cunning and sticking together, and punishments they'd taken for breaking the rules. He told it all in a very amusing style so that she couldn't help laughing and yet she sensed a certain sadness behind the light words.

"You must have missed each other when you left."

Tamar gave a lopsided smile. "Well, I missed him for a bit. But there you are. Typical of the old man to die so inconveniently. Didn't you know Dax as a child, too?"

"Yes, a little. I lived with my aunt, Lady Shelby. We spent summers and Christmastides at Gore Park, which marches with Dacre Abbey land, so we all spent a lot of time together."

The dance came to a close and she sank into a curtsey.

Tamar bowed in return, and placed her hand in his arm. "And now I believe it's supper. Was that not well-planned of me?"

"Yes, it was," said Dax cheerfully, seeming to materialize on her other side. "I've found us all a table in the dining room. Lady Wickenden is defending it from all comers. Did he stand on your toes?"

"No," Willa replied. "More amazingly, neither did I stand on his."

"I believe I saved her from a fate worse than death," Tamar said provokingly. "Dancing with her own husband."

"How very brave of you to step in," Dax said. He was clearly bantering, and yet beneath that, Willa sensed he wasn't quite pleased.

But Tamar was suddenly distracted. "Lord, Dax, do you remember our duel at school?"

Dax grinned, any ill-nature apparently forgotten. "Dawn in the dorm, with swords. Well, carved sticks with sharpened points."

"They were lethal, looking back. It's as well we were rumbled, and old Sour Face stopped it."

"I don't know, I was about to stab you in the sword arm."

"You *did* stab me in the sword arm. I've still got the scar."

"I've got one in my side I owe to you," Dax recalled. "We were pretty evenly matched in those days."

"Well, I gather you've surpassed me in affairs of honor since then."

"It's not the same with pistols," Dax said carelessly. "It's over too quickly." He glanced down at Willa's no-doubt appalled expression, and nudged her with his elbow. "It's just nonsense," he said, a little too quickly. "Don't take us seriously."

WATCHING HIS COUSIN WILLA go into supper surrounded by fashionable and titled people, all of whom seemed to be making a quite unnecessary fuss over her, Sir Ralph Shelby felt more outraged than ever. She had run away, with *Daxton*, the most infamous rake in the country.

Admittedly, Daxton had taken him by surprise by actually marrying Willa, but nevertheless, respectable people should have shunned her. Instead, Wickenden himself, quite a leader of London society, had danced with her. Lady Wickenden and even the damned vicar's wife, seemed to have made a friend of her. Of course the vicar's wife was the notorious Kate Crowmore, so one could expect no better of her!

But still, somehow, his scheming little minx of a penniless cousin had turned her disgrace into a shining social success, one that even his mother's missing purse had done little to tarnish. Yet...

The purse, of course, was another grudge, for although it was Haines who had managed to lose it, he found it easier to blame Willa and Daxton for the whole sorry mess.

"Your pardon, sir," said a tiny voice at his side. "May I pass?"

Instinctively, Ralph stepped back and found a small, rather mousy young lady smiling timorously. "Thank you. I lost my brother in the crush and I think he must have gone into supper without me."

She touched her hair nervously as she hurried past, and the bright candle light glinted off a large, diamond bracelet on her wrist. Mousy and wealthy, he judged, just as his lost heiress, the Duke of Kelburn's daughter, had been reputed to be.

"One moment, ma'am," he said, hastily stepping after her. "Let me help you find your brother. It is quite daunting to enter such a crowded place alone. My name is Shelby. Sir Ralph Shelby, at your service."

"How do you do, sir?" she twittered. "I'm Lydia Tranter. Perhaps you know my brother? Robert Tranter?"

"I shall find him for you," Ralph soothed as he conducted her onward in gentlemanly fashion. "Do you live in Blackhaven?"

"Oh no, we have brought our mother here for her health, but it is a charming place, is it not? And informal, so different from what I've been used to…"

"And what is it you are used to?" Ralph inquired pleasantly.

"Oh, you know what is like with old names and large, established houses, all tradition and uncomfortable formality…"

"Tell me more," Ralph said. At last, it seemed, his luck was turning.

WITH HER HUSBAND once more at her side, Willa found supper the most fun of all. Growing in confidence, she relaxed and joined in the quick-witted banter that flew back and forth across the table, and not just among the men. She found she liked both Lady Wickenden and Mrs. Grant, who were nothing at all like the ladies who called on her aunt and cousins.

"You and Dax must come to dinner at the vicarage tomorrow evening," Mrs. Grant said idly as they walked together back to the main ballroom.

"Thank you," Willa said in some surprise. She cast a slightly shy smile at the other woman. "You and Lady Wickenden are being very kind to me."

"Oh, Gillie's kind to everyone."

"And you are not?"

Mrs. Grant's lips twisted slightly. After a moment, she said, "Unhappy people are often unkind through carelessness. Through concentrating too much on their own unhappiness and not enough on those around them."

Willa regarded her more closely. "Are you talking about yourself?" she asked bluntly. "Or Dax?"

Since they entered the ballroom, Mrs. Grant had a good excuse not to answer. In truth, Willa wasn't sure she wanted to know, but perversely, she pursued the issue.

"Do you imagine Dax is unkind to me?" she blurted.

"Well, marrying you at the border is a somewhat scandalous start to a marriage. To some. I was married by special license myself, so I can say nothing against it."

"You feel sorry for me." It was a bit of a jolt. She'd imagined they were almost friends, that the other women liked her.

"Oh goodness, I feel sorry for everyone who is a pawn in marriage."

"Pawn?" Willa repeated indignantly. But, of course, she was. She was Dax's means to his inheritance and she was pretty sure Mrs. Grant knew that, too. "Dax is not the only one who benefits from the marriage, you know. My life was not—" She broke off, appalled at saying so much.

Mrs. Grant sat down, catching Willa's hand to draw her into the next chair. "Not very tolerable," she guessed. "I can see that. And I know it's none of my business. You and Dax seem to understand each other better than I'd hoped. I *like* Dax, but no one could call him stable. Perhaps you're just what he needs, but... Equally, you've lived a sheltered life and you may not be entirely aware of what you've taken on as his wife. Don't look like that, Willa, I'm not insulting you or him. I just want you to know you have friends. Please don't cut me, and please *do* come to dinner."

Willa couldn't help laughing at Mrs. Grant's comical expression, and she was aware her initial umbrage was not deserved. Mrs. Grant was right. She was very hazy on Dax's misdeeds and exactly what constituted a rakehell.

She had married a charming rake on impulse, in the hope that she could win his love and save him from his dangerously ruinous lifestyle. But she should be prepared for that never to happen. It was at least as likely—more likely—that she would have to live in unhappiness and hide it from him, from everyone.

"To the devil with fashion," Dax said, standing before her with his hand held out. "Will you dance with me, new wife?"

She took his hand and stood. "I believe I will, new husband."

She did it largely for Kate Grant's benefit. But as they walked across the room to the opening strains of the waltz, she said, "Is it really not acceptable for married couples to dance together?"

"I'm told not. Except at wedding parties, of course, and we haven't yet had one of those, so perhaps no one will ostracize us."

"Ostracize!" Willa repeated, startled.

Dax laughed. "I was joking. *Laugh at us* might be more appropriate."

"We don't have to dance," she said reluctantly.

He paused. "It's up to you. Personally, I don't care who sniggers, or who even notices, and I want to dance with you. But I'm happy to do anything else you wish instead."

She met his gaze, curiously. "I don't remember you being this accommodating."

"I'm not. I'm a selfish bas—I'm selfish."

She smiled and began to walk again. "Then I would love to dance."

He laughed. "I've never been rewarded for selfishness before."

"I doubt that's true. You just haven't noticed."

"Ouch."

"Oh, I wasn't criticizing," she assured him as they arrived on the floor, and he whisked her into the dance.

"I know," he said ruefully. "You are quite wonderful, aren't you, Willa Blake?"

The new flush to her cheeks might have been due to the sudden exertion of the dance. "I don't see why," she muttered.

"It might be something to do with the way your eyes laugh," he mused. "Or perhaps the dimple."

"What dimple?"

"I can't show you here. People would definitely talk. But I like that I can still see my fun little friend in the beautiful woman you are tonight."

She tore her gaze from his, to stare instead at the buttons of his coat. "I suppose that is flattery. You don't need to say such things to me, Dax."

"Then what shall I say to you?" he asked softly, and it came to her at last, belatedly, that he was *flirting* with her.

Her gaze widened as it returned to his. "You could tell me exactly what a rakehell is," she said breathlessly.

A shout of laughter escaped him, causing several curious heads to turn in their direction. Dax didn't appear to notice, merely swung her around with a trifle too much exuberance.

"I suppose he's a fellow who kicks up a lot of trouble," he said. "Drinking, gambling, that kind of thing."

"*All* gentlemen do those things, don't they?"

"True. Rakehells just take them to extremes, usually in low dens rather than respectable establishments."

"And get into fights?"

"Frequently."

"Duels?" she hazarded.

"Occasionally."

"Womanizing?"

"Are we talking about me or rakehells in general?"

"I'm not perfectly sure," she confessed. "I'm just trying to understand what your life is like."

"Hectic and hedonistic," he said flippantly. "Which is why I married you."

"Well, it's very kind of you to say so."

Startlement leapt in his eyes. "*Kind?* I'm not known for it. Willa, I was excessively drunk and I behaved badly to you, but I *am* glad I married you." A smile flickered across his face. "And I'll do my best to see that you don't regret it too much. Was Kate warning you about me?"

"I believe she meant it kindly."

"I suppose there's a lot to warn against," he said ruefully. "But we can be friends, can't we?"

She nodded dumbly. Being friends was a beginning, but she wanted so much more and so badly, that she could barely breathe.

His thumb moved against her gloved hand in an absent caress. "And we waltz pretty well together."

"I let you lead."

"Then maybe it's your turn."

"Really?" In spite of everything, laughter caught in her throat.

"Really."

So she did, and it worked well for almost a minute before he had to practically lift her off the ground and swing her around to avoid crashing into a staid couple who danced with no panache whatever.

"Sorry," Willa said. "I can't see over you!"

"All part of the fun," he assured her.

And bizarrely, it was.

THE DAXTONS LEFT the Assembly Rooms together, in perfect charity with each other, having promised to go to the Grants' for dinner tomorrow evening. They walked back to the hotel arm in arm, Willa listening to the hasty beats of her heart as she gazed up at the sky. Its glittering beauty seemed to reinforce her happiness. Like Dax, she would live in the moment and simply enjoy his presence at her side, and the strange excitement it brought her.

In companionable silence, they entered the hotel and made their way to their rooms. A lamp burned low on the side table. Dax turned it up and took off the shade to light a few candles from it.

A bump from behind the door of the servant's bedchamber told Willa that Clara had taken possession. But she kept to her room, and there was no sign of Carson. Willa was glad. She peeled off her gloves and dropped her gauze shawl—yet another gift from Dax—onto the sofa.

Dax, having brightened the room, walked back to her. The candle flames spread golden light across his handsome face and hair. And yet as he moved, she was aware of the shadows too, beneath his fine cheekbones and across his determined chin. They made him a stranger, as dangerous, perhaps, as everyone said, but one she was beginning to know, one she *wanted* to know.

"I enjoyed this evening," he said, coming to a halt only inches away from her.

She could smell him, the pleasant oil from his soap, a hint of wine behind the distinctive, earthy scent she'd come to associate with him.

"So did I," she managed.

"I'm glad," he said softly. "I think we deal pretty well together."

"I hope so," she replied with more calm than she felt.

He leaned closer, filling her with fright as well as longing. But he only took her hand, raising it to his lips. His kiss lingered on her skin, sweet and thrilling. And then he turned her hand over, unfastening the bracelet, and again, pressed his lips to her wrist.

He lifted his head, his thumb caressing where his lips had been. "I can feel your pulse racing," he said huskily. "Is that for me?"

Heat suffused her. It came with embarrassment as well as yearning. And yet she could only ever be honest.

"Yes," she admitted.

A smile flickered across his shadowed face. "I'm glad. One day...one day, when you're used to me, I'd like to see if I can't make it beat faster yet."

She was afraid to breathe. His gaze slipped from her eyes to her lips. She couldn't speak, to encourage or even to make light of his words.

"Good night, Willa," he murmured and released her hand.

Disappointment flooded her, especially when he stood back, walked to the table, and picked up his hat. With a last smile that melted her exposed heart, he sauntered to the door—not his bed-chamber door, but the passage door.

But where are you going? Stay here with me. The words in her heart stayed buried. But with the click of the latch behind him, she wanted to weep.

OF ALL THE SIGHTS Sir Ralph Shelby expected to see in Miss Pinkie's house of ill-repute, his mother's missing purse was certainly not one of them.

But there it was in the lap of some ill-bred fellow in an obviously new but badly made suit of clothes. He looked like a working man aping the fashions of the middling classes. He was good-looking in a rough kind of a way, but had the air of a man who'd knock his fellows down without much regret.

Which was the trouble with establishments like Miss Pinkie's. They admitted anyone who could pay, regardless of birth or breeding. Someone like Daxton might have been comfortable rubbing shoulders with riff-raff and rogues, but Ralph's standards were higher.

However, even he had to assuage the desires of the flesh, and so Miss Pinkie's was a necessary service.

The man with his purse was bestowing largesse liberally on the girls who sat on either side of him—presumably as a tip, since he immediately stood and strolled away toward the door.

Ralph followed him into the hall. "Your pardon," he said haughtily, and the man turned to him in surprise. "I couldn't help noticing your purse, for I have one just like it."

The man's eyes shifted tellingly, but he only said jauntily, "Good for you, mate."

Ralph curled his lip. "I ought to say, I *had* one just like it. It was stolen from my servant in the Blackhaven Hotel."

"Never," the man marveled.

Ralph stepped closer. "I see you like to have a little easy money, to facilitate, no doubt, the finer things in life. New coats, women, a little respect for your wealth."

The man's eyes narrowed. "Who wouldn't?"

"Exactly. And so, I have a choice to lay before you. I could summon the Watch, and you should know there are many respectable witnesses in Blackhaven who can declare that that purse is mine. Or—" He held up one finger to silence the furious and pointless denials about to erupt from the fellow's mouth. "Don't bother. You're known here and, I suspect, all over town. It would be easy for local magistrates to track you down. But I am a generous man. I would rather reward you. Or at least, employ you."

Clearly intrigued, the man came nearer. "In what capacity?"

"Breaking the law," Ralph said. "As you're clearly so good at it."

The man grinned. "If it pays well enough."

"If you get rid of my particular problem, and I do mean get rid—permanently—it will pay you very well indeed. Unless it ever comes back to me."

Chapter Eight

THE FOLLOWING MORNING, Willa broke her fast alone, served by Clara, who was thrilled to show her the new riding habit which had been delivered from Madame Monique, along with another two day dresses. Willa admired them enthusiastically, and was disgusted with herself that as soon as Daxton's bedchamber door opened, all her attention flew immediately in that direction.

However, it was only Carson who emerged, whistling. "Morning, m'lady," he greeted her.

"Good morning, Carson. Is his lordship within?" she asked casually. She hadn't heard him come back last night, but then she'd slept like the dead from the moment her head touched the pillow.

"No, m'lady. He'll be back shortly, though."

Stupidly, her heart sank. She'd always known what Dax was, and what life with him would be like. She didn't expect him to stay in or to attend only the most respectable social functions with her. Fashionable husbands and wives lived largely sperate lives outside the home, and she would have died rather than constrain Dax to be with her through guilt or duty. She would have to learn just to enjoy her moments with him and find her own way for the rest of the time so that he didn't feel obliged to look after her. And after last night, she had invitations to call on several local ladies. Lady Wickenden had even spoken of arranging some expedition of pleasure in the countryside.

Her gaze fell on the new riding habit draped over the back of a chair. "Carson, where does one hire a horse in Blackhaven?"

"Livery stables," said Dax, breezing in through the outer door just in time to hear her question. "And I've found you a beautiful little mare."

Her heart skipped a beat, as it often seemed to around him. She couldn't help being pleased that he wore well-fitting buff breeches and a blue coat, rather than last night's black evening clothes as she'd more than half expected.

"Oh, thank you, Dax! How did you know that riding was exactly what I wanted to do today?"

"I guessed from the new habit," he said with a quick grin.

"Do I have to take a groom?" she asked.

"Not if I'm with you."

"But you're not allowed to ride," she protested, indicating his injured arm.

"We won't go far and I'll only use one hand."

"I'm not sure that works," she said doubtfully.

"Well, if it opens the wound, we'll just have to get the quack back. Hurry and change."

IT WAS TOO easy to forget Daxton's injury as they rode along the beach under the turreted castle they could see from all over the town, and then up the path to the hills beyond it.

"That must be Braithwaite's pile," Dax observed. "Wonder if he's at home?"

"Is he a friend of yours?"

"Not anymore," Dax said. "He told me off for compromising his sister."

"Oh dear," Willa said uneasily. "You didn't, did you?"

"No, it was a fuss about nothing. We danced together a few times at some party—possibly more than the requisite twice. I don't perfectly recall, to be honest, expect I was foxed—and the old bore they'd betrothed her to took exception to my *singling her out.*"

"Did you apologize?" Willa asked.

"Lord, no. Told Braithwaite they shouldn't tie such a lively girl to such a dullard. It was asking for trouble. And that if she was happy about the marriage, she wouldn't be flirting with me."

"I don't expect he liked that."

"He didn't. If we had been in his house, he'd have thrown me out. Since we were in mine, he had to make do with stalking out. He hasn't spoken to me since."

Now that he told the story, she realized she'd heard something similar being discussed among her cousins just before she'd left for Blackhaven. She looked at Dax, preparing for pain. "Were you in love with Lady Serena?"

"Good God, no," he said with satisfying astonishment. "And before you ask, she ain't in love with me, either. She just wanted a little amusement at a very dull party. Look at the view from here. Isn't this another of Tamar's scenes?"

"Yes, I believe it is. He caught it very well, I think."

"He was showing me some of his other paintings last night. I never expected him to have such a talent."

"Did you see him after the ball, then?"

"Yes, we drank contraband brandy in a seedy tavern and once the sailors started to fight, we backed off and went to his studio instead. He lives there among paints and canvasses. You have to see the place."

"I'd love to," she said warmly, delighted not so much by where he'd been but that he'd told her.

After a very pleasant and companionable ride, they returned the horses to the livery stable on the edge of the town and walked the rest of the way to Lord Tamar's studio. This was little more than a one room fisherman's cottage by the shore, though with spectacular views.

It was impossibly cluttered. Tamar seemed perfectly happy to sweep all the tools, sketches, and canvases off the sofa and onto the floor so that Willa could sit. Not that she wished to for very long. She preferred to flit about the room, examining all the paintings.

Only one was covered up with a paint-spattered cloth. Willa peeped beneath and found a portrait of a young couple. The lady had a refined sort of quiet beauty and she wore hazy spectacles that reflected the light, giving her a faint impression of mystery and a rather sweet vagueness. The man beside her was ruggedly handsome, with hard blue eyes. He looked restless and impatient, although his hand rested protectively on the back of the lady's chair. Behind them was the sea view from Tamar's studio window, but he'd painted it in such a way it might have been from a ship's large cabin window.

"I'm not sure whether that one's finished or not," Tamar offered, dropping onto a rug on the floor and reaching for a sketch book. "Sometimes it makes me angry because it's not right, and other times I think it's the best portrait I've ever done."

"Who are they?" Willa asked curiously.

"The Honorable Mr. and Mrs. Alban Lamont," Tamar replied. "Otherwise known as Captain Alban and Lady Arabella Niven."

"Really? Oh, I don't think Ralph ever stood a chance with her, Dax, do you?"

Dax strolled over to look. "No, she's got too much character," he pronounced. "How would you paint us, then, Rags?"

Tamar, busily sketching, said only, "Haven't decided yet."

"Do we get to decide?"

"No. But you have a right of veto."

"Fair enough. Shall we go, Willa? I think we've lost him to his muse."

Tamar grinned. "Ah, no, you *are* my muse. Or at least Lady Dax is. But go away, by all means."

"He was always the best of hosts," Dax observed.

MORE THAN THREE hundred miles away, stood the very different seaside town of Brighton, which the Prince Regent had made fashionable and overcrowded. Here, in the house she'd taken for the summer, the Countess of Romford was indulging in a fit of the vapors.

Fortunately, she did so before no larger an audience than her husband, who watched proceedings with growing irritation. Eventually, with a curse, he threw down the letter that had caused all the trouble.

"Oh for God's sake, my lady, pull yourself together!" he snapped.

When she paid him no heed, he strode to the wall and pulled the bell.

"What are you doing?" the countess demanded quite clearly.

"Ringing for your maid. I won't have this damned racket in my presence. When you've recovered, we'll talk again."

"Oh no, Romford, wait! I don't want the wretched maid. It's just the shock."

"Well, it's a shock to me, too," her husband retorted. "But you don't see me making a scene that can probably be heard in the damned Pavilion."

"Oh, stop being such a bear," the countess said crossly. "We have to put our heads together and decide what can be done about this disaster."

"Done about it? Nothing! He married the damned girl, whoever she is, to spite me. Now he can live with his own folly."

"She's Sally Shelby's niece."

Lord Romford snorted. "Well, at least he didn't marry the housemaid."

"He might as well have. Her mother's birth is unexceptionable, but George Blake was some fly-by-night flim flam merchant who abandoned them both within a year. When the mother died, the Shelbys took the child in."

Romford scowled. "Well, it could be worse, I suppose."

"No, it couldn't. I was never more taken in in my life. I remember Willa Blake as a lively, polite young girl with a lot more sense than the rest of them. She thinks she'll take my place one day as countess!"

"Well, she will," Romford said brutally.

"Over my dead body," the countess said grimly before turning on the servant who'd answered the bell. "Go away!"

The footman effaced himself.

"Gretna Green," the countess said disparagingly. "A paltry, shabby

business and easy to have overturned. All I need is Charles's cooperation."

"Why the devil would he cooperate?"

His wife regarded him with pity. "Because if I know our only son,
he's done this in a fit of drunken rage and is already regretting it. We'll
have it annulled on the grounds of nonconsummation if nothing else.
How well do you know the archbishop?"

"What archbishop? He's irrelevant if the marriage took place in
Scotland. Besides, there are no grounds for annulment in non-
consummation, only in the lack of the *ability* to consummate, and no
one's going to believe that of Daxton!"

"I'm not sure you're right about that. In any case, you must look
into the legalities. I will ensure Daxton's cooperation in shaking off this
ridiculous mésalliance."

"And how will you do that?" her lord inquired with heavy sarcasm.
"I suppose he is known for his amiability and desire to please us."

Lady Romford whisked herself to the study door. "He is known for
pleasing himself. And so, I shall go to Mrs. Holt's party."

AT THE EVENING PARTY, Lady Romford's quarry was easily discovered,
since she was her hostess. Helena Holt was beautiful, accomplished,
intelligent and, in Lady Romford's opinion, utterly amoral. It was no
wonder Daxton had been drawn to her.

Since Lady Romford had made no secret of her disapproval of her
son's relationship, no one was more surprised than Mrs. Holt when
she found herself welcoming the countess.

"We must have a cozy talk," the countess said playfully, tapping
her fan against the wrist of her son's lover.

Mrs. Holt looked understandably appalled, but as the countess had
fully intended, curiosity ensured that her host sought her out before
too many minutes had passed.

"I hear I am to congratulate you on Lord Daxton's nuptials," Mrs.

Holt drawled, as they took a turn together around the drawing room.

"I don't consider it a matter for congratulation," the countess said frankly, "and neither, I imagine, do you."

"It is immaterial to me whom he marries."

"I suppose you quarreled," Lady Romford guessed. "That will have contributed to his anger. Not that I blame you. A saint would quarrel with Charles if he's in the wrong mood. Can we at least agree that this is not the right time for him to marry anyone?"

A faint frown marred Mrs. Holt's beautiful brow. "It is done."

"And if it could be undone?"

Mrs. Holt's frown deepened. "I don't understand. What is it you want of me?"

"I want you to remind my son just why he doesn't wish to be married…at this time."

DAX DIDN'T PAY much attention to the theatre. He normally attended such establishments with the dubious intention of getting drunk with his cronies and ogling the actresses and dancers. It was quite a novelty for him to sit through an entire performance sober and actually enjoy himself.

It had been Willa's idea. Apparently, she loved the theatre, but had barely had the chance to enjoy it in the past, being kept well to the back of her aunt's box as a kind of maid to take care of shawls and such.

In Blackhaven's small theatre, Dax was quite diverted by the farce and tolerated the tragedy, but his main enjoyment came from watching his wife's rapt expressions. Leaning forward, she clearly got caught up in the whole experience, living each moment with the characters, laughing at the jokes and even wiping the odd surreptitious tear.

Her emotions ran deeply, he realized, and she'd clearly been starved of both fun and affection at the Shelbys. But in her company, it was easy to keep his anger in check, even when he saw that the Shelbys were present, too. Ralph, who was escorting his mother and sister, barely concealed his ill-grace.

With rare patience, Dax awaited his moment. Eventually, during the final interval, Ralph left his box and appeared a few moments later in the pit with more congenial company.

Since two local ladies and one of Willa's male admirers were visiting their own box, Dax took the opportunity to slip out and downstairs.

It had been Kate Grant who'd warned him that Lady Shelby had been whispering her disappointment with her niece and alluding to a purse which had vanished on the same night as Willa. Perhaps it was a measure of Dax's new maturity but he actually contemplated leaving the rumor to run its course, for surely the truth would out before long without his help. But he found he valued his wife's happiness and he didn't want anything to mar it.

He was acquainted with all of the men in Shelby's group—in fact, the young woman in the lowcut gown looked familiar, too. Strolling directly up to them, he exchanged cheerful greetings and a few jokes about the play. Only then, did he turn to Ralph, who stood stiffly beside him, acknowledging his presence by little more than a curl of the lip. Perhaps it was meant to be a smile, though Dax doubted it.

"A word, Shelby," he said easily. "Excuse us, ma'am, gentlemen. Family matters, you know." With that, he seized Shelby's arm and jerked him away from the group, toward the door to the back stairs.

"Get your hands off me," Shelby said between his teeth.

"Gladly," Dax said, releasing him. "But I'm more than happy to make this public if you don't come with me."

"Make what public?" Shelby demanded.

Dax pushed open the door and politely ushered his enemy through before following and letting the door fall back behind him.

Since the stair led to the boxes above, they were well lit, but quieter than the main staircase from the foyer.

Dax wasted no time. "It's come to my attention that your mother is spreading lies."

"If you're trying to insult my mother—"

"I'm not. I'm insulting *you* who fed her the lies. Understand, you won't hurt Willa with this nonsense. If I catch so much as one more whisper, I'll start reminding people who won that purse from you, and who gave it back to you via the hotel staff, who returned it to your mother's maid."

Under the candlelight, Shelby flushed darkly. "Left it behind, did you?" he blustered.

"Yes. Willa asked me to return it to your mother. So, you'll see why it's so paltry of you to be trying to accuse her of the crime that is entirely yours. That can easily be made public knowledge, too. The hotel staff already know. If you want to make such figures of yourself and your family, just carry on whispering your lies. I will know."

With that, Dax simply climbed the stairs away from him. He imagined he'd said enough.

FOR WILLA, THE WEEK following her marriage was the happiest of her life. There was a delicious novelty in doing exactly as she pleased, when she pleased. She had new and interesting friends who swept her along on expeditions of pleasure and improvement and invited her to all the social gatherings Blackhaven had to offer. She even had male admirers, who vied to walk with her, fetch her things, and sit beside her as well as dance. It was all rather intoxicating for a girl who'd lived most of her life in genteel drudgery.

But the best parts were the times she spent with her husband.

Dax occasionally accompanied her on her outings with Lady Wickenden and Mrs. Grant, whom she now called Gillie and Kate. And he escorted her to evening events, although he hardly lived in her pocket, especially as her acquaintance and her confidence grew. But nearly every day they had their own expeditions—riding or walking or enjoying an al fresco luncheon in the sunshine.

One evening, instead of going out, they sat together in their sitting room, each reading their own book and occasionally watching the sea which could be glimpsed over the rooftops from their window. Once, she glanced up and found him watching her.

"What?" she asked, as once before. "Have I a smut on my nose?"

"No. I was just thinking what a restful person you are. I can't remember the last time I just sat in peace."

"Is that good?" she asked lightly, suddenly afraid that she was boring him.

He smiled. "I think so."

Of course, he went out later on, but the peace and the closeness stayed with her.

Often, they spent time with Lord Tamar, who worked every day on their portrait. Usually. Once, when they arrived by appointment, he'd already been imbibing brandy with some disreputable friends who welcomed Dax among them like a long-lost brother. Willa found them fun and amusing, and they soon lost any awkwardness in her company. Neither she nor Dax considered the afternoon wasted. In fact, Dax seemed both surprised and delighted that she'd enjoyed meeting his wilder cronies.

"Damn me if I won't be taking you with me to gaming dens and the like," he grinned. "I daresay, you'd bring me good luck."

"I suppose you'll have more money to lose at such places now," she observed.

He glanced away, a little ruefully. "I suppose I shall."

Willa understood that he was "being good" for her sake. Part of her was warmed by it and part was afraid, because she didn't want him to spend time with her through guilt. She didn't want him growing to resent her. She knew, too, that it was only a matter of time until he "broke out". Although he seemed quite content, and his more moderate lifestyle was clearly good for his health, she was aware she could not change his character and did not wish to.

On the evening a week after their hasty marriage, they dined with the Wickendens at Gillie's childhood home. There, they met Gillie's brothers—one a strapping lad of twenty summers, the other a baby of no more than six months—and her stepmother. Mrs. Muir was an elegant Spanish lady with a haughty demeanor that seemed to betoken shyness rather than disapproval.

The Grants were present, too, for it was something of a celebration as well as a farewell dinner. The Wickendens were leaving for their estate the following day, and Gillie, blushing, imparted the news that she was to have a child in the New Year.

Willa was sorry they were leaving, for she liked Gillie very much, but she supposed it would not be long now before she and Dax left Blackhaven, too.

They didn't walk directly back to the hotel, but strolled along the beach from the harbor, talking now and again. It was peaceful, companionable. And yet Willa had never been so aware of anyone as she was of Dax, sauntering at her side in the moonlight. Her hand was tucked loosely in the crook of his elbow, and she felt his every step brush against her skirts.

She gazed at the dark, rippling sea, constantly in motion, and yet somehow calm. Reflecting the silver moonlight, it was incredibly beautiful and just part of the wonder that was her new life. She'd never been so happy before. It flooded her, bringing sudden tears that she tried very hard not to release.

She didn't realize Dax was watching her, until one gentle finger brushed the corner of her eye.

"Tears, Will?" he said softly.

She shook her head. "Only because it's so beautiful here. And I'm so happy, suddenly."

He paused and turned her toward him, searching her face. A smile began to play around his lips. "I believe you are."

His hand cupped her cheek, drawing her a pace closer as he bent his head over hers. Her heartbeat quickened, depriving her of breath. She couldn't look away from his lips as they slowly parted and drew nearer to hers.

Her eyelids fluttered, trying to close, but she wouldn't let them.

His mouth closed on hers, gentle and sweet. She was afraid to move, but from some instinct, her lips clung to his until he lifted his head.

"That was sweet," he murmured. "For me, at least."

"You can do it again, if you like." Her voice wasn't quite steady.

A smile flickered across his lips as he lowered them once more to hers, brushing in a soft caress before sinking and claiming.

She gasped at the force of it, and he took advantage, deepening the kiss. Just like in the carriage that first time, she felt his tongue and teeth, and everything in her leapt to meet him. His hand tangled in her hair, holding her head steady for his ravishment, while his other arm swept around her, pulling her hard against him.

Heat flooded her, seeming to melt her very bones. Every inch of her thrilled under his mouth, to the hardness of his body which held few secrets through her flimsy gown. It was almost like those heady moments in the carriage after their wedding, only sober, he was more sensitive, a shade gentler. Compared with that experience, she sensed a hint of restraint in his passion that somehow inflamed her even more. She wanted to make him lose it, although she hadn't much idea what that would entail. She just knew that when the kiss ended, she wanted more and stood on tip toe, snaking her arms around his neck to take back his mouth.

He gave it, and she responded with shy but eager passion.

"I think we've done this before," he murmured against her lips. His voice, like his breath, was uneven, adding to her excitement. "I remember your lips, your kisses." He detached his mouth, leaving it hovering over hers. "Don't I?"

She hedged. "How can I know what you remember and don't?"

"Did I make love to you in that hired chaise?"

"Does it matter?"

"Well, yes, because if I don't remember such a gift, it's almost enough to make me forswear the bottle."

"You kissed me," she admitted. "And then you laid your head on my breast and went to sleep."

His lips brushed hers. She felt the soft graze of his teeth. "Are we still leaving each other a way out, Willa?"

"We still have one, if you want it."

"Do I?"

A breath of laughter stirred her lips.

"I don't think I do. I'm tempted—very tempted—to take you here on the beach, with the moon as witness."

Her heart thundered. "Why don't you?"

He seized her mouth in a hard, almost bruising kiss that was over before she could even respond. "Because the damned sand gets everywhere. And because then you'd be stuck with me before you even know what I'm capable of."

"You might be capable of badness," she said. "But you're not a bad man, Dax."

His hand swept down her back, pulling her hips into his. She gasped with shock and sudden, surging desire as the hardness of his erection dug into her abdomen.

"Yes, I am," he whispered. "Never doubt it." His kiss was hot, melting, utterly devastating. And when it was over, it turned into another. His heart thudded against hers.

And then, very slowly, his arm fell away. His hand slid down her wrist to take her fingers and he began to walk on.

Since her hair was loose and tangled by then, she drew the hood of her cloak up over her head before they took the path back up to the town. Anticipation kept her breathless as they walked back to the hotel.

Briefly, by the door, she was distracted by the sight of a man she seemed to recognize. She must have seen him around town a lot, but she couldn't place who he was.

In any case, she didn't truly care. Excitement, longing, and just a little fear flooded through her veins, intensifying as they entered the hotel and walked upstairs to their rooms.

As usual, one lamp was left burning, but there was no sign of either Carson or Clara. Her heart thundered as he led her straight to her bedchamber door, without lighting any more candles.

"Good night, new wife," he murmured, kissing her hand, and then, softly, her lips.

Until he released her hand and stepped away, she didn't properly realize that he was leaving her. For an instant, dazed disappointment cleaved her tongue to the roof of her mouth. Then as he turned away, she blurted, "Dax. You don't need to go."

He paused but didn't turn his head. His breath was labored. "Oh, I do," he said at last. "Trust me, I do. Good night, Willa." And then, as if his feet were made of lead, he walked to the passage door and left, closing it quietly behind him.

JEM BROWN, CLARA'S rejected suitor, had discovered ambitions well beyond the confines of inheriting the lease to Black Farm. He much preferred the easy money paid to him by gentlemen for doing the things they couldn't be seen doing themselves. And Jem thought he was pretty good at it.

Not that he'd actually done anything yet to earn that other, prom- ised purse full of money, but the gentleman, Sir Ralph Shelby, was more interested in discretion than speed, and so he'd spent several days watching his victim's habits.

The beauty of the situation was, his victim turned out to be the man employing Clara, who'd never gone home after Jem's failed abduction. It was Daniel Doone who'd told him she now worked for Lady Daxton. Generously, Jem wished her well. He even wished Dan well until the fellow began to get in his way.

Because finding out his victim's habits turned out to be impossible. He didn't have any. He was totally erratic. The man never left the hotel at the same hour two days running, or went to the same places. He didn't see anyone at regular hours but was rarely alone, and when he was, he moved so quickly that Jem had trouble finding him, let alone killing him.

This job, clearly, was not going to be quite as easy as he'd imagined, not least because Dan Doone seemed to be hanging about Lord Daxton as well. To be near to Clara, Jem supposed, although he'd heard Dan say he was paying off a debt to his lordship.

And yes, when Jem entered the tavern, there he was again, standing by the counter with a pint of ale, making occasional conversation with the tavern keeper and the tap boys. Meanwhile, Lord Daxton roistered at the back of the tavern with several other nobs, all clearly the worse for wear.

There were possibilities, of course, in Daxton staggering home in his cups, only the bastard rarely staggered, however much he put away, and if he parted from his friends before the hotel door, there were nearly always other people around. Often Dan.

Jem betook himself to the counter and requested a mug of ale. Then he turned and regarded Dan, as though surprised to see him there. "Dan."

"Jem," Dan said warily.

"What you doing in this den of vice then?"

"Having a pint of ale. What are you doing?"

"Thought you'd have taken Clara home by now. Since you balk at Scotland."

Dan regarded him with hostility.

Jem smiled winningly. "No hard feelings, mate. I reckon she isn't for either of us. But I want you to know I withdraw from the contest. As far as I'm concerned, she's all yours."

Dan smiled sourly. "If only it were that simple."

"What's she doing here in Blackhaven anyway? Why doesn't she go home?"

"Because you ruined her reputation," Dan retorted. "And because Lady Daxton took a shine to her and gave her a position as her maid."

"Aye, I've seen her running after the woman. What about *him*? You working for him, too?"

"No," Dan said with dignity. "Well, not really. I shot him by accident, if you must know, so I'm just helping out."

Jem sniggered, hiding the fact that he was impressed, and looked across the smoke-filled room to where Lord Daxton was arm wrestling the local carter while his friends cheered him on. "He doesn't look shot," he observed, "I admire a man like that. He's not looking for any more help, is he?"

"Not that I know of and in any case, Lady Daxton wouldn't let you within a hundred yards of her household. Clara told her everything, and she's not one of the usual ladies who don't give two pence for their servants."

There went another possibility. It seemed he couldn't infiltrate the household and get to Daxton that way. He'd just have to continue watching and waiting for his opportunity.

Which came sooner than he expected. Without warning, Lord Daxton hauled himself to his feet, seized his hat, and sauntered away from his table with no more than a casual farewell. His friends called after him in disappointment, but his lordship didn't pay any attention, merely lurched through the door to the street, swaying slightly in the fresh air.

And Dan had gone to relieve himself.

Jem drained his mug, threw a few coins on the counter, and sauntered after Lord Daxton. This was a real possibility. Jem reached into his capacious coat pocket and wrapped his fingers around the knife he carried there. Once they passed the drunken sailors and whores hanging around the tavern door, the road was quiet. When Daxton turned the corner, before he reached the lights and probable traffic in High Street, Jem could slide in the knife. Tavern scum would be blamed. Some poor bastard would probably be arrested and hanged. That wasn't Jem's problem.

Jem moved swiftly, judging his timing to a nicety. Daxton wasn't weaving up the street exactly, but walked with the amiable expansiveness of the slightly bosky. This should be easy. Shelby would give him more money. There would, no doubt, be more jobs from him and from his friends. And then even more money. In a few months, Jem could be set up for life. All because he stole that purse from the maid's pocket.

Jem began to run silently. In his condition, Daxton should barely be aware of him. And as he ran past, it would be easy just to slide the knife between his ribs. It would be like stabbing butter, if he judged it right.

Except, just as he withdrew the knife from his pocket, his legs suddenly vanished from under him and he fell to the ground with such force that the knife skittered across the road. Daxton kicked it further away before dropping a sovereign on the ground beside Jem's bemused face.

He hit me! Damn it, he kicked my legs from under me!

"Next time, just ask," his lordship suggested and sauntered off. Jem, hearing pounding footsteps behind him—probably Dan's—was forced to roll under a hedge into someone's garden and take off round the back of the house before he was recognized.

And he'd lost his bloody knife.

Chapter Nine

A LTHOUGH WILLA DIDN'T quite understand why Dax had left her, by the following morning, she had decided that it was a good thing. He was holding back out of gentlemanly respect for her position. He would not take advantage until he was sure it was what she wanted. She was sure now that he cared a little, that in spite of everything, he'd wanted her as Willa, not just a conveniently available female.

Her heart sang as she rose and breakfasted in the sitting room, for at last, she truly believed that a lasting happiness was possible for them.

"Is his lordship here?" she inquired of Carson, as he emerged from Dax's bedchamber with a bag of laundry.

"Sleeping it off, m'lady," Carson said cheerfully.

"Oh."

It was a little thing. Gentlemen overindulged, and Dax was…well, he was Dax and she'd never wanted to change him. And so, she dressed for the day, with Clara's help, and sallied forth to meet Kate and some other ladies of the parish who were raising funds to help injured soldiers returning from the war.

When she came back to the hotel after luncheon, there was no sign of Dax or Carson. Clara told her they'd gone out, though she didn't know where. Willa hid her disappointment—she'd been looking forward with new excitement to seeing Dax again—and settled down to read her new book from the circulating library.

Clara blurted, "I saw Jem in town, m'lady."

Willa dropped her book into her lap. "Did he threaten you? Try to abduct you again?"

"Well, no, he didn't even see me. I ducked into the draper's shop until he was past."

Willa nodded approval. "Maybe you shouldn't go out without Carson, for now. Or Dan if he's still here."

"He is. He seems to think he has to serve his lordship until his wound is better."

"I don't think that can be his reason," Willa argued. "No one would know his lordship had ever been wounded, he pays so little attention to it. I suspect Dan stays because of you."

"It'll do him no good," Clara said stubbornly. "It's over between us and so I've told him."

"Very well," Willa said peaceably, picking up her book again. "Just be careful when you go out, and if Jem gives you any trouble, we'll set the magistrate on him."

Half an hour later, a knock sounded at the outer door. Clara went to open it and admitted a young woman who moved with such languid elegance Willa was surprised she didn't fall down.

Willa rose, accepting the card Clara conveyed from her visitor. Mrs. Helena Holt. Never having heard of her, Willa walked forward with her usual friendliness.

"Mrs. Holt," she greeted her. "How do you do?"

"How do *you* do, Lady Daxton," the visitor replied, smiling. Truly, she was dazzling—a little like Kate was, only fair where Kate was dark. And her eyes, although warm and curious, gave little away. "Forgive the intrusion, but when I heard about your marriage, I just had to come and congratulate Dax. We have known each other forever."

"You are very welcome, ma'am, only I'm afraid Dax isn't here. I'm not perfectly sure where he is!"

"Indeed, how could you be?" the lady soothed, although Willa hadn't actually felt in need of comfort on that score. "You must tell me all about yourself!"

"There is little to tell. May I offer you tea? Clara, see to it, will you?"

Politely, Willa invited her visitor to take one of the chairs by the occasional table, and took the other herself.

"How kind you are," Mrs. Holt drawled, her darting gaze falling on the table in front of her, and the diamond spiral pendant which lay there. Dax must have dropped it there when he unfastened it for her yesterday, and neither she nor Clara had picked it up. Clara was not really a very good lady's maid by most standards, but then she was only learning. The spiral seemed to entrance Mrs. Holt for she gazed at it for some time. "That's a pretty thing," she said at last. "Let me guess, it was a gift from Dax."

"Everything I have is a gift from Dax," Willa said candidly.

"Oh, how sweet you are!"

"Not remotely," Willa assured her, which won her a peel of musical laughter from her beautiful visitor.

"Why, you are delightful. Dax must absolutely adore you."

Everyone called him Dax. There was really no reason for Willa to take exception to Mrs. Holt's frequent use of his nickname, and yet for some reason, it grated. Nor could she think of a suitable reply to the lady's latest remark, so she was quite relieved when the outer door opened once more—presumably Clara with the tea.

However, it was not Clara but Dax himself who strode in like a gust of sudden wind, kicking the door carelessly shut behind him.

"I say, Will, you'll never guess what—" He broke off, his eyes widening as he took in Willa and Mrs. Holt. He even started to swear, she was sure, before he bit it back. No one could have accused him of being pleased to see Mrs. Holt, and yet Willa found that no comfort at all. She had a terrible feeling she knew why he looked quite as appalled as he did.

"Mrs. Holt has kindly paid us a visit," Willa said mildly. "I understand you are old fr—"

"Dax," Mrs. Holt interrupted her efforts to cover for Dax's rudeness, by rising to her feet and extending one languid hand. "How wonderful. I congratulate you on your adorable bride. You must bring her to my soiree tomorrow evening."

"Soiree? Where the devil are you staying?" Dax demanded. Although he'd taken her hand, he dropped it again almost immediately. Fury flashed in his eyes, held his lips unnaturally thin and rigid.

"Why, here at the hotel. I didn't know there *was* anywhere else to stay, for even the Braithwaites aren't at the castle, are they?"

"I don't believe so," Dax managed.

"Well, I shall throw open my rooms to visitors. The world and his wife do appear to be in Blackhaven this month. Goodbye, Lady Daxton!"

"Mrs. Holt," Willa rose and bowed as amiably as she could while her husband opened the door for their departing guest. He not only opened it but followed Mrs. Holt outside.

Stricken, Willa sank back into her chair, staring out of the window.

In her heart, she'd always known this little idyll with Dax had been an illusion. She'd known it would, eventually, crash around her ears, because of who she was, and who he was. Only she'd been so content, and last night had been so thrilling, so promising that she'd allowed herself to hope…

But Mrs. Holt was undoubtedly his mistress, and she'd undoubtedly come here to make sure of her claim. Willa could not compete, not with that kind of unsurpassable loveliness, elegance, and sophistication. He would never even *see* Willa now. And honestly, it had always been a faint hope.

As soon as the door closed on Willa, Helena reached up one arm to his neck.

Dax caught her by the wrist and yanked her arm down again. "What the devil do you think you're playing at?"

She laughed in her most provoking manner. "What do you think, darling?"

"I think we concluded our business in London," he said deliberately.

"You were very rude," she recalled.

"I was," he agreed. "We were never good for each other, Helena. I don't know what brought you up here, but whatever it was, I'm not part of it, and neither is my wife."

"*My wife,*" she mocked, although her eyes flashed with a spurt of venom. She wasn't used to playing second fiddle to a mere wife. "Are you warning me off, Dax?"

"Yes, I am."

"Oh, very well, I suppose it was bad form to visit her, but I was so very curious. And she clearly has no idea who I am."

"Let's keep it that way," Dax said grimly, for he didn't want his wife hurt, especially now when she was beginning to care for *him* rather than the boy he'd been.

"I am the soul of discretion," she assured him. "But remember," she added, walking away down the empty passage. "You don't need to wait until tomorrow evening to visit me."

Since a door opened further along the passage just then, he refrained from answering her, merely reentered his own rooms. He closed the door with a definite thud, wondering how he could have stood the wretched woman for all the months they were together.

Because they had never really been *together*, he realized. They'd flirted at parties and he'd visited her for discreet pleasures a couple of times a week. She had never been his only lover, though, and he was fairly sure he'd never been hers.

Willa seemed to have been gazing out of the window somewhat blindly, for she gave a sudden start and stood as he walked across the room to her.

"London seems to be descending on Blackhaven," he observed as lightly as he could. For he felt the weight of his old, familiar life pressing down upon him, trying to squeeze out the new, intriguing closeness he'd begun to find with Willa. In sudden panic, he felt her slipping through his fingers, before he'd even properly grasped her. He didn't want that. He didn't want it at all.

"Shall we leave for Daxton tomorrow?" he blurted.

She glanced at him in surprise, searching his face. A faint smile curved her lips and he longed to kiss them as he had last night.

"You can't always run away, Dax," she said vaguely.

He frowned. "Run away?"

"You don't need to. I don't mind. I expected it, really."

She was talking about Helena. Of course, she'd worked out who and what Helena had been to him, had seen his horror and embarrassment at the whole situation. He opened his mouth to assure her that it was over, only she was already walking away from him. He had the feeling he'd just sound like a guilty husband making excuses to a long-suffering wife. The thought of either of them in such paltry roles appalled him.

He closed his mouth again, gazing after her, totally perplexed.

I don't mind. I expected it, really. Damn it, was she giving him absolution or permission? *Why* the hell didn't she mind?

"In any case," she added over her shoulder. "You should see Dr. Lampton again before you make any long journeys."

As PLANNED, LATER in the afternoon, Dax and Willa walked to Lord Tamar's studio for their daily sitting. Willa behaved as if nothing had happened earlier, which Dax supposed optimistically was true. She'd merely met someone from his past, and she'd always known such women existed.

After Tamar released them from their pose, Dax wandered over to watch what he was doing, while Willa examined some paintings at the far end of the studio.

"Got something on your mind, Dax?" Tamar murmured, no doubt because Dax simply stared at the canvas without really seeing what was there.

"Helena turned up," Dax said abruptly. "Helena Holt."

"Your mistress?"

Dax shrugged impatiently. "She was. We parted before I even left London. The thing is, she's healthy as a horse, so it ain't the waters she's here for."

Tamar cocked an intelligent eyebrow. "You think it's you?"

"I'm afraid she's here to cause trouble, though why she would bother is beyond me. I found her closeted with Willa in our rooms."

"Did she upset Willa?"

Dax glanced at her, as she stood back to better admire a seascape. "I think she did, but Willa's hiding it. I don't want her anywhere near Willa." He brought his gaze back to Tamar.

"I'll do what I can," Tamar said doubtfully.

It was as they walked back to the hotel that Helena's presence began to make sense of a sort. A barouche passed along High Street, bearing two middle-aged ladies and came to halt just in front of them. Dax glanced at the occupants without much interest, and then stared, coming to an abrupt standstill and swearing.

"Sorry," he breathed to Willa, squeezing her fingers on his arm. "I'm afraid it's my mother."

IT SEEMED TO be a day for shocks. And certainly, if Willa could have chosen a time to meet her mother-in-law for the first time as Lady Daxton, it would not have been now. However, since there was nothing she could do about it, she merely turned with Dax to greet the occupants of the open carriage.

There were two middle-aged ladies within, one rather mousy who wore an expression of alarm mingled with gratification. The other, tall and willowy with deceptively drooping shoulders, was Lady Romford.

The countess didn't appear to have aged one jot in the eight or nine years since Willa had seen her last. The only change appeared to be the steeliness of her eyes, which had never used to regard her with quite such revulsion. Well, as the Shelbys' poor relation, she had been a creature worthy of condescension and kindness. Lady Romford had always treated her much as she'd treated the Shelby children. But having the temerity to marry Daxton, clearly changed everything.

"Mother," Dax greeted her, stepping up to kiss her proffered cheek. "What an unexpected pleasure."

"Well, it shouldn't be. I have come to visit Cousin Harriet. You do remember Cousin Harriet?"

"Of course," Dax said with easy but clearly untruthful civility. "How do you do, Cousin?"

"Cousin Harriet lives a bare five miles from Blackhaven, so it was quite a co-incidence to receive your letter just after I'd written to her to accept her invitation."

"Yes, that is an astonishing coincidence," Dax marveled in clear disbelief. "Allow me to present my wife, whom I'm sure you must remember."

There were clearly to be no affectionate kisses, embraces, or even handshakes for her. Not even insincere ones. Instead, Lady Romford bowed, very slightly and coldly.

"Wilhelmina," she uttered in such freezing accents that it might have been an accusation. It probably was.

Willa curtsied to the countess and to Cousin Harriet. Since there was nothing she could say to make this marriage palatable to Dax's family, she could only hope that Dax himself could win his mother around by familiarity with the situation.

"Dax, may we not invite Lady Romford and Mrs. Wicks to dine with us tonight?"

"Of course we may," Dax said, clearly trying not to look appalled. "The hotel dinner is quite tolerable."

"Oh, I'm sure," Lady Romford said, "but I shall spend the evening quietly with Harriet. You'll call on us tomorrow, Daxton."

"Well, I might," Dax said doubtfully. "If you tell me—*remind* me—of Cousin Harriet's direction."

Cousin Harriet twittered something about her gratification, looking even more alarmed, and Lady Romford instructed the coachman to drive on.

"Well," Dax said, walking on toward the hotel, "that went well."

Willa stared at him. "It did?"

Dax gave a quick grin. "She didn't cry or insult us. And she didn't accept your foolhardy invitation to dine. I wonder who the devil Cousin Harriet is?"

"Presumably some distant relative whom she can use as an excuse to visit Blackhaven and discover exactly how disastrous this marriage is. Or to overturn it."

"I wouldn't be surprised," Dax agreed. "And I must say, it's suspicious that she turns up here on the same day as Helena Holt."

As soon as the words were out, he scowled, as if he'd have taken them back if he could. Willa pretended not to notice.

"Are they friends?" she asked calmly.

"Good God, no. Quite the opposite, I'd have said. Still, it's worth thinking about."

"I'm sure they each have their own reasons for wishing you'd married elsewhere," Willa murmured. "Or not at all. Do you suppose your father is here, too?"

"Lord, no, my parents are happiest with several hundred miles between them."

Willa knew a guilty relief at that. Perhaps meeting them both at once would have got all the unpleasantness over with more quickly, but the countess seemed quite formidable enough on her own.

THEY DINED IN the hotel that evening with the Grants as their guests. And Willa had to admit it was a lot more convivial than it would have been if the countess had joined them. Mr. Grant, it turned out, had been a soldier before he became a clergyman. Dax revealed he, too, had once wished to obtain a commission under Lord Wellington.

"My father wouldn't have it," Dax said carelessly. "I was his only son, and he seemed convinced I'd be killed immediately."

"I didn't know that," Willa said in surprise. It was probably another reason for his wildness. Thwarted in his ambitions, he'd needed another outlet for his considerable energies.

The meal was almost finished when a flutter seemed to circulate around the dining room. Willa, in conversation with Mr. Grant about his charity for injured soldiers, couldn't help a quick glance to the door to discover the cause of the commotion.

Helena Holt sailed into the room, quite alone, a bowing waiter scuttling before her as though she were royalty.

Willa looked away almost immediately, and back to Grant who, however, stopped talking just in time for her to hear Kate speak to Dax in a low, irritable voice.

"Please tell me you did not bring her here."

Daxton's reply, whatever it was, got lost in Willa's slightly desperate question to Grant about how he was trying to find paid work for the injured soldiers.

For Willa, the evening was spoiled. Not just because of the nagging suspicion caused by Kate's words, but by the fact that she couldn't help admiring Mrs. Holt. It was a brave thing to defy convention and dine in public alone, unescorted by a gentleman of one's family. And Willa could see all too easily why Daxton had been attracted to her. She had all his courage and impatience with pointless society rules.

It came to her too, just how chafing it must be for Dax to be constantly considering those rules now for Willa's sake. She wished Mrs. Holt anywhere but here, but she couldn't change it. Nor could she bring herself to make a friend of the woman. All she could do was pretend not to care.

And so, as they left the dining room, she inclined her head to Mrs. Holt and laid her hand on her husband's arm. Dax cast the faintest of careless bows in his mistress's direction, then escorted Willa from the room. They parted from the Grants in the foyer, and made their way to their own rooms.

It was not late, and the candles were all lit. Carson and Clara effaced themselves, leaving their employers to enjoy a companionable evening. Trying not to feel the tension between them, Willa sat by the lamp and began to read.

But this was not like the previous evenings they'd spent together in this way. Willa was too churned up to concentrate on the words, and Dax too restless to settle at all. He paced the room for a bit, gazing out of the window, kicking up the carpet, and smoothing it down again. After about twenty minutes of that, he came to a halt in front of Willa.

"I'm going out," he said abruptly. "So, I'll say goodnight." Peremptorily, he held out his hand and she gave him hers, hiding her sinking heart. He kissed her fingers, gave her a quick flash of a smile, and was gone.

She'd grown used to him leaving. She hadn't minded until now, when his departure inspired suspicion and misery. Her happiness, so bright and new and hopeful, was falling apart around her.

Chapter Ten

I N THE MORNING, Dax looking slightly rough and rather adorably rumpled, joined her for breakfast in the sitting room. Or at least, Willa ate breakfast. Dax drank copious cups of coffee.

"Either you're up very early, considering," Willa observed, "or you haven't yet been to bed."

"Oh, I've had a few hours' sleep," Dax assured her. "I wanted to be up early and get this visit to my mother over with."

Willa made to rise. "I'll be ready momentarily."

He caught her hand, keeping her beside him. "You actually *want* to visit my mother?"

"Well yes. She is your mother."

His lips twisted. "I wish I could send you instead of me."

"Well, I will, if you like, but I feel you should—."

"I was joking, Will. I need to make this visit on my own."

It felt like a slap in the face. She dropped her gaze. "Whatever you prefer."

His hand tightened on hers for an instant. "It would be best."

"Of course." She slid her hand free, reaching for her cup. "Then I shall finish my coffee before I go out."

"What will you do this morning."

"I haven't decided," she said, deliberately cheerful. "Give my duty and regards to Lady Romford."

DAX DOUBTED HE would get enough words in at this meeting to pass on Willa's message. Which was why he didn't want Willa to come in the first place. Until he had made his mother understand, he didn't want her anywhere near his wife.

He drove himself in his curricle, leaving the town by the southern road, then following the left-hand fork as he'd been directed.

Cousin Harriet, whoever she was, lived in a small manor house set in modest estate that seemed to be squashed between the Earl of Braithwaite's land and that belonging to Haven Hall. Or so Cousin Harriet informed him as she welcomed him and rang for tea, and kept him company in a flustered kind of way until his mother deigned to emerge from her bedchamber and join them. Cousin Harriet then effaced herself.

"Your wife does not join us?" Lady Romford drawled.

"She wished to pay her respects, but I insisted on coming alone."

"I'm not surprised. It must be such a burden to a young man of your…energies. What were you thinking of, Daxton? Did you really imagine this would hurt your father more than yourself?"

"If I'd wanted to really hurt him I'd have married the housemaid," Dax retorted. "And to be frank, I wasn't thinking of very much at all, except getting my hands on Grandfather Winter's money. For the rest, I was dead drunk, as I'm sure you know."

"Well, I've spoken to your father—who is not best pleased by this ludicrous start of yours, but I doubt I need to tell you that. However, he is prepared to help. He has approached the Archbishop personally—"

Dax scowled and leapt restlessly out of his chair. "He has no need and less right," he flung at his mother as he paced to the window. "The marriage will not be annulled."

"Of course, it will. No one will hold such a mistake against you. At least not for very long."

"They'd hold it against Willa, though, wouldn't they?" he retorted.

"And that will serve her as she deserves! Vulgar, scheming, hussy, exactly like her father. Blood will out."

Dax swung on her. "Don't speak of Willa that way. It was I who schemed and treated her very ill."

"Because she's Ralph Shelby's cousin?"

"Of course not," Dax said impatiently. "She was just there. I was glad to see her again and in my cups, I imagined marrying her would help both of us."

"It has certainly helped *her*," Lady Romford observed tartly. "And whatever you imagine, she was well aware of it. What are you thinking, Charles? That she loves you and depends upon you? That you are responsible for her?"

His lips twisted. "Well, two out of the three." He was working on the other.

"Well, it's nonsense! You know perfectly well such a marriage is a disgrace to your family and your name—"

"I know no such thing," he retorted. "The Shelbys may be bad blood, but it is perfectly respectable blood in the eyes of the world. Willa is undoubtedly a lady. But it's of no consequence. The marriage will not be annulled."

His mother changed tactics smoothly. "Then it is you who are being unkind. Will you really force her to put up with your mad starts? Your women and your drinking and all the other bad behavior?"

Annoyingly, Dax felt a faint flush rise beneath his skin. "No. I shall do better."

"Really?" his mother marveled. "Even with the beautiful Mrs. Holt under the same roof?"

Dax curled his lip as he strode past her. "I knew it. It *was* you who brought her here."

"I might have mentioned to her that you were in Blackhaven."

"And did it never enter your head that that was unkind to both Willa and Helena?"

"No," his mother said frankly. "I was thinking of you. And Willa will be fine. We'll set her up with a small allowance somewhere quiet. No doubt, in time, she will marry someone more suitable and—"

"No, she won't," Dax interrupted. "She's married to me. There will be no annulment."

"If you mean you have consummated the so-called marriage, that needn't matter. I shall talk to Willa and make her options clear to her."

"You shall do no such thing," Dax said between his teeth.

His mother blinked. "Charles, I want what is best for you! And Wilhelmina Blake is *not*. When you are ready to settle down, there are any number of girls of excellent family for you to choose from. You cannot stay married through mere guilt, to some scheming, ill-bred hussy! If you would just think about it, you'd know perfectly well she took advantage of your condition and your anger to try and make herself a viscountess! And a countess one day when you inherit the earldom."

Dax had rarely tried so hard to keep his temper in check. He clenched his fists hard at his sides. His feet positively itched to kick poor Cousin Harriet's furniture.

He drew in an uneven breath. "Mother, I take leave to tell you, you're talking rubbish. And so, *I* shall talk now. What I came to say was, you and my father must accept this marriage, for I shall not forswear it. What is more, you will treat Willa with all the respect due to her as my wife and the future countess. If you cannot manage that, if you cannot refrain from trying to interfere, then don't come near us. At the first hint, Mother, I shall cut us off from you and speak only through solicitors to obtain my inheritance. Do you understand?"

She stared at him in disbelief for a moment, then, inevitably, sank onto the sofa with a moan of misery. "What have I done that you should speak to me so? What has *she* done to you that you turn your back on your own parents?"

"I haven't and I won't if you behave," Dax said severely, and then, because he couldn't help it, he grinned. "Who'd have thought those words would come *from* me rather than *at* me? Seriously, Mother, I don't want to quarrel, and neither does Willa. I know eloping was a bad start, but truly this is what I want, and I wish you and my father to accept it."

"Of course, you do," she said sorrowfully. "Now. I shall do as you wish, of course, but you will see soon enough that you have been blinded. Willa Blake is very far from the angel you think she is."

"Oh, balderdash, Mother!" Dax said irritably, snatching up his driving gloves from the table. "Good day!"

Although he felt a bit of a cur for leaving his mother weeping on the sofa, he knew that if he showed any weakness at all on the subject, she'd consider it permission to interfere. Not that she needed permission for that. He only hoped he'd been forceful enough to discourage her. In any case, now that both his mother and his one-time mistress were in the vicinity, Blackhaven no longer seemed quite such an attractive place to waste a couple of weeks. Maybe, they could travel down to Daxton by easy stages.

Lost in thought as he bowled along the bumpy road toward Blackhaven, he was aware only of his horses, paying little attention to his surroundings. The sharp crack of a gunshot took him entirely by surprise.

The horses took off immediately, neighing wildly and tossing their heads. Dax, bumped mercilessly along the less than perfect road and had to concentrate all his attention on calming his team, soothing them to a gentler pace before the curricle overturned or simply shook his bones to pieces.

It was only later, once the horses were trotting peacefully once more onto the coast road, that he wished he'd given a piece of his mind to whoever let off that shot. Whatever they were shooting, rabbit, fox, or even deer, he hoped they missed.

ENTERING BLACKHAVEN, HE found a welcome relief in the site of several of his cronies perched on rocks on the beach playing cards, oblivious of the oncoming tide. Paying one street urchin to hold the horses' heads, and another to run and fetch Fergusson, his groom, he jumped down to join his friends, who greeted him like a long-lost friend and passed him a bottle.

Inevitably, he lost track of time, went fishing, and ended up in the tavern. It was a most convivial afternoon, although it came to him eventually that something was missing. *Willa.*

Of course, he couldn't bring her to a place like this but did feel a certain longing for her company, and looked at his fob watch somewhat owlishly.

"What the devil?" he said, startled. "That's never the time!"

"It's only just past eight in the evening, old boy," someone reassured him. It was true he didn't normally care much about the time, even if it was eight the following morning. But he wanted to take Willa to dine.

Despite the protests of his friends, he grabbed up his hat and gloves and strode back to the hotel. The fresh air sobered him up somewhat and he began to anticipate Willa's delighted smile at his sudden appearance. He looked forward to dining with her, hearing about her day, and making her laugh with the tale of his bolting horses and the card game on the beach. He hoped she hadn't given up on him and had dinner brought to their room.

He all but barged into their sitting room, calling, "Willa!"

But there was no sign of her. Crossing to the bedroom, he gave one brief knock and threw open the door. The maid, Clara, looked up from the dressing table with surprise and not a little alarm.

"Where's her ladyship?" Dax demanded.

"She went to a soiree, my lord," Clara answered nervously.

He frowned. The word soiree held ominous connotations for some reason. "Where?"

"Just here in the hotel, my lord. A Mrs. Holt, I believe. Her card is on the mantel shelf in the sitting room."

The blood drained from Dax's face so fast he felt dizzy. "Jesus," he uttered, swinging away and striding to his own chamber. "Carson!"

WILLA HAD NOT at first intended to go anywhere near Mrs. Holt's party. For one thing, she hadn't really taken to the lady, for another, and more importantly, her connection with Dax made her company utterly unpalatable.

But then, Dax was gone all day. From Carson, she learned he'd been back in Blackhaven since midday, although the valet was vague on the details of where he actually was.

With her?

Surely, he would not be so unkind, not when they were staying under the same roof and everyone would know...

But he was a notorious rake and, by his own admission, appallingly selfish. He'd married Willa to get his hands on his inheritance and he'd never pretended to care for her in that way.

Yet the memory of his kisses haunted Willa. Why would he kiss her like that if he hadn't wanted their relationship to be more than chaste? And he would need an heir one day. Perhaps he'd been testing the waters, as it were, and found her wanting. After all, a man who'd come from Mrs. Holt's beautiful and sophisticated arms would hardly be satisfied with plain, naive little Willa who'd adored him from afar since childhood. She was probably more like a puppy to him than a wife, someone to be looked after and petted when he remembered.

"I'm not a puppy," she said to her face in the glass as she changed for dinner.

"Of course you're not, m'lady," Clara said in astonishment.

Willa, who'd forgotten she was there, coughed in embarrassment and hastily looked around for jewelry. The ruby and diamond pendant would suit the gown best, but somehow Helena Holt's interest in it made it less appealing. She stopped looking for it. Perhaps she would wear no jewelry after all. It might start a new, natural fashion.

She stood and went to wait for Dax in the sitting room. But her pride disliked what she was becoming, revolted at simply hanging on his arm and his life, waiting for rejection. She'd had her fill of that when she'd discovered how little her aunt and cousins actually cared for her when they were all she had. She refused to make that mistake again. She refused to be either a pathetically clinging wife or a complaining shrew insisting on his escort.

In fact, she refused to be seen that way by anyone. No one, for example, would ever see that she cared two straws about Mrs. Holt's relationship with Dax. Mrs. Holt herself would never guess. Willa would not run away from this as Dax had wanted her to.

In fact ... in fact, she might just step up to Mrs. Holt's room to prove it to anyone who cared. Surely, when the party was in the hotel, she did not need an escort? She was a married woman now, a viscountess and well above the rank of most people she was likely to encounter there. She would just look in for ten minutes, whether Dax was there or not, and leave as though fashionably bored.

She gave Dax another half hour to join her in the sitting room, but once the idea had taken root, it would not be denied. Eventually, fetching her shawl and matching reticule from her bedchamber, she informed Clara where she was going and left the room.

Mrs. Holt's door was wide open, the hum of chatter spilling out and along the passage as Willa approached. She steeled herself to discover Dax in the room, to greet him with careless pleasure and pass on to speak to someone—anyone—else.

Fixing a smile on her face, she stepped into the room.

In her heart, she had been prepared for some slightly less vulgar version of the gaming party which had flung her into Daxton's path. But the two events could not have been more dissimilar. Only the most respectable of the fashionable world were there, many of them women, although the men considerably outnumbered the fairer sex. There was no sign of any card table, and while champagne and brandy were being served, no one seemed to be the worse for drink.

Willa's first glance found her aunt, Elvira, and Ralph, but not Dax. Or at least not yet.

Then Mrs. Holt was approaching her, hand held out with languid grace. "Lady Daxton, how marvelous." And her eyes gleamed with what looked like amused triumph.

I shouldn't have come. But it was too late for such panicked regret. She could only take Mrs. Holt's hand as briefly as was polite and smile.

"Is Dax not with you?" Mrs. Holt asked, as though expecting him to leap out from behind Willa's skirts. Or at least saunter after her into the room.

"Oh no," Willa said carelessly. "I expect he'll look in later on."

She had the impression this didn't quite please Mrs. Holt, whose eyes narrowed as though finding an insult Willa hadn't even intended.

"He'll be avoiding the poetry readings, if I know him," Mrs. Holt said. "Come, who shall I introduce you to? Or do you know everyone already?"

"You must introduce *me*, ma'am," a gentleman said, materializing at their hostess's side. He was young, personable, immaculately dressed, and his eyes held frank admiration as he gazed at Willa.

"Why, of course," Mrs. Holt said at once. "Lady Daxton, allow me to present Sir Jeremy Leigh." She tapped Sir Jeremy's forearm with her fan. "Behave, or Dax will shoot you."

"So, you are Daxton's bride," Sir Jeremy observed, bowing over her hand with perfect grace as Mrs. Holt wandered off to greet yet more guests. "Now I understand perfectly."

Willa narrowed her eyes. "What is it you imagine you understand, sir?"

"How Dax was tempted away from his determined bachelordom. And why he did it so quickly before the rest of us could get a look-in."

"I don't care for flattery, you know. Are you also a friend of my husband?"

"I'm not sure I can claim friendship, though certainly we have spent several convivial evenings in the same company. I'm afraid I have neither the youth nor the stamina to move in Daxton's closest circle."

"Most people don't," she agreed without thought, for her eyes were darting around the room in search of Dax.

Mrs. Holt's greeting implied he was not there, but she did not trust the woman. Feeling Sir Jeremy's gaze upon her, she dragged back her gaze to find his amused regard on her face. "What?"

"Oh, nothing. It's refreshing to encounter a bride with so few illusions about her new husband."

"I like Dax," Willa said dangerously.

He threw up his hands in mock surrender. "Everyone likes Dax! Very likeable chap—unless you get on the wrong side of him," he added as they passed her cousin Ralph, glowering at her from his conversation by the drinks table. A small, timid looking young lady was gazing up at him worshipfully, which gave Willa few qualms. Had Ralph found himself a new heiress to court? She just hoped he would treat her with respect...

Sir Jeremy's voice broke in to her uneasy reflections, perhaps seeing the direction of her gaze. "May I offer you champagne? Lemonade?"

"Champagne, if you please," Willa said recklessly.

In one of the inner rooms, chairs had been set out in rows and the bed, pushed against the wall with cushions to make it resemble a large sofa.

"This must be where the readings happen," Sir Jeremy observed as they wandered in with several other people.

"Ah, yes. Mrs. Holt did mention poetry."

"Do you enjoy it?"

"For the most part, yes," she began.

"Then I hope you will enjoy mine," someone said beside her—a frail-looking, willowy young man with a pale complexion.

"Mr. Yoeville," Sir Jeremy murmured. "One of Mrs. Holt's favored poets. Yoeville, this is Lady Daxton."

Mr. Yoeville regarded her, apparently entranced. "Beauty to his beast, light to his darkness," he said. "My lady, you speak to my muse."

"I beg your pardon," she said tartly, since she didn't quite care for the implications of his words. "I shall endeavor not to do so in the future."

"You cannot help it. You possess the most beautiful, speaking eyes I have ever seen...Does she not, Walter?"

Walter turned out to be another poetic-looking gentleman, clearly a bosom friend of Yoeville's, who vied with him to recite the best verse to her beautiful eyes. Sir Jeremy then joined in, waxing lyrical on the subject of her nose until her laughter drew the attention of other gentlemen who approached and quickly joined in the game of improvising poetry to her beauty. It varied drastically in quality, but since Willa took none of it seriously, she thoroughly enjoyed the repartee.

Thus, without intending to be, she was the teasing center of an attentive group of young men when she suddenly caught sight of Dax.

She was already laughing at some nonsense of Sir Jeremy's, but as soon as her eyes met her husband's, her smile widened spontaneously. And Dax swung back to Mrs. Holt as if he hadn't even seen her. His attention was rivetted on his mistress.

Something inside Willa broke into a thousand pieces.

But he'll never know. None of them will ever know.

At that moment, she didn't think her pride would last longer than enough time to get her out of the room, but somehow, she kept smiling and then Mrs. Holt announced that Mr. Yoeville would read his new poem and everyone began to file into the rows of chairs.

Almost blindly, Willa did so, too, with Sir Jeremy ushering her along. She sat, gazing expectantly toward the lectern where Mr. Yoeville was setting out his notes.

Sir Jeremy nudged her, and when she glanced at him quickly, he nodded significantly to her other side. She glanced around and her heart turned over, for her husband sat beside her, eyeing the front of the room with pronounced misgivings.

"Dax," she exclaimed.

"Dash it, Will, have I been inveigled to a poetry evening?" Dax demanded. "I know that fellow, don't I?"

"Mr. Yoeville," she murmured faintly.

He sat forward. "Quick. If we squeeze out now, no one will notice."

On one level, it was funny, as a couple of surreptitious grins around him testified. Willa had to fight back half-hysterical laughter. But at the same time, she suspected Mrs. Holt of doing the inveigling, and refused to be dragged away just because her errant husband suddenly wished to go.

"Oh, no, Dax, I want to hear it," she said. "But I shall be fine, so go if you wish."

She expected him to do just that, even if it was only into the main room with Mrs. Holt in attendance. But, scowling, he settled back in his chair and stretched his long legs out in front of him, crossing them at the ankles. She caught a whiff of wine from his breath as he sighed and closed his eyes as though about to enjoy a nap.

Although inventive, Mr. Yoeville was not the finest poet alive. In fact, some of his imagery and more obscure word choices made Willa want to giggle. Surreptitiously, she glanced at Dax whose shoulders were shaking, apparently in his sleep.

She nudged him and he opened one eye so full of wicked laughter that she had even more trouble controlling her own.

"YOU MANAGED THAT very ill," Helena Holt murmured to Leigh. The first poetry reading was over and her guests were mingling once more. Since the Daxtons were both still in the reading room, she'd accosted Leigh while she could. "You were meant to bowl her over with your overwhelming charm and have her eating out of your hand. Instead, you made her the center of an admiring court! Dax couldn't have been more pleased when he walked in."

"I don't know that he was. He tried to take her away immediately, only she dug her heels in. As for the rest, she's hardly as foolish and naive as you gave me to understand."

"If it's too difficult for you, I'll give the task of ruining her to someone else," Helena retorted.

Leigh's smile was twisted. "Oh, no, it will be my pleasure. But it will not be accomplished in an hour by anyone. He has a hold on her, as he has on you."

Leigh strolled away, leaving her fuming. How dare anyone suggest a mere man had a hold on her? Men were interchangeable, like gloves, and she was damned if she would let a mere glove cast *her* off. Even without Lady Romford's encouragement, she wouldn't have let Dax off the hook so easily.

There was, of course, a certain cachet in having the wild Viscount Daxton as one's privately acknowledged lover. Besides which, maddening and volatile as he could be, he was by far the best lover she'd ever enjoyed. If she were to be honest, she missed him. And she would not give him up to a mere wife. Certainly not to an innocent, naïve nobody...

"Mrs. Holt," Sir Ralph Shelby said, accosting her as she made her way across the room. "What a charming party. A most pleasant change in this rather dull little town."

"One does one's poor best," she drawled. She was about to pass on, when she remembered who he was, the new Lady Daxton's cousin. What's more, there was some kind of enmity between him and Dax. She stayed where she was. "Besides, I find Blackhaven a most...surprising place. Where else would I encounter Lord Daxton with a bride in tow? Your cousin, no less. You must be thrilled by the match."

Tactfully, she did not mention the unorthodox nature of the wedding.

Shelby's smile was somewhat fixed. "Unutterably. It is, of course, a more brilliant match than we could ever have hoped for, but we feel very let down by the manner of it."

Open hostility, she thought with astonished glee. *How marvelous.* Aloud she said comfortingly, "Oh the world will make allowances for Dax. It always does. No one will refuse to receive Lady Daxton."

"I'm afraid my mother will. Certain items of hers vanished the night my cousin ran off."

"Really?" How interesting. Perhaps Leigh was right. And perhaps the girl was not the innocent Helena had believed her. Of course, she'd never been good at reading women. Men, on the other hand, she knew very well, and Shelby, she guessed, was out to damage both Dax and his wife. And she was more than happy to help him with the latter.

Laying her hand on his arm, she began to promenade around the room. "How terrible."

"Well it was. My mother took her in when her own mother died, and brought her up as though she were her own daughter. To have housed such a viper is clearly devastating for my mother, for my whole family."

"I can imagine…"

Chapter Eleven

WILLA AND DAX left before the second poetry reading, mainly because Willa was starving and the champagne she'd drunk made her head spin just a little.

"Thank you for a charming evening," Willa said to Mrs. Holt as they left. It wasn't even disingenuous. She knew she'd been a social success, and it was, besides, the first she'd accomplished on her own, without either Dax or the benefit of his friends looking out for her.

"What were you thinking of?" Dax demanded as they made their way along the passage and downstairs toward their own rooms. "Going there without me?"

"Well, you weren't here to go *with* me," Willa said reasonably.

He blinked, clearly forced to acknowledge the truth of that, if not the logic.

"Besides," she admitted as they approached their door. "I thought I might find you there already."

He paused, staring at her for an instant before pushing open the door and almost yanking her inside by the wrist. Fortunately, there was no sign of Carson or Clara, for he kicked the door closed behind them and spun her against it, towering over her. Her heart lurched, with more than a hint of fear, for she'd never been on the receiving end of his anger before.

"You know who she is?" he said abruptly. "What she was to me?"

"I guessed," she managed. She took a deep breath "The necklace you gave me—you bought it for her, didn't you?"

"Yes," he admitted. "But we had one quarrel too many and I never gave it."

Still, Willa could swear Mrs. Holt had recognized it.

"Throw it away," he said impatiently. "I never expected to en-counter her here. There seemed to be no harm in your wearing it."

"Is there harm in it now?" she blurted. "Will it offend her?"

Dax frowned. "I don't care," he said deliberately and bent his head, swooping to catch her lips with his.

It was an invasive kiss, hungry and possessive. She clutched his shoulders, then slid her fingers up into his hair, opening to him as he demanded. His hips pushed into her, pinning her to the door while he devoured her mouth. Nothing in the world had ever been so thrilling as his kiss, his hard, urgent body against hers, his hands in her hair, then roaming wildly down her side from breast to waist and thigh.

"When I kiss you," he said huskily against her lips, "I could almost imagine you loved me, just a little." He raised his head. "Do you?"

Already befuddled from his kiss, she almost blurted out the truth. *Of course I love you. I always have, and now it's so overwhelming it frightens me.* But her tongue wouldn't move. She could only stare up at his hot eyes, darkened with lust, and his beautiful, sinful mouth.

A rueful smile flickered across his face. "Of course, you don't. You have no idea what binds a man and a woman. I think it might be time I took you to bed and showed you."

Another wave of heat thrilled through her. She stood on tiptoe, pulling his head back down to reclaim his lips. His body caressed hers as he kissed her, and she thought she might burn up in bliss and need that she barely understood.

And then a loud knock thundered in her ear, making her jump and gasp. Half laughing, Dax whisked her up in his arms and strode with her into her bedchamber, where Clara waited, openmouthed with shock.

This was a situation Willa had never even thought of. What did one do with one's maid when one's husband visited?

"Go away," Dax growled. "Her ladyship will ring for you." He didn't appear remotely embarrassed. In fact, he didn't even wait for the door to close before he buried his mouth in Willa's and lowered her to the bed.

He came with her. There was an instant when she felt his full, glorious weight upon her. He groaned, lifting himself a little so that he could kiss her throat and shoulders. Beyond the sitting room, the urgent knocking at the outside door stopped abruptly.

Willa was glad. Trembling and desperate, her fingers tangled in her husband's hair. Somewhere, beyond the pleasure, she was aware of Clara's voice denying Lord and Lady Daxton to their caller.

"I know they're at home, so stand aside," Lord Tamar's voice said. And then, closer. "Dax? I know you're in there. Come out."

Dax raised his head, swearing beneath his breath. A violent conflict raged in his eyes. Then, reluctantly, he eased himself off her. "I'll get rid of him," he muttered, standing and straightening his coat before he strode out of the room.

Willa sat up slowly. She could still feel the imprint of his kisses and his hands on her shaking body, but at least without his overwhelming presence she could think again. Was this truly the time to become his wife in every sense? He'd spoken of love, but it was hers, not his, he'd been concerned with.

She'd never expected him to bring up the subject of love, certainly not this evening when they'd just come from his mistress's rooms. And even if he truly imagined he was finished with Helena, it didn't seem to Willa that Helena was finished with him.

The door opened again and her eyes flew to Dax. She knew at once he wasn't staying, for he didn't come in, merely stuck his head around the door.

"Sorry, Will, I have to take care of something. Why don't you order us a light supper? And I'll be back in an hour."

"Of course," she said easily. She should have been relieved, but in truth, she was horribly disappointed.

LEAVING WILLA AT that moment was one of the hardest things Dax had ever forced himself to do. It had been a spontaneous rather than a planned seduction, but her instant, melting response to his kiss had inflamed him almost to the point of no return.

But perhaps Tamar's intervention—*damn him*—was for the best, for though Dax no longer felt drunk, he *had* been drinking all afternoon and one was not at one's sensitive best in such a condition. For Willa, he should take account of such things. He'd never had a virgin before. All his lovers—and since he'd been in his teens he'd known them from all classes—had been experienced women of the world, skilled in physical love. Willa, he was afraid of hurting with his lust.

In any case, he couldn't ignore what Tamar had just told him.

"I've just come from Helena Holt's. No, I wasn't invited, but she claimed she would have sent me a card if she'd known I was in Blackhaven these days. I suppose I'm still a marquis, albeit a poor one. Anyway, there doesn't seem to be much wrong with her health. She was quite thick with that Jeremy Leigh chap."

"Yes, he was sniffing around Helena in London," Dax remarked. "He's probably her latest flirt, to call it no plainer. He was also very attentive to Willa. I'm not sure I like that."

"I don't," Tamar agreed. "For I think your Helena's up to something. She spoke quite a lot to Shelby, and to his mother and sister. And *they* are still spreading the story of Willa stealing from them. The purse is no longer mentioned, just *missing items* which disappeared with Willa on the night you eloped, making it sound as if the purse—which everyone knows Shelby lost to you—was just one of those items."

"An alliance between Helena and the very proper Shelbys? Who'd have thought it. I suppose I'd better go and call Ralph out."

"You're very casual about it," Tamar observed, as Dax swept up his hat and gloves and strode to the door. "And Dax? You really don't want to drag your wife's name into it."

"Since when did you become this model of propriety?" Dax demanded.

"I suppose I must have absorbed it somehow," Tamar said thoughtfully. "Though to be sure, I never pay a blind bit of attention on my own account. Never been married or likely to be."

"It does make you stop and think," Dax said ruefully. "Which in my case, is probably a good thing. I was pretty much going to the devil."

"According to most people, you'd already gone," Tamar contributed.

"Oh no, one can always go further. But I can't really drag Willa with me. Wouldn't be right."

Tamar's lips twitched. "No, it wouldn't," he agreed gravely.

Dax eyed him without favor. "Stop laughing at me or I'll shoot you, too. Where is Shelby? Still at Helena's?"

"No, he left just after you did. My guess? Pinkie's place."

"What the devil is Pinkie's place?"

"The brothel," Tamar said candidly. "We met outside it last week. Pinkie won't like you picking a fight, though."

"Oh, I'll be discretion itself," Dax said savagely.

PINKIE'S WAS APTLY named. The Madam, presumably, was called after her favorite color which was reflected in her gown and in the décor of the establishment. Apart from that, the public room into which Dax and Tamar were shown, could almost have been some society drawing room.

A young woman in a flounced yellow gown played upon the piano forte and sang rather beautifully, while several other women circulated amongst the gentlemen, refilling glasses and making conversation. As Dax sat, taking it all in, one gentleman rose with the lady beside him and discreetly left the room. A moment later, another middle-aged gentleman came in and sat down with a smile upon his face. Dax had rarely seen anyone look so pleased with themselves.

"What brings such a handsome man as you to our establishment?"

a girl asked, sitting beside him. Her accent was local but not so thick that he couldn't understand her. And she was eye-catchingly pretty with jet-black hair and smoldering dark eyes.

"I'm glad you asked," Dax said. "In fact, I'm looking for someone."

She smiled cheekily. "Is it me?"

"I wish it was. I understand he's become a frequent visitor here over the last week or so. Shelby is his name."

The girl's smile vanished, which was when Dax knew the bastard hadn't changed. "Is he a friend of yours?" she asked.

"Not exactly."

"Perhaps there's something I can do for you while you wait. A glass of wine, perhaps?" She picked up a nearby bottle and poured him a glass, which he accepted. "And some company?"

"I like your company and if I was looking for a girl, it would be you," Dax said frankly. "Sadly, I'm only here for a word with your other…guest."

"Are you sure?" she asked, laying her warm hand on his knee. "I can tell," she said, her hand gliding upward over his thigh, "when a man is in need of love."

"I expect you can," he said ruefully, catching her hand and holding it on his leg before it could roam any higher. "Only it isn't always the kind you pay for that's needed."

"No," she agreed, "but it's better than nothing. And if you pay, you're not being unfaithful."

Dax laughed. "Definitely I would have picked you," he said, just as Ralph Shelby strolled into the room as if he owned it. Dalliance could do that to a man, but Dax was more than happy to burst his self-congratulatory bubble. He stood up.

Shelby came to an abrupt halt, staring at Dax in surprised alarm before the inevitable sneer settled on his face. "Surprised to see you here, Daxton. Conjugal bliss worn off already?"

Dax refused to be riled. "Didn't come to sample fleshly pleasure, just to see you."

"Should I be flattered?"

"God, no. I was a trifle bosky on the night I left for Scotland, so the memory's been coming back to me in flashes. Tonight's flash was you accusing me of cheating. I've come for your apology."

Sudden silence filled the room. Neither the gentlemen clients nor the ladies of pleasure were the center of anyone's attention any longer. Even the girl in the yellow gown stopped playing the piano.

Shelby wouldn't apologize in public, whatever he might have done in private. It was one of the reasons Dax had approached him here.

"Apologize?" Shelby sneered. "The brandy has addled your brain, Daxton. Certainly your memory is faulty."

"Not in this case," some helpful gent said from across the room. "I was there and heard you say it, Shelby."

Shelby shrugged irritably. "Well, I don't recall it, so I'm damned if I'll apologize for it."

Daxton smiled. "Then I have no choice but to challenge you." Tamar materialized at his side. "Lord Tamar will act for me." He nodded curtly, then turned to kiss the hand of his black-haired companion. "*Enchanté, mademoiselle.*" And he strolled out, leaving the pink house and walking round to the tavern, where he expected Tamar to join him.

Barely ten minutes later, the impoverished marquis slid onto the bench opposite him. "It's arranged for tomorrow morning, so you'd better stop drinking."

"I shoot better in my cups."

"No, you don't. And he has chosen pistols. At dawn on the beach beyond the town. Apparently, the tide will be out. One shot each and honor is satisfied."

Daxton nodded.

Tamar hesitated. "He's not a bad shot, I hear. He practices at Manton's."

"So, do I. And he's never fought a duel before. Plus, he's a damned coward."

"You think you can make him apologize?"

"I think I can make him shut himself and his mother up about

Willa's so-called theft. Though I'm contemplating killing him anyway and doing the world a favor."

"Would Willa like that?" Tamar wondered.

"I don't know." Dax shifted restlessly. "He's still her cousin, but she don't like him much. Which isn't to say she'd condone his killing."

"Neither would the magistrate," Tamar warned. "One more thing. He's chosen Sir Jeremy Leigh and some chap called Tranter as his seconds. I can't vouch for their discretion."

"Which is why I'm offended by him calling me a cheat and not by his calling Willa a thief."

"Tongues will wag," Tamar warned.

"I don't pay attention to that," Dax said impatiently.

"Does Willa?" Tamar countered.

Dax gave a slightly twisted smile and pushed his beer mug aside. "Let's hope not, since the poor girl is married to me!"

WILLA WOKE TO AWARENESS of someone else in the room. For her, that was nothing unusual. It had happened so often in her aunt's house as someone came to rouse her to deal with a trivial want. Half asleep, she lay perfectly still and hoped they'd go away, which is what she'd tried to do at her aunt's when she was totally exhausted. It had never worked, just given her a few extra seconds.

The knowledge that she was no longer with her aunt, swam slowly through the clouds of sleep. Clara? Was it morning already? She was about to speak when something touched her hair in a gentle caress. Her breath caught, because she sensed him now, his touch, his scent. *Dax.*

He'd come back last night just as she was finishing her solitary supper and joined her in wolfing down what was left. His mood had changed completely from amorousness to cheerful companionship, but since the servants were in the room that was rather more comfortable. Unusually, he'd shown no signs of going out again, so when

Willa had retired as normal to her own chamber, undressed for bed and dismissed Clara, she'd lain awake for some time, wondering if he would join her at last.

He hadn't. But he was here now. She could hear his even breath as he stood by the bed, gazing down at her. She was afraid to move in case she spoiled the moment. Yet, she *should* speak, let him know she was awake.

She opened her eyes. The room was in total darkness, for he carried no light. All she could make out was a man-shaped patch of blacker darkness beside the bed. Longing surged, thrilling through her whole body. She wanted him to lie with her again, hold her as he'd done before the wretched Tamar had interrupted them. She wanted her arms around him, feeling the hard strength of his body, stroking his hair and naked back. She wanted his mouth on hers, his hands...

For a moment, the whole world seemed to stand still. Then he moved, turning and walking away from her. The door hushed across the floor and quietly clicked shut.

Disappointment flooded her. *Why didn't I take his hand? Speak to him? Why didn't he wake me? Why did he just stand there?*

In truth, the last was so very unlike Dax that she began to wonder if she'd dreamed the whole thing. She wanted him there so much that she'd imagined it in her sleep, and when she'd wakened properly, he'd vanished.

Perhaps. But listening, she was sure she could hear him beyond her door, moving quietly across the sitting room. On impulse, she rose and sped through the darkness to her door, all but wrenching it open. But everything was dark there, too. No light shone beneath his bedchamber door that she could see. No one spoke to her.

She swallowed and turned back into her own room, closing the door and gingerly feeling her way back to bed.

DR. LAMPTON, ALTHOUGH HE'D come in answer to Tamar's summons, scowled ferociously at Dax in the lantern light.

"I should have known it was you. Haven't you been shot enough?"

Dax grinned. His wound barely troubled him at all. In fact, it was almost healed.

Dawn on the beach was beautiful, spreading a grey, eerie light over the sea. Dax had walked down to the beach with his seconds—Tamar and, somewhat bizarrely, the vicar Tristram Grant.

"I thought we needed God on our side," Tamar had said irreverently.

"Well, He isn't," Grant had retorted, "There are enough people blowing each other's heads off in war. Why would He support two more trying to kill each over some imagined slight to their vanity?"

"Harsh," Dax commented. "And convincing. I'm surprised you couldn't negotiate an apology and reconciliation."

"He tried," Tamar said. "He tried very hard. I almost apologized myself. But surprisingly, Shelby would not consider it. He really hates your guts, Dax."

"I should have brought the Watch," Grant muttered as bobbing lights heralded the figures of Shelby, Leigh, and Tranter hurrying down the path to the beach and walked across the sand toward them.

"I wish you had," Lampton said grimly. "I wish *I'd* thought of it."

"I imagined you must have attended dozens of such affairs, with the barracks being here," Dax said.

"If the officers decide to shoot each other, they use their own doctor," Lampton retorted. "Although right now, the vast majority of them, including the surgeon, are on the Peninsula, being killed for king and country instead of for nothing."

"You're bad for morale," Dax observed. "Come on, let's get this over with."

Tamar and Grant went again to consult with Shelby's seconds, but again apology was ruled out. Tamar suggested moving further down the beach away from the path, but Shelby said impatiently, "Here is fine. Just get on with it!"

Since the sun wasn't yet risen, looking into it was not an issue. The seconds placed lanterns strategically so that both men would be able to see in the poor light, but not be blinded.

Seizing his pistol, Shelby stood facing the sea. Dax strolled over and stood back to back with him, facing the shore.

"Twenty paces, gentlemen," Leigh said quietly. "Then turn and fire."

Dax had fought several duels before this. The excitement, the actions, were all familiar to him. But he couldn't remember ever feeling this grim before. Almost...nervous. Afraid. Of course, he'd generally been bleary from lack of sleep, or even still foxed from the night before, but he'd never thought of himself as a fearful kind of man.

Perhaps it was fate. Perhaps he really would die today, failing to protect Willa's honor. Willa... He wanted to live for Willa. In previous duels, he hadn't much cared whether he'd lived or died. If he'd thought about it at all, he had a blind and quite unreasonable faith in his own survival. Plus, he was a good shot and he never aimed to kill, although such things tended to be in the lap of the gods.

Something glinted above the path. He thought they were about to get interrupted, but it was too late to stop now.

"Twenty," said Leigh, and Dax turned, his side to the sea, his right arm stretched out as he took aim and fired.

The crack of the gunshots was familiar, too, though the sharp pain in his shoulder was quite unexpected.

The bastard hit me!

The "bastard" in question had gone down, so at least Dax had hit him, too.

Dax threw his pistol on the ground and ignoring all etiquette, strode across the sand toward Shelby, who lay on the ground, his coat ripped off his right arm, bright red blood staining the shirt beneath. His face was white, his eyes wild with pain and fear.

"Here, Dax," Leigh protested. "Go away, old man. Let the doctor in."

"I will," Dax assured him, fixing his erstwhile opponent with his scowl. "I'm still standing, Shelby, so you lose. If there's a next time, I'll sue you in court and see which of us hates *that* more. Or I might just kill you." He turned away. "He's all yours, Dr. Lampton."

"Sit down before you fall, man," Lampton growled. "You're hit in the shoulder."

"Nonsense," Dax said, striding back toward his friends who were hurrying to meet him. He was only half way there before the blood singing in his ears rose to a crescendo and the sand rushed up to meet him.

Chapter Twelve

WILLA WOKE EARLY as usual and lay still, thinking over the events of yesterday evening and last night. It came to her that Dax really was beginning to care for her as more than the adoring little friend who'd followed him around and been on his side during most of the games played with the Shelbys and other local children. It was a sweet thought.

Unusually, there was movement beyond her door, in the sitting room. And it wasn't Clara. She heard lowered voices conversing. One of them was surely Dax. Another might have been Lord Tamar. She couldn't really tell. Then she heard footsteps and the sound of the passage door opening and closing. And all was quiet.

Either Dax was up extraordinarily early—for it was not yet quite dawn, judging by the light—or he had not yet been to bed. He'd certainly never gone out this early before. Rising, she padded across her chamber and opened the door to the sitting room. Clara was straightening cushions and yawning.

"You're up early, m'lady," she observed. "Shall I bring you hot chocolate? Or coffee?"

"It seems there's coffee here already," Willa said as the maid stood aside, revealing the pot and three cups.

"It's still warm, and only one cup's used," Clara said. "I'll bring it to you in bed, if you like."

"Yes," Willa said faintly. "Yes, please…Was his lordship up and drinking coffee at this hour?"

"With the vicar and Lord Tamar, though Lord Tamar didn't have any. They both called for his lordship, and Carson already had him up and dressed, and off they went together."

Willa frowned at the strangeness of such behavior and accepted the cup of coffee from Clara. Dax was up to something, and it made her uneasy. He would hardly have taken Tamar and the vicar with him on a tryst with Helena Holt, but there was more dangerous mischief than dalliance. What had Dax told her about rakehells? Womanizing, gambling, drinking, dueling –

"No," she uttered, sitting bolt upright in bed. A little coffee sloshed out of the cup and into the saucer. He wouldn't, would he? Distractedly, she raised the cup to her lips, drinking the coffee while she remembered his rushing off with Tamar instead of returning to their sudden intimacy in her bedchamber. He'd said he was going to take care of something. And then, last night, he'd surely entered her chamber again and merely watched her sleeping before he'd left again without trying to wake her. He hadn't known she was awake already.

"Where were they going, Clara?" she asked with foreboding.

Clara, who was picking clothes from Willa's ever-increasing collection, merely shrugged. "They didn't say. Fishing, maybe? Or sailing. I heard them mention sand. Perhaps they were going for an early walk on the beach."

"To watch the sunrise?" Willa said skeptically. "I'm not sure his lordship is quite so romantic." Not with Tamar and the vicar at least. Though when she thought about it, the presence of Mr. Grant was actually comforting. How much trouble could he get into with the vicar? Surely no one would take a vicar to a duel…unless to administer some kind of blessing or last rites?

"Oh no." She thrust the cup aside. "Hurry, Clara, I need to get dressed right away."

WITH CLARA TROTTING after her, Willa sped down to the harbor, from where you could see most of the way along to the castle beach. The sun was rising on another beautiful late summer's day, but she could make out no one on the beaches on either side.

"Blackhaven Cove," Clara suggested. "It's mostly hidden from the town. Smugglers land there sometimes."

"Lead the way," Willa commanded.

She knew at once this was the place. Two closed carriages with their placid horses stood at the side of the road, just next to the path down to the beach. Willa hurried in that direction, but the door to one of the carriages was open and with sinking heart she recognized Dr. Lampton sitting on one bench and leaning over a patient stretched out on the other.

The patient was not Dax. She saw that right away because his hair was dark brown not golden. Then, as Dr. Lampton caught sight of her and straightened, frowning, she saw that his patient was her cousin.

"Ralph," she whispered. "Oh God, he isn't dead, is he?" If Dax had dueled with Ralph, if he'd killed him…

"No, he just fainted," said quite another voice when the doctor didn't answer her, merely returned his attention to the patient. The speaker was Sir Jeremy Leigh, whom she'd met last night. He stood at the other side of the coach, looking in. "What is Shelby to you?"

"My cousin. What happened to him?"

"Just an accident," Leigh soothed.

"Don't let her go down to the beach," Dr. Lampton ordered. "Not until I've seen to her husband."

With a cry, Willa fled without listening to the words the doctor called after her. Vaguely, she was aware of Clara scuttling after her as she slid down the path. "Oh wait, m'lady, please wait. Let me go down there."

And the deeper voice of Sir Jeremy Leigh: "Lady Daxton, wait. It is not fitting…" She didn't hear the rest of that either. She was aware of his pounding feet in the sand behind her. He even caught her arm at one point, but she shook him off with a strength that must have surprised him, for she'd already seen the figure on the ground. Lord Tamar and Mr. Grant were crouched on either side of him, though both rose hastily as they saw her approach.

"He's alive, Lady Dax, don't fret," Tamar said, trying to ward her off.

She swerved around him, throwing herself onto the sand beside her husband. They'd taken off his coat, revealing a bloody shirt and a gory hole in his shoulder.

"Oh, Dax," she whispered, dragging her appalled gaze from the wound to his pale face and closed eyes. She took his face between her hands. "Don't you dare die, Dax, don't dare!"

His lips moved. "Of course, I'm not going to die," he growled. Then his eyes opened and one of his most dazzling smiles lit his whole face. "Willa." He reached up his left hand and pulled her face the rest of the way down to his, kissing her lips with a strength and thoroughness that certainly lent credence to his statement that he wasn't going to die.

"Careful there, Dax," Tamar said sardonically. "You'll get blood on Lady Dax."

Dax released her with flattering reluctance to peer at his wound instead. "Where's the damned quack?"

"Here," Dr. Lampton intoned dryly from behind Willa. "Stand back, if you please, so that the damned quack might at least see his other patient."

Willa stumbled to her feet to let him in.

"How is Shelby?" Mr. Grant asked.

"He'll live," Dr. Lampton said. "No thanks to you. I had to dig a ball out of his side. I suppose we should be grateful it didn't hit anything too vital. As for you, you've lost a lot more blood this time. Sit him up there, will you?"

Whether he needed the help or not, Tamar heaved Dax to a sitting position while the doctor examined the even bloodier back of the wound. "The ball went straight through him," he said slowly.

"From the back?" Mr. Grant asked.

"The back?" Sir Jeremy repeated at the same time as Tamar. "How can it be from the back?"

"I don't know, but it can't have been Shelby who shot him." Mr. Grant passed a pistol somewhat gingerly to Sir Jeremy, "This is Shelby's pistol and it hasn't been fired."

Sir Jeremy stared. "Hasn't been...?" He took it, examining it with care.

"Then who the devil shot me?" Dax demanded.

"Someone behind you," Dr. Lampton said. "Grant is correct. The ball entered your shoulder from the back. And it will need a stitch or two. Here." Unexpectedly, the doctor handed Daxton a flask which Dax sniffed before a quick smile flitted across his lips and he drank.

"Good brandy," he observed. "There's a lot of good brandy in Blackhaven. Very well, Doctor, do your worst."

Thoughtfully, Sir Jeremy walked back up the sand, pocketing the pistol. The coach with Ralph in it appeared to have left without him.

With tight lips, Willa watched the doctor work. Dax seemed quite stoic about the whole procedure, although his skin was alarmingly pale and he had recourse to the brandy a couple of times. Mostly his eyes remained fixed on Willa's face.

"How did you track us down?" he asked.

"Clara heard you mention sand. And I knew, I knew you were up to some mischief or other. How on earth did this happen?"

"He accused me of cheating, remember? You were there."

"That was more than a week ago!" she protested.

"I just recalled it," Dax said firmly.

With neat efficiency, the doctor bound his wound. Tamar and Grant had walked up to the road and were investigating the rough tree and brush-covered ground on either side.

"Someone who was not Ralph tried to kill you," Willa said shakily.

"You do make a lot of enemies, do you not?" the doctor observed. "Everyone and his brother seems ready to shoot you. In fact, if I'm called out to you again, I might do it myself, properly this time."

"What a comfort you must be to your many patients."

"My many patients need me," Dr. Lampton retorted. "Frivolous shootings are not my priority."

Dax blinked. "Frivolous?"

"Frivolous," Dr. Lampton repeated, and Dax actually laughed with what seemed to be genuine amusement. "Can you walk, or shall we summon your friends back?"

"I can walk." Leaning on the doctor more than on Willa, Dax rose to his feet and they walked slowly up to join the others.

Dr. Lampton addressed Willa. "This time, he *should* stay in bed. Today and tomorrow at the very least. Here is some laudanum for the pain. I'll come back and change his dressings tonight. He must not use the arm and give that wound an excuse to open again, which is why I've placed his arm in the sling. It has to stay there, as still as possible. Are you hearing this, my lord?"

"He shot my shoulder, not my ears," Dax retorted.

"He'll be fine," the doctor said dryly. "Send for me if there are any signs of fever."

"I will. Thank you, Dr. Lampton."

FORTUNATELY, IT WAS still early morning and the hotel was quiet. Dax in his torn and blood-stained clothes was able to enter and walk upstairs more or less surrounded by Willa, Tamar, and Grant without anyone seeing his state. Not that it mattered, for the news of the duel would no doubt be all over Blackhaven before luncheon.

Carson was discovered pacing the sitting room and he hastily took over the burden of his master. "My God, you're injured!" he exclaimed.

"This never happened before?" Willa asked.

"A graze once or twice, but—"

"Help me get him into bed," Willa instructed. The doctor says he is to stay there today and tomorrow."

Carson groaned. "God help us all."

"And if you hit me, I'll dismiss you on the spot," Dax warned.

"No, you won't," Carson said with confidence. "All the same, don't make me hit you! You do exactly as her ladyship tells you."

In the end, Willa left the men to it, and in no time, Dax was ready to hold court from his bed. He looked ridiculously young and rakish with his rumpled fair locks and his arm in a sling, a clean white shirt thrown around his wounded shoulder.

"Forgive me," Grant said, "but I must leave you to it. I have duties to attend to. I'll ask Kate to call later on, or send earlier if you need anything at all."

"He's a good fellow for a vicar," Dax observed when the outer door had closed behind Mr. Grant.

"He was in the army," Tamar volunteered. "Fought in India and the Peninsula before he took Holy Orders. And actually, it was he who first thought the gunshot came from behind us. It all sounded like one loud bang to me. But Grant had the gumption to check Shelby's pistol. No wonder he kept calling for it."

"Did he?" Daxton frowned.

"I heard him as they carted him off the beach to the coach, then he fainted."

Willa gazed from Tamar to Dax. "Then...you think Ralph knew? You think he was responsible for the other shooter?"

Dax rested his head back against the pillows propping him up. "I think he didn't want us to know his pistol hadn't been fired. And not all doctors are as perceptive or as attentive as Dr. Lampton."

"Also, you turned and shot pretty fast," Tamar remarked. "Which might have taken him by surprise. He might have meant to shoot you in the conventional way, with his hidden man as reinforcements. Perhaps a signal was missed, and his man shot too late to save Shelby a ball in the side."

"Whatever, it's entirely dishonorable," Dax pronounced, looking at Willa. "And you don't seem terribly surprised, let alone indignant about the accusation."

"I'm not," Willa agreed. "It's a long time since I've believed my cousin had any honor at all."

Dax looked as if he would say more, but in the end, he closed his lips, apparently turning his mind back to the duel. "Do you know, Lampton's right. Everyone and his brother does seem to shoot at me. Even the other day, driving back from my cousin's house after seeing my mother there, someone shot from close enough to startle the horses. And then there are footpads leaping out of nowhere!"

Willa stared at him. "Someone is trying to *kill* you?"

"No, no, just thinking aloud," Dax said quickly. "It's a lot more likely Shelby hired someone just to save him from the duel. The other shot will merely have been some local shooting rabbits. And in truth, the footpad wasn't much of a threat."

"But this is Blackhaven," Willa said. "Not the London underworld! Who on earth could Ralph have hired for such a purpose?"

"You'd be surprised," Tamar said. "There are some very unsavory characters that haunt the Blackhaven tavern. Villains in hiding, escaped prisoners, navy deserters, invalided and desperate soldiers and sailors. Most of them would pick your pocket, and a few wouldn't mind slitting your throat while they were about it. I'll ask around. Pretty sure Grant will already be doing the same. And he knows everyone in this town."

Lord Tamar left a little later, promising to return tomorrow, if not before. "But send to me if he gets difficult," he instructed Willa.

"Why, what are you going to do about it?" Dax challenged.

Tamar grinned. "Call you out, of course.

Willa pointed silently to the door.

The rest of the day passed rather pleasantly, considering all that had gone before. Willa entertained her husband with a mixture of childhood games and chatter. She read to him, including a couple of poems from the book of his own works which Mr. Yoeville handed in, until Dax cried for mercy, possibly because his wound was paining him too much when he laughed. Kate Grant called in and sat on the edge of Dax's bed as if he were her little brother.

Some of his drinking and cardplaying cronies also made a call, blatantly trying to learn the details of the duel.

"What duel?" Dax said aggressively, and they lapsed into silence.

To everyone who didn't already know, they maintained the fiction that he'd slipped on the wet rocks at Blackhaven Cove and injured himself.

In the early evening, Willa and Dax enjoyed a companionable dinner together. The only friction between them came when he tried to take his right hand out of the sling to eat, and Willa insisted he use his left. But even this had childishly hilarious consequences as his left hand was awkward in the task.

A little after dinner, Dr. Lampton came to change Daxton's dressings and pronounced the wound clean enough, although he didn't like the redness forming around the stitched area. He slathered more of the muddy ointment upon it before he bandaged it up again. By then, Dax had a couple of reddish patches on his cheeks.

Dr. Lampton said abruptly that someone should check on him during the night and that if the fever didn't abate, she should send for him before morning.

"Try and keep him calm," he added as she walked with him to the outer door.

"I'm perfectly calm," Dax insisted when she returned to his bedchamber. "You're a very calming person, Willa Blake." He frowned. "Though I suppose that is Willa Dacre now."

She smiled. "I seem to be Lady Dax to most people."

"Hope you don't mind that. My friends are somewhat informal."

"No, I like it," she said, passing by the bed toward the window seat.

But he patted the bed beside him. "Come, sit by me here. I want to talk to you."

"What about?" Obligingly, she changed course, and perched on the bed next to his good shoulder. She liked being so near him. It made her whole body tingle and her heart beat faster.

"About Shelby," he replied, taking her by surprise.

She frowned slightly. "What about him?"

"What did he do to hurt you?"

The direct question threw her. He'd just fought a duel with Ralph.

What more could he do?

Dax took her hand. It jumped and then lay still in his, letting his fingers close warmly about it. "Look, I know he's a boor. And if he has any power or authority over anyone, he'd rather hurt their feelings than not. I'm sure you came into that category. But I think there's something more."

Willa thought of deflecting the question again. But he was her husband, and if she wanted honesty and openness from him, she had to return them. So, she opened her mouth to tell him, then closed it, overwhelmed by the difficulty of putting it into words. She swallowed and tried again.

"One day, in the spring, he cornered me in the breakfast room and wouldn't let me go."

Daxton's fingers tightened on hers. "What did he do?"

"He pulled me against him, put his hands on me. All over me. He tried to kiss me but I had my head strained so far away that he just slobbered over my face. That wasn't very nice either."

But for once Dax wouldn't be distracted by humor. "Did he hurt you?"

"He was rough," Willa admitted. "I was a little bruised. But not as badly as he was."

Daxton's brow twitched. "You got away from him? How?"

"In a very unladylike manner. I rammed by knee between his legs and shoved," she said candidly. "He made a great fuss about it, and in truth, I did not realize that could be quite so painful for gentlemen. It was luck on my part because my knee was one of the few parts of me that was free to move at the time."

She hesitated, but she'd begun now and had to finish. "While he was doubled up and rolling on the carpet, I told him if he ever touched me again, I'd tell his mother about him and Haines—my aunt's abigail."

He put his arm around her shoulders, drawing her into his side. "You bested him. And he's been punishing you ever since. That's why he got you to bring him the money the night we played dice."

"I'm sure he meant to humiliate as well as inconvenience me. And in front of you, too, because you punched him for pushing me into that wall."

His arm tightened around her. "Well, I know it can't have been very comfortable for you, walking into such a party, with all eyes upon you, too. But I find I can't be sorry for it."

She smiled. "Neither can I."

For a time, they sat in companionable silence, Willa very aware of his closeness, the warmth of his arm and his shoulder. Then she said, "Ralph has hated you ever since you punched him when we were children. I don't think you cared or even knew. Yet now, *you* hate him. Why? What happened?"

This time it was Daxton's turn to hesitate. "It's not a very edifying tale, particularly not for a lady and my wife to boot."

"Tell me anyway."

"Ralph kept a mistress, an opera dancer called Julia. She was beautiful, graceful, and I became obsessed with her. I think I was all of nineteen years old. But she liked me, let me visit her, and before long I could tell she was unhappy with Ralph. More than that, he ill-treated her, beat her, indulged in...pleasures, shall we say, which were no pleasure to her. So, I took her away from him, gave her my protection instead. And there was nothing he could do about it without appearing sillier than he already looked for losing her to a nineteen-year-old boy in the first place."

Willa's heart welled with pity. "What became of your Julia? Do you still see her?"

He smiled. "Lord, no. After a few months, she went off with an American sea captain and I haven't seen her since. To be honest, it was a relief, for my youthful infatuation was wearing off."

Willa couldn't help being glad of that.

They spoke desultorily of other things that were more comfortable and pleasant, and gradually, Willa's eyes began to close. It had been a long, anxious day. She was warm and comfortable and contented. It wasn't surprising that she fell asleep with her head on his good shoulder, and the heat of his body seeping through her flimsy clothes.

Chapter Thirteen

S HE WOKE TO DARKNESS and the gentle thrill of fingers caressing her arm and shoulder and coming to rest, finally on her hip. Something—someone—warm snuggled close into her back.

Dax. I fell asleep in his bed...

The realization brought a surge of delicious heat, especially as his hand began to move on her hip, stroking the curve as far as her thigh. His quickened breath stirred her hair, caressed her ear. His lips touched the delicate skin behind her lobe and slid down her neck. She could almost believe he was smiling. His hand began to roam toward that part of her which seemed to radiate all the heat and tingling that was melting her.

And then he stopped. For several moments he didn't even seem to breathe.

He's asleep, she thought, stricken. *He doesn't know it's me.*

But it seemed he had wakened up. His breath came out in a rush, whispering her name. "Willa."

Afraid to move, she lay perfectly still until gently but insistently, the hand on her hip began to pull her onto her back.

"Dax," she said shakily, "I—" The rest was lost in his mouth as it sank on hers in a kiss that was slow and hot and utterly irresistible. His hand caressed her other hip now, roaming upward to her breast where it lay heavily before beginning to move, sweet and arousing.

"Willa," he said against her lips. "Tell me it's time. Let me love you."

Through her deep, sensual haze, she knew what he meant. "You're my husband," she got out.

"I am, and if we do this, you'll never get rid of me."

Her laughter was half-sob. "Dax. I never wanted to be rid of you."

She felt his smile as he kissed her mouth again. "But do you want me, now, like this?"

"You know I do," she said shakily, throwing both arms around his neck.

With one tug, it seemed, her clothing all fell away from her upper body. He must have unlaced everything while she slept. While *he* still slept. Perhaps the implications of that should have appalled her, but she'd always known what he was, and in reality, it made her want to laugh. Except that his mouth on her naked skin, her throat, her breasts, flooded every other emotion with pleasure and need.

Only once did common sense intervene. "Your shoulder!" she exclaimed. "You mustn't—"

"My shoulder is as desperate for you as the rest of me," he growled. "And none of me will be denied."

Clearly, to keep him calm as she'd been instructed by the doctor, she had to give in. Although there was nothing calm about his all but panting breath, or his feverish, turbulent eyes blazing in the darkness, and certainly not in his increasingly wild caresses. The only clothing he wore was the shirt dangling from his good arm, tangling around their bodies. His naked skin was hot and smooth under her hands, the hard muscle rippling beneath in instant response to her every caress.

When he entered her body, she stilled, gazing at him in shock. And yet the trust was still there. His fingertips glided over her lips. "It's a dance of love," he whispered. "Hold on and follow me."

She did, until it no longer hurt but filled her with fierce, new desires that flowed from inside her with his every, sensual stroke.

"And like the waltz," she whispered, lost in the pleasure. "I may not lead?"

"Oh, you may," he said fervently, which thrilled her even more, only right now it was all she could do to follow where *he* led, for all the hunger and bliss seemed to be coming together in one rolling, fevered wave that broke over her with stunning, impossible joy.

She clung to him, reaching for his mouth with astonished grati-tude. He gave it, groaning deep in his throat as he thrust hard within her and collapsed on her, his hand fisted in her hair. It seemed the storm had taken them both.

In time, as the world came back, she realized his lips were smiling against hers.

"Now you really are my wife," he said unsteadily.

"And you are my injured husband. How badly have you hurt your shoulder?" She eased out from under him, rolling him gently onto his back, gasping as he left her body. She felt rather than saw his wicked grin.

"My shoulder is as happy as the rest of me," he assured her, but she insisted on lighting the candle and checking the bandage for signs of blood. She could see none, although the magnificence of his naked body quickly distracted her.

"I never realized men were so beautiful," she said in wonder. "But perhaps it is just you."

"Well, you're not to go looking to find out," he said dryly.

She laughed and, greatly daring, kissed his good shoulder. "Why would I do that?" she wondered. "I have everything I've ever wanted, more than I ever imagined, here, in you."

His hand cupped her cheek. A smile played around his lips. "I would live up to that." He pulled her back down into the bed beside him, his good arm holding her close against him.

"Your skin is so hot," she said with sleepy contentment.

"That is your fault," he replied.

AS BECAME CLEAR in the light of day, it wasn't entirely Willa's fault. His skin was still hot and his cheeks somewhat hectically flushed. Worse, there was a strange glitter in his eyes when he woke that caused Willa to send Carson scurrying for Dr. Lampton.

Dax, apparently annoyed by all the fuss, only tried to entice Willa back into bed with him. "I've a few more things to show you before luncheon," he promised. "And I might even let you lead."

She flushed, with both memory and desire, but guilt and good sense were too strong now to give in to that temptation. "Wait until the doctor has been," she soothed, evading his grasping hands to seize his discarded robe and put it on while she gathered her clothes and hastened back to her own chamber to dress before Dr. Lampton arrived.

Worry for him put something of a damper on the new wonder of her body and all the things Dax had done to it last night. Beautiful as it had been, it would hardly be worth his illness or, unspeakably, his death.

Dr. Lampton, however, did not appear unduly anxious, or even terribly surprised. He changed the dressings, applying yet more of the muddy ointment, and gave him a tonic to drink that would help bring down the fever.

On the way out, he paused and looked closely at Willa. She had the ridiculous notion that he could see in her face what she and Dax had done last night and was about to tell her off.

"Don't tie yourself entirely to his sick room," he advised. "Get some fresh air, occasionally. And don't worry yourself sick about your husband. He's strong as an ox, despite the way he mistreats his body, and is most unlikely to die at this point."

"At *this* point?" she repeated in dismay.

"Well, we must all die at *some* point," Dr. Lampton said wryly. "I predict Lord Daxton's to be well in the future. If he does as he's told."

Accordingly, after breakfast, Willa went out, taking Clara with her, and bought some things at the market—a few lengths of ribbon for herself and a pair of gloves for Dax. It was while buying the latter that she found herself beside Sir Jeremy Leigh.

"Lady Daxton," he said in apparent surprise. "How does your husband?"

"He is confined to bed, which does not agree with his temperament! I was looking for something to entertain him with."

"Jackstraws," Sir Jeremy said at once. "Come with me."

"But that is a children's game," she protested, following him across the market to another stall full of toys.

"Exactly," Sir Jeremy agreed. "And now he has an excuse to behave like one again."

The stall keeper presented him with a box of Jackstraws and Sir Jeremy paid before presenting the box to Willa. "With my compliments to the patient. It's the least I can do."

"*You* didn't shoot him," Willa protested.

"No. Apparently neither did Shelby, which is rather worrying."

"How is my cousin?" she asked. If he died, after all, Dax would be in trouble.

"The doctor said he would be fine. I confess I haven't seen him since we took him back to the hotel yesterday."

"Why not? I thought you were his friend?"

"Acquaintance," Sir Jeremy corrected. "And I'm afraid I find myself suspicious of his involvement in Lord Daxton's quite dishonorable shooting."

"Why, do you have proof?" Willa demanded. "Do you know who it was?"

"No," he confessed. "But perhaps we should put our heads together and discuss it."

"Come and visit him," Willa suggested. "Though perhaps not until tomorrow."

"I will, but I wouldn't want to worry him with this business when he's already injured. I was thinking you and I might see more clearly going over it all together."

"Of course. When you come to see Dax we can talk. Lord Tamar and Mr. Grant also have…" She broke off as someone she recognized stepped out of a familiar barouche which had stopped at the edge of the market. Lady Romford.

"Excuse me," she said hastily to Sir Jeremy. "Thank you for the gift, and I look forward to seeing you tomorrow…" She was already hurrying away toward Lady Romford who, with another middle-aged lady, was strolling past the stalls at the front.

Willa didn't really wish to encounter her mother-in-law, but in this case, it had to be done, so she approached her head-on.

"Good morning, Lady Romford."

Daxton's mother glanced up from the flowers she was examining. Immediately, her nostrils flared with distaste. She didn't as much as incline her head in recognition.

"I know you don't wish to speak to me," Willa blurted. "But I do have to tell you something. About Dax."

Anger spat from Lady Romford's eyes. "There is nothing *you* can tell me about *my* son!"

"There is, ma'am. Please." She stepped back, away from the crowd and after an instant's indecision, Lady Romford said something to Cousin Harriet, and followed Willa.

Lady Romford raised one supercilious eyebrow. "Well?"

"You have to know that Dax fought a duel yesterday and though he is very much alive, he *was* shot in the shoulder."

Lady Romford whitened, swaying slightly so that Willa caught her by the wrist to steady her.

"Why does he *do* these things?" Dax's mother demanded. "You must let me see him."

"Of course," Willa said in surprise. "Come back with me to the hotel now. Or later, if you prefer. He is not desperately ill. I just didn't want you to hear the rumors that have no doubt spread all through the town before you learned the truth of it."

Lady Romford's eyes focused on her for a long moment. "You were never an ill-natured girl," she recalled.

"I hope not," Willa said humbly.

"Who did he fight, and why?" the countess demanded.

"My cousin Ralph. Over some card game when Ralph accused him of cheating. Or at least that's the reason he gave. I wouldn't be surprised if there was more to it."

"There is bad blood between him and Ralph Shelby."

Willa said nothing. His mother had probably heard the tale anyhow from other sources than her son.

Lady Romford raised her voice. "Harriet! Let's walk to the hotel."

Unfortunately, the first person Willa saw in the hotel foyer was her aunt, who stormed across to her without appearing to see her companions.

"It's your fault, you viper!" Lady Shelby accused. "Your fault that my son lies dying in his bed. Our sole support! I know they were fighting over you, you nasty, vindictive hussy!"

"One moment, madam," Lady Romford interrupted icily. "I make allowances for a mother's natural anxiety, but you will not speak so to my daughter. Your son and mine made their own beds and must lie in them. I gather they will both survive the ordeal. We may talk later when you are calmer. Good morning, Lady Shelby."

And Lady Romford sailed rather magnificently onwards, just as if she knew the way, leaving Willa and Cousin Harriet to hurry after her. Willa remembered to bow politely to her aunt on the way past.

"Insufferable woman," Lady Romford remarked as they caught up. "I'm sorry for it, since she's your aunt, Willa, but I'm afraid I have always found her so."

Willa, still stunned that Lady Romford had referred to her as her daughter, could only smile understandingly and lead the way up to the rooms she shared with Dax.

Clara was discovered in the sitting room, telling off Carson and Daniel Doone. Clara lapsed into silence the moment they walked in, and Carson and Dan attempted to efface themselves.

Willa said calmly, "Carson, is his lordship fit to be seen?"

"Yes, m'lady. He's washed and shaved and mostly dressed."

"Tell him Lady Romford will be in to see him in a moment," Willa instructed. "Clara, perhaps you'd arrange tea."

"Of course, m'lady."

"I don't know why Charles insists on employing that man." Lady Romford scowled after Carson's retreating back.

"I know he's unconventional for a valet," Willa excused, "but actually, he looks after him very well. And he is utterly loyal."

Lady Romford snorted and swung on the hapless Dan, edging toward the door after Clara. "And who is this?"

"Daniel Doone," Willa said. "He's been... er... helping us out with extra work."

"In return for my mistake," Dan blurted. "I'm the one who shot him. The first time."

"It was an accident, a misunderstanding and not remotely serious," Willa said hastily. "The merest graze. Go away, Dan. Or help Clara or something."

To her surprise, Lady Romford was regarding her with something close to amusement. "You are very accepting of the madhouse that follows my son."

"I like it," Willa confessed. She couldn't quite read her mother-in-law's expression.

Carson came out of Daxton's bedchamber, throwing the door wide. "His lordship is receiving," he said cheerfully.

LADY ROMFORD WASN'T a woman who admitted easily to making mistakes. But like her son, she acted very much on impulse and feelings. On first hearing of Daxton's marriage, she had been furious that he did not make one of the brilliant matches she had so hoped for and worked for. Not that she'd ever disliked Willa as a child. Quite the contrary, in fact, she had always found her to be a natural and well-mannered girl, her innate sense of fun tempered by good sense as well as by good nature. But never in a million years could mere Willa Blake be considered a suitable bride for the future Earl of Romford. His birth, his heritage—and the fact that his mother loved him ferociously—all demanded he have the very best of everything. In the matter of marriage more than anything else.

And so, she'd allowed nothing to get in the way of her determination to end that hasty mésalliance.

But then, despite her unkind treatment, Willa had forced herself to do the right thing, to tell her about Dax's injury before she heard rumors from other sources that might have worried her even more. And the countess had remembered the kind child she had been rather than the malicious, designing temptress of more recent imagination. Her worry for her injured son had made her less careful than usual, and when Augusta Shelby had attacked Willa, she had defended her, more from instinct than anything else. And as usual, she'd gone too far. Words like "my daughter" couldn't easily be taken back.

But there had been a certain look in Willa's face, behind the natural diffidence of accosting a hostile parent-in-law. A care and concern, overlaying a new happiness that she saw reflected in Charles. Willa's birth and fortune might have been all wrong, but in every other way, she seemed to suit Charles very well. She'd clearly handled him, his untamed servant and his chaotic lifestyle with natural skill.

The countess left their rooms very thoughtful. Her anxiety eased by her son's bright manner and confidence in his own speedy recovery, she felt guilt and shame rise up from her toes. She got as far as the hotel front door before she turned and walked back to the desk.

Presenting the clerk with a card, she said, "Please have this taken up to Mrs. Holt."

A few minutes later, she was following a maid back up the staircase, beyond Daxton's floor and to another set of rooms.

Helena Holt was alone. She sat at an escritoire, busily writing, although she stopped and rose as soon as Lady Romford entered.

"Are you come to check up on my progress?" she inquired with a hint of sardonic humor.

The countess could see what had drawn Charles to her—beyond her beauty, of course. She could also see that she didn't hold a candle to Willa in any sense.

"No," Lady Romford said with a sigh. "I have come to apologize for my insolent request and to ask you to disregard it."

Surprise widened Helena's beautiful eyes. "May I know why?"

"I have just met my son. He is quite…content. And therefore, so am I."

"I see."

"So you will give up whatever schemes you've made at my foolish request?"

A spurt of anger flashed across the younger woman's face. "Hardly. You should know I was never doing it for you in the first place. You only put the idea in my head. Dax and his milksop bride may be content—for now—but I am not."

"But he will not give her up. What can you hope to achieve?"

"Oh, he will. She may have given him temporary contentment, but I can give him much more. As to what *I* hope to achieve, you know that perfectly well. Holt will not live forever, and I have no intention of ending up like poor Kate Crowmore, tied to some nobody like her country vicar. I have a fancy to be a countess."

"Then find another earl's son—or another earl, it is immaterial to me," Lady Romford said tartly. "Have a duke if it will make you happy. But please, do not interfere any further with my son's life. I have withdrawn my permission."

"Madam," Helena said insolently, "I never needed your permission before and I certainly don't now. I have no wish to quarrel with my future mama, but you should know where we stand."

"I do. And I won't have it," Lady Romford said with dignity. "More to the point, neither will my son." She bowed and left the room.

Helena Holt's voice followed her, confident, amused, and unperturbed. "We shall see."

WHEN WILLA QUIETLY entered her husband's sick room, he was fast asleep. Part of her was relieved, for she was no longer sure of the meaning of last night's dalliance. Had he made love to her because he was fevered and not in his right mind? Or had their lovemaking caused the fever? Or, at least, made it worse. The rest of her was worried that his mother's visit had exhausted him, that he was worse now than when Dr. Lampton had come this morning.

Thrusting aside her own pettier concerns, she went to him immediately, touching his forehead with the palm of her hand, and then feeling just inside his shirt. She didn't think he was worse. If anything, surely, the hot tightness had receded a little.

Without warning, his hand closed over hers on his chest, and her gaze flew up to his face. His eyes were open and fixed on hers. They still looked slightly fevered, although that might have been the laudanum.

"Your hand is cool," he said. "I like that. Although I liked it when it was hot last night, too,"

She flushed, drawing her hand free. "Then you remember last night?" When she was too innocent, or too lost in her own desires to be able to tell that his own heat came from fever.

A wicked smile parted his lips and glinted in his eyes. "Every delicious detail. Come back to bed with me, Wife."

"Not until you're well," she said firmly. "I'm afraid our... your...the...what we did made you ill. Too much exertion—"

"Sweet exertion," he said, and despite her best intentions, desire surged with the memory. "Besides, if I can support an unexpected visit from my mother, I can support an hour of delight with my wife. Or two hours, or three..."

"Drink this," she said, with a hint of desperation, thrusting the glass of the doctor's tonic into his hand. He dipped his head and kissed her wrist before she could take her hand away, but at least he drank it.

"What did you do with my mother, by the way? She asked me if I wanted to annul our marriage. I said no, and she changed the subject."

"Is that bad?"

"No, I think it's good. Only why the devil did she come up here— and at the same time as Helena Holt, too—if she didn't mean to upset the marriage?"

"Perhaps she changed her mind," Willa suggested.

Dax scowled. "Or she's biding her time."

"I'm sure she was genuinely worried about you. Her manner changed immediately when I told her what had happened. And do you know, she defended me and called me her daughter when my aunt accused me of causing your duel."

Dax looked thoughtful as he drank the rest of the tonic. He wrinkled his nose. "Why are doctor's potions always so nasty?"

"To make you avoid the necessity of taking them, I suppose." She took the glass from him and set it on the bedside table. "Shall I read to you?"

"Yes, if you can spare the time. Willa?" He reached out and caught her hand as she would have gone to fetch the book from the window seat. Her heart beat quickened as she allowed him to draw her back to the bed. He held her gaze. "It wasn't the fever last night," he said deliberately.

Warmth flooded her. She couldn't help smiling. Impulsively, she drew his hand up to her cheek and then to her lips. This time she let him pull her down onto the bed and settle her head against his chest while he stroked her hair. Her heart felt so full she wanted to weep with happiness.

Chapter Fourteen

THE FOLLOWING MORNING, Dax looked so much more like himself that Willa was glad she'd insisted on returning to her own bedchamber to sleep. Not that Dax had tried to prevent her, for he'd already been sound asleep himself.

They enjoyed a comfortable breakfast together in his room, and were arguing over whether or not he should get up from his bed that day, when Dr. Lampton arrived together with Mr. Grant and Lord Tamar.

"Her ladyship is right," the doctor said, even before he'd changed the dressings. "Bed for at least one more day."

Dax tried to argue the point until he got bored, but Willa saw she would have her work cut out to keep him contented and rested for another day. Grant and Tamar helped, once the doctor had left, lounging about the bedchamber and entertaining him with amusing anecdotes, as well as engaging his mind with the mystery of who the devil had shot him.

"Neither of the coachmen saw anyone on the rocks above the beach," Grant said. "So, I poked further around until I think I found where the shooter lay—considering your position and where the ball hit you. What's more, it would have been easy to slide down to a cattle track lane that leads directly to the market road. He could easily have been long gone before the doctor even got to you."

"But who would have done that?" Willa demanded, distressed.

Tamar shrugged. "Someone in Shelby's pay. We checked up on his servants, though. The coachman stayed with his coach and his valet was cowering in the hotel, afraid that Lady Shelby would find out about the duel. We looked for strangers, at first, London villains, since Grant says there's been some trouble with such before. But it seems to us, this fellow knew Blackhaven."

"The town is full of old soldiers, hungry for work and not necessarily fussy what it is," Grant added. "But I know most of them and I can't imagine any of them who might have been both able and willing."

"Maybe it's nothing to do with Shelby," Dax said thoughtfully. "Maybe it's someone else I annoyed."

Tamar stared. "You'd have to *really* annoy someone before they'd shoot you in the back! A duel is one thing, but there's no honor in *murder*."

Willa said, "There's that man I see skulking outside the hotel sometimes. I've seen him at the stables and the theatre as well. I always have the impression he's watching us."

Dax frowned at her. "He probably is. Well, watching you, at any rate." He shifted restlessly. "I need to get up."

"Tomorrow," Willa soothed. "Providing you don't exert yourself today."

Grant went off about his own business just a little later. Tamar, who'd brought his easel and canvas, made them pose for him and worked on his portrait, in a discontented kind of way.

"The light's all wrong in here," he grumbled. But he condescended to eat some luncheon with them before he, too, went off.

Willa then played jackstraws with her husband, which turned out to be both hilarious and almost impossible on the bed. They were thus engaged when Carson announced Sir Jeremy Leigh, and Dax called cheerfully for him to come in.

"Thank you for returning me to my childhood," Dax said to him with a grin, indicating the collapsed heap of straws. "Now, you're obliged to join in."

Willa left them to play and sent Clara to fetch tea. Although now reconciled with her parents, the maid showed no wish to go home, and Willa had asked her to think about a permanent position with her. She was hardly a conventional, let alone a trained abigail, but Willa, who'd never had a lady's maid before in any case, had grown used to her and would miss her if she left.

Carson went off with Clara, presumably to help bring the tea things, and Willa settled on the sofa with her book. She didn't want to be constantly hovering over Dax, especially when he had other people to entertain him. Now that her anxiety for him had eased, hope and happiness had seeped into her. Even Lady Romford seemed to have relaxed her opposition. The future with Dax seemed bright, filled with fun and laughter. She'd never have imagined such a thing remotely possible before she'd come to Blackhaven.

About half an hour after tea was served, Sir Jeremy emerged from Dax's bedchamber and closed the door.

"Did you win?" Willa asked lightly, rising to meet him.

"Handsomely," Sir Jeremy replied.

"I'm not sure I believe you!"

"Well, Dax will no doubt give you the same answer." Sir Jeremy took her hand, as though taking his leave, then asked instead, "How are you bearing up?"

"Oh, I am quite well now that he seems to be doing better."

Sir Jeremy handed her to the sofa, and since he clearly wished to discuss something, she sat expectantly. He lowered himself beside her, gazing at her with an intensity that made her suddenly uncomfortable.

"How is my cousin?" she asked, a shade nervously.

Sir Jeremy shrugged. "Recovering, I believe. I'm sure it will be no time before he's telling the world how he shot Daxton in a duel."

"Do you know yet who did shoot Dax?" Willa asked directly.

"No," he said, frowning. As though distracted, he picked up her hand again.

Willa, unused to the pursuit of men, assumed he was in need of comfort, or imagined she was. "What is it?" she asked anxiously. "What is it you know?"

His gaze never left her face. For several seconds, he said nothing at all, then, abruptly, he rose, drawing her with him. "Come. There's something I need to show you. Bring your bonnet."

"Oh. If it's important…let me just look in on Dax—"

"He's fallen asleep," Sir Jeremy said. "That's why I came away to speak to you."

After only a moment's hesitation, Willa picked up her bonnet and pelisse and preceded him out of the door. "Where are we going?"

"Not far, but it is important."

Intrigued, wondering if it would finally solve the mystery of who had shot Dax, she accompanied him from the hotel. It was a busy time of day, and the street was filled with pedestrians and vehicles. For the first time, Willa wondered if it was quite proper for her to be abroad with no one but Sir Jeremy Leigh for escort, but she was more interested in what he had to show her, in how it would help to save Dax from any further attacks.

And in truth, Sir Jeremy maintained his gentlemanly conduct throughout. He didn't walk too close, or change his manner in the slightest, merely making amusing and rather witty small talk as they walked the length of High Street and around the corner, where he paused outside a tall house.

"Where are we?" she asked bluntly.

"Outside my lodgings."

Willa frowned. "Well, I don't think I should go in there. Whatever it is you wish to show me, you should bring it to me, or take Dax when he's better."

Sir Jeremy's lips twisted. "You really don't understand, do you? Do you believe in my innate goodness? Or do you truly not realize the temptation you present to a man?"

She stared at him for a moment, a flush of anger mounting to her cheeks. This was all he had ever intended. He had enticed her away from Daxton for this. Had he really imagined she would just give in? Certainly. He made no effort to force her into the building.

She said intensely, "I had thought better of you." And she turned on her heel.

Sir Jeremy sighed behind her. "I know. I'll escort you back to the—"

"There is no need," she interrupted, without even turning her head or adding any words of farewell. She was far too furious, both with her own naivety and with Leigh's utterly dishonorable conduct. But then, what else should she have expected from anyone with a claim to friendship with Ralph?

At least he made no attempt to drag her back or accompany her. She'd have imagined he was ashamed if he hadn't had the gall to bait her this far, away from her wounded husband's sick room, with the aim of seduction. Any number of people must have seen her in his company, too. Had his aim been to hurt Dax? To ruin her?

Her first instinct was to pour out everything to Dax himself. But, of course, that would be foolish. Dax would inevitably charge from his sickbed to knock Leigh down, or worse. No doubt there would be another duel, before he'd even recovered from the last—with the same assailant free to take an extra shot at him in case Leigh missed.

Was Leigh the true villain, then? Had he employed the gunman? She wondered what grudge he could possibly have against Dax.

Any number. Who would know?

Kate Grant.

Since she was still too angry and churned up to go straight back to the hotel, she turned her steps toward the vicarage.

Of course, the day's lesson was that you couldn't trust anyone, not even Kate, whom she liked, so she couldn't even pour out the whole tale to her. Instead, once they were settled in the vicarage drawing room drinking tea, she merely asked Kate about Leigh's reputation and his relationship with Dax.

"You think Leigh is the culprit?" Kate said in surprise. She thought about it. "I never imagined him quite so villainous. Or dishonorable. On the other hand, he is, I think, quite besotted with…a certain lady from Daxton's past."

"Helena Holt," Willa said bluntly. She thought about that quite hard for a while, until she became aware of Kate's gaze on her face.

"Don't look so troubled," Kate said lightly. "I do mean his past. I have never seen Daxton as he is with you."

She tried not to ask but she couldn't help it. "What do you mean?"

"I mean you and he are both so natural and accepting of each other. I won't go into the signs of obvious affection since it would only embarrass you."

HELENA HOLT WAS thoroughly bored with Blackhaven and couldn't wait to return to London—or Brighton at the very least. But she needed to do with it with Daxton's escort. And with luck, the impediments to that were being dealt with at this moment, even as she replied to the letters of friends in the south, with her version of the duel rumored to have been fought between Daxton and Shelby.

The offence was trumped-up, of course, she wrote. *My own belief is that it was over his bride, despite her apparent propriety.*

A knock on the door interrupted her, and her maid announced Sir Jeremy Leigh.

"Well?" she demanded as he strolled in. "Is it done?"

"You needn't look so eager for me to be making love to other women."

"Don't be so mealy mouthed. Did you bed her?" Helena asked bluntly.

Sir Jeremy smiled in a way she didn't quite like, and flicked some imaginary dust from his sleeve. "No, I didn't. She is, you know, quite tiresomely devoted to Dax."

"But you at least got her into your rooms?"

Leigh sighed. "No, I didn't. I couldn't."

Helena narrowed her eyes with irritation. "You couldn't or you wouldn't?"

Leigh met her gaze. "I wouldn't. It seems I'm not yet completely lost to gentlemanly conduct."

"So, what, you just tamely brought her back to the hotel?"

"No, she walked away from me. I followed her to make sure she got home safely—since you and I are clearly not the only ones out to harm the Daxtons. But she didn't come back to the hotel, she went into the vicarage."

Helena rose to her feet. "Then I have to act quickly. Go home, Sir Jeremy. It seems I have to do everything myself."

WHEN LEIGH HAD left him, Dax laid his head back against the pillows and listened to the muffled sounds of his wife's voice in the next room as she conversed with their departing guest. He smiled, for he liked just to hear her voice.

Then the outer door closed and he waited for her to come in to him. He was feeling so much better and his body ached for her. A little afternoon love with Willa was just what he needed, and with an urgency that had him shifting about in the bed. Intoxicating thought. She was his wife. He could have her whenever he liked, and God knew he liked. He liked more than he'd ever imagined possible.

But she didn't come in. And the room beyond was silent. He couldn't even hear her moving in there.

He slid out of bed rather more carefully than usual, and walked quite steadily to the bedchamber door.

The sitting room was empty and there was no sign of Carson or Clara either. She must have gone out and taken the maid, he thought, until the passage door opened and Clara and Carson entered together. He couldn't tell if they were arguing or flirting and frankly didn't much care.

"Where's her ladyship?" he snapped.

"I thought she was here," Clara said in surprise, going hastily to her mistress's bedchamber and looking inside. "No, she must have gone out, for the green bonnet and pelisse aren't here. I suppose she won't be long if she didn't tell you."

Dax was aware his annoyance was both unreasonable and childish. Willa hardly needed his permission to go out, though he was slightly piqued she hadn't said goodbye. He was slightly more piqued that she must have left with Leigh, for he'd only heard the door close once.

He groaned internally. *I'm going to be one of these awful husbands who guard their wives jealously. Or at least I'll want to be, which is just as bad.*

"Anyway," Carson said accusingly. "What are you doing out of bed?"

"Looking for her ladyship, of course."

"Well, you'd better get back to bed before she comes home or we'll all get it in the neck."

Dax couldn't help grinning, delighted to see Carson afraid of somebody at last, and proud that it was Willa. All the same, he'd more than had enough of bed and his robe. "Get me dressed, Carson, and I'll make sure it's only *my* neck under the axe."

Carson looked mutinous for a few moments. But then, probably suspecting—correctly—that if he didn't help, Dax would simply do it alone, inevitably harming his wound further, he gave in and followed Dax into the bedchamber.

Half an hour later, Willa still hadn't returned and Daxton's unease had increased. For some reason, he was convinced she was unhappy and needed him. Pacing the sitting room, from the window to the door and back, he knew he was going to have to go and look for her.

"My hat," he barked at Carson, just as a knock sounded at the door.

Since he stood right beside it, he opened it and blinked at the unexpected sight of Helena Holt, smiling lazily at him from the passage. She took advantage of his bemusement, sailing past him into the room.

Dax turned to face her, though he didn't close the door. She looked like a breath of autumn in flowing browns and reds and dark greens. "What do you want, Helena?"

"I see marriage hasn't improved your manners," she observed, apparently amused. "Or does the wound make you such a bear? I have to say you look very dashing." She waved one languid hand to indicate his sling and the coat loose about one shoulder. At least Carson had manhandled him carefully into his shirt and tied his cravat for him.

"Helena," Dax repeated dangerously.

She smiled provokingly. "What I want, Dax, is to help you."

"You," he mocked, "wish to help me? On the contrary, you *wish* me to perdition."

"You're wrong. Dax, I know exactly what's going on, why you're pacing the room like some wounded beast, desperate for your good little wife to come home."

"Helena," he warned.

"Oh, be calm, Daxton, get your hat, for I know exactly where she is. I'll take you to her."

Fear twisted through his stomach. "Where is she, Helena? Is she well?"

"Of course she is *well*," Helena soothed, while her eyes danced with amusement. Once the contrast had beguiled him. Now, he found it annoying. "She's perfectly well and happy, I imagine. Are you fit for a short walk?"

"No," Carson said baldly behind him, though he gave him his hat.

"Yes," Dax said, allowing Carson one glare as he snatched the hat and followed Helena out of the room.

"I'll just tag along," Carson announced. "Catch you when you fall over."

"You do that," Dax said.

They left the hotel together, Carson trotting a pace or two behind Dax and Helena.

Dax was barely aware of his wound as he strode up the high street. The ache was quite subsidiary to his fear for Willa, because he knew perfectly well Helena was up to something. But he had to get to Willa, and right now. Helena seemed to offer the best means. He'd deal with her motives after that, if he had to.

A few people hailed him on the way, their faces alive with curiosity, no doubt about Helena as much as about his wound. If he could have done this without Helena, he would.

At the end of High Street, she turned left and walked a little way up the quiet street to a tall house with a green door that opened onto the street. She rapped on it with the handle of her parasol.

She smiled at Dax, but, glowering, he refused to give her the satisfaction of asking where the devil they were. A middle-aged woman in a mob cap opened the door and scowled.

"Thank you, Mrs. Jones, I remember the way," Helena drawled, sailing past into the house. Dax followed her, Carson at his heels.

"Very well, Helena, you win," Dax said impatiently, climbing the stairs behind her. "Where the deuce are we?"

"Mrs. Jones's house. She rents out rooms to ladies and gentlemen of quality."

"Quality!" Mrs. Jones muttered behind them as she waddled back into the depths of the house. "Ha! No better than they should be, any of them!"

Helena tapped on the first door at the top of the stairs and stood back a little, smiling at Dax with a strange but worrying mixture of triumph and malice. The door flew open quite suddenly and there, in his shirt-sleeves, stood Sir Jeremy Leigh.

"Helena," he began with a hint of frustration, and then, catching sight of Dax, his eyes widened. Abruptly—and quite without manners—he made to slam the door, an act which suddenly blasted all the pieces of the mystery into place for Dax.

With a curse, he hurled himself at the closing door, all but falling inside with the force of it.

Helena followed him, calling out with clear mockery, "Lady Daxton! Oh Lady Daxton! Come out, come out, wherever you are."

"Lady Daxton is not here," Leigh said. "For God's sake, Helena, you *know* that."

"Gone already, has she?" Helena drawled. "You must be losing your touch, Jeremy." She threw open a door on Daxton's left, clearly Leigh's bedchamber, and walked familiarly inside.

Dax, enraged by this whole charade against his wife, swung on Leigh for an explanation. The man had turned white, though, slipping into the chamber after Helena. The pair almost raced in an undignified manner to the unmade bed, where something glinting on the pillow caught Daxton's eye.

It was Helena who got to it first, seizing it up in triumph and swinging it around to dangle it in front of Dax.

It was the diamond spiral pendant, the one he'd bought for Helena, and in the end, given to Willa. Helena hadn't planted it there. It had already been on Leigh's pillow when they entered.

Blood sang in Daxton's ears. He felt as if the world were folding in on him, burying him. Only his rage fought its way out. Without thought, he lunged and with his good, right hand, struck Leigh a massive blow on the jaw.

If he touched him again, he'd kill him. Barreling past Carson, he bolted out to the stairs. The word *No!* seemed to be ringing in his head so loudly that he stopped half way down, panting with fury.

"No." A frown tugged its way across his entire forehead. Then he turned, staring at Carson.

"She wouldn't, sir. She just wouldn't," his valet uttered.

Dax ignored him because he had to. With much more dignified steps, he returned to Leigh's room. Helena stood outside the bedchamber looking very pleased with herself. Leigh, on his feet and nursing his jaw was scowling at her before he spun around to regard Dax in fresh alarm.

"Blackhaven Cove," Dax said. "At dawn, the day after tomorrow. No seconds. Just you and me. And pistols. And a priest if you want one. Thanks," he added to Helena, plucking the pendant from her nerveless fingers. "I know you stole it the day you visited my wife." He caught her expression, one of slightly annoyed amusement, before he turned and walked away down the stairs and across the hall to the front door.

Chapter Fifteen

B Y THE TIME WILLA returned to the hotel from the vicarage, she had herself well in hand, and breezed into her rooms as though nothing had happened. She would tell Dax of her stupidity one day when it didn't matter, or at least when he was recovered enough from one duel to be fighting another. But for now, this was one secret she had to keep to herself.

And in the interim, perhaps she could wean him off his penchant for such challenges.

There was no sign of Clara or Carson in the sitting room, so she passed on to Daxton's bedchamber, in spite of everything looking forward to seeing him as she always did.

She scratched briefly on the door before entering. She didn't want to knock and wake him if he was still enjoying a healing sleep. But when she opened the door, his bed was empty. Her heart missed a beat. Then she swung around and looked in all the rooms before pulling the bell. Rushing to the window, she looked down into the street for any sign of him, worried sick that he was doing something foolish—riding or playing cards on the beach and no doubt drinking, which would bring on his fever again.

She would have to find him. She only hoped Carson was with him and that one of them had had the sense to tell Clara where they were going.

Thankfully, it was Clara who answered the bell first.

"There you are, ma'am! His lordship was anxious for you and I couldn't tell him where you were."

"Oh dear," she said in dismay. "I thought he was asleep!"

"He must have wakened up, for he made Carson dress him, and then they went off with Mrs. Holt."

Willa's jaw dropped. "Mrs. Holt?" she repeated dumbly. "Mrs. Holt was here?"

"Yes, and they went together to find you. Don't worry, m'lady," she added anxiously. "Carson will make sure he comes to no harm."

No harm? With Helena Holt just waiting to get her claws into him as soon as he was led to believe Willa was not the faithful wife he imagined her to be. Of course, Willa had not committed the ultimate foolishness of entering that house with Sir Jeremy, but any number of people had seen them together. And with Helena dripping her poison, Dax might be somewhat susceptible in his anger. Who could blame him? Willa was nobody, with little idea of his world or the adulterous games that went on in it. Helena knew everything and was more beautiful than anyone she'd ever met, except possibly Kate.

But it's not Helena who's good for him. I am...

Except for blithely wandering through the town with an acknowledged rake who was most definitely not related to her. Her foolishness would cause him a relapse, or another duel, or both.

"Thank you, Clara," she managed. "That will be all."

After all, there was no point in looking for Dax now. Unless Carson came home and told her what mischief he was up to. And if that happened, the mischief would no doubt be with Helena, and she would have to live with that... Or she could walk away.

I won't, she decided fiercely. *I'll never give him up to that scheming...hussy. He is my husband and I will win him in the end.*

Despite her determination, she couldn't help shedding a few tears as she sank down on the sofa, for it had been an anxious few days and just as everything seemed to have been coming right, there was *this*. Whatever *this* was.

A knock on the door interrupted her self-indulgent tears. Hastily, she wiped her eyes on her sleeve, in the style of childhood, while Clara, who'd only retreated as far as her own chamber, opened the door.

"Afternoon, Clara," came Lord Tamar's casual voice. "Is her ladyship receiving?"

"Come in, my lord," Willa said, hastily, jumping to her feet, and barely waiting for the door to close behind him before she demanded, "Have you seen Dax?"

"Dax should be in his bed," Tamar replied.

"Yes, he should, but he's gone out. I was hoping you'd seen him on his way back when you only asked for me."

"You're better company," Tamar said with a grin. He peered at her. "Willa, have you been crying?"

"No," Willa lied, but the mere mention of weeping seemed to bring it on again before she could flee. She tried to hide her face in her sleeve, but Tamar's comforting arm wrapped around her shoulders, and she wept into his coat instead.

It was a few moments before she managed to raise her head and apologize. "I'm so sorry. I'm not usually such a water spout, I assure you."

"Dax would drive any woman to tears," Tamar said lightly, although there was a hint of genuine grimness behind his eyes. "He's a thoroughgoing scoundrel and a great fool besides, and so I shall tell him."

"Oh, don't do that," she said with a slightly watery chuckle. "I don't want him involved in any more duels. Besides, this is nothing to do with Dax."

"Of course, it is not," Tamar soothed, without any noticeable belief. "Shall I go and fetch him for you?"

Willa shook her head violently.

Tamar drew out a handkerchief and wiped around her eyes for her. He paused, gazing down at her. "You know, even when they're full of tears, you have the most beautiful eyes."

"Is that a fact?" Daxton's most dangerous voice said from the other side of the room.

Tamar couldn't have closed the door properly when he entered, and Dax had come in without anyone hearing. He stood now, just inside the door which he closed with a decided click.

Startled, Willa tried to jump apart from Tamar, who, however, hung on to her firmly. After all, neither of them had done anything wrong, and Dax should know that.

Fully dressed, with his coat hanging loose over his wounded shoulder, Dax threw his hat onto the side table, his hard, unblinking stare shifting deliberately between her and Tamar. Willa's stomach dived. She hadn't seen him look like that since the night he'd played dice with Ralph.

"Unhand my wife," Dax commanded. "And then, since you're an old friend, you can explain your conduct."

"Oh, get off your high horse, Dax," Tamar said, releasing her. "You know perfectly well I'm not hurting Willa *or* you."

Dax came further into the room. There was blood on the hand hanging by his side. He'd been fighting again, though her anxious gaze could pick out no other injuries. His face was a little white, perhaps, but she thought that was probably anger.

Dax said deliberately. "Do I? Then why were your arms around her?"

"I was comforting her," Tamar retorted. "Which is your business, only *where were you, Dax?*"

Daxton's lips thinned and his eyes flashed with fury, but he didn't answer. Because he couldn't, she realized dully. He'd been with Helena. Tamar had seen him or knew from some other source. That's why he'd come here.

"A word," Dax said stiffly and walked back to the door.

Alarmed, Willa opened her mouth to forbid them to fight in any way, but she found she couldn't speak to Daxton's rigid back. In any case, she was well aware neither of them would listen to her.

Tamar gave her a comforting grin as he sauntered toward the door and closed it behind him. Willa immediately bounded after him and flattened her ear to the wood.

"...making a mistake, but if you insist," Tamar was saying in his usual casual way. Unforgivably casual if they were talking about blowing each other's brains out for absolutely nothing. "I presume it's dawn at Blackhaven Cove?"

"Dawn is too early for me," Daxton drawled, "Make it an hour later."

"Suit yourself. I'll bring the weapons."

"You do that."

The handle rattled as one of them, presumably Dax, took hold of it and Willa bolted back into the room, keeping her back to the door as it opened behind her.

"You should rest," she managed.

"Yes, I probably will."

"Shall I send for Dr. Lampton?"

"On no account. Unless you need him?"

"Of course not."

Finally registering that he didn't sound angry any more, she turned slowly to face him. He didn't look angry either, although the turbulence still lingered in his eyes. Instead, he looked...distant. And that was almost worse.

His lips quirked. "There's another ball at the Assembly Rooms tomorrow evening. Shall we go?"

"You won't be up to that, Dax—."

"We can call in for an hour or two, if you'd like? Good. I've left Carson to buy the tickets. I'm going to lie down for a little while."

She followed him into his bedchamber to help, but it seemed lying down on his bed was all he meant to do. Without a word, she fetched a cloth and bathed his knuckles.

"I was foolish," she blurted. "He said he wished to show me something and I assumed it was to do with who shot you because that's what we'd been talking about, but he only ever meant to take me to his rooms. But I never went in there, Dax. You didn't need to hit him and you certainly don't need to let him shoot you."

"Everything will be well," he said vaguely, as if he was thinking of something else entirely. Even so, his eyes followed her as she rose and walked to the door to let him sleep.

WILLA WOKE IN DARKNESS the following morning. Normally, she would have closed her eyes and gone back to sleep. But this morning, knowing about Daxton's duel—or duels, since he'd told Tamar he was engaged at dawn—she sat up and lit the candle. She'd deliberately left her bed curtain open and the bedchamber door slightly ajar so that she'd hear anyone coming or going from the room.

Exactly how she meant to stop the duel—or duels—she had no definite idea, but she was quite prepared to send for the Watch or the magistrate if necessary.

She donned her robe and sat up in bed, waiting.

She'd barely seen Dax since he'd come back to the hotel. He'd slept until evening, and then risen, bolted his dinner in her company, and retired to his bedchamber to write letters. He'd displayed no anger toward her. In fact, he'd barely seemed to notice her, which made her more miserable than anything.

Perhaps his growing affection for her hadn't been deep enough to survive the irritation and suspicion of yesterday. But surely he couldn't believe her guilty of liaisons with both Leigh and Tamar! Or with either one of them. It was ridiculous. He must know that. So why was he so distant? Was his mind simply on other matters, such as his upcoming duel? Or duels.

The grey light of dawn began to seep beneath the window curtains and slowly, gradually, began to brighten. People began to move about the building beyond her rooms—hotel staff and the servants of guests. Footsteps sounded along the passage outside, crockery rattled. But nothing stirred in her own rooms. No one knocked on the outer door. Daxton did not emerge.

Maybe his flurry of letters last night had been to prevent the duels, to reconcile somehow, although she couldn't imagine him apologizing. Except, perhaps, to Tamar. Or perhaps she'd simply misunderstood. There had been no flurry of seconds—or anyone at all, in fact—visiting him yesterday afternoon or evening.

But then again, perhaps he was simply so ill that he'd slept through everything.

Worried now on quite different grounds, Willa slid out of bed and padded out of her bedchamber and crossed to his. She scratched lightly and opened the door. The curtains were drawn around his bed, so she approached and drew them apart.

Dax lay against the pillows, sound asleep, breathing deeply and evenly. His golden eyelashes fanned across his lean cheeks, a lock of unruly hair fell forward across his face. His angelic beauty caught at her breath all over again. Reaching out, she touched his forehead for signs of fever and found none.

He was right. Everything was fine.

Only, it was not. A lump rose into her throat and she turned and walked out of the bedchamber.

LADY ROMFORD AND COUSIN HARRIET joined them for dinner at the hotel that evening. The countess, once more gracious and cordial as Willa remembered her from childhood, had decided to attend the ball also, a favor she clearly imagined Blackhaven should be grateful to receive.

"Lady Shelby," she offered over dinner, "is giving out that she and Elvira won't be attending the ball because her son is too ill to escort them. Too embarrassed, more likely!"

"Well, it will be more comfortable without them," Dax observed.

Willa agreed wholeheartedly, although when she first walked into the ballroom she was almost sorry. For, almost immediately, Kate introduced her to Lady Arabella Lamont, formerly Niven, whom Ralph had once had in his marital sights. Ill-naturedly, Willa wished Ralph was present to meet her, too, for she was very far from the woman he'd led his family to expect–an aging, plain spinster who would have been grateful for any offer of marriage from a man under forty with all his limbs and most of his teeth intact.

In fact, Lady Arabella was a rather lovely and amiable lady, a trifle vague, perhaps, but with an unexpected sense of humor that appealed instantly to Willa. Her husband, the heroic Captain Alban, was much more saturnine and forbidding, although he and Dax seemed to get on famously. In fact, they went off to play cards together.

When she found the opportunity, Willa said quietly to Mr. Grant, "Dax isn't up to something is he?"

"Such as what?" Grant asked evasively.

"More duels? I know he's quarreled with Lord Tamar."

"Tamar?" Grant said, plainly startled. "I don't think you *can* quarrel with Tamar. You shouldn't worry on that score."

As she sat quietly with Kate, watching the dancers, her attention was drawn to a pretty, vivacious girl flirting with one of the wealthy town worthies as they danced.

"Who is that young lady?" she asked Kate, trying to place her.

"I don't think I know her. Why?"

"I've seen her before...With Ralph," Willa remembered, finally placing the memory. "Only, she was different, then. Quiet and almost mousy. Perhaps she's had too much champagne. Miss Tranter."

Kate blinked. "Tranter? Well, if she's related to Robert Tranter, I imagine she's as much of a chameleon as he is. He's an inveterate fortune hunter."

"Oh dear, and you think she's cut from the same cloth?"

"She probably discovered the Shelbys weren't as wealthy as they pretended. Since she isn't either," Kate added flippantly, "it could have been a match made in heaven. Perhaps she's just preserving her options."

Shortly after that, Lord Tamar sauntered in and came almost immediately to ask Willa to dance. Willa might have been more circumspect were it not for the fact that Helena Holt entered the ballroom at that moment, escorted by a stranger, and Willa refused to be seen sitting alone waiting for her husband to notice her again.

So, she stood up with Tamar. It was quite difficult to hold a private conversation during a country dance, but she did manage to say to him bluntly, "Did Dax challenge you?"

"Don't be silly," Tamar said cheerfully.

"That isn't an answer," she pointed out.

"I'd never hurt him or you," Tamar said.

Toward the end of the dance, she glimpsed Dax emerging from the card room and immediately looked away, smiling at Tamar. When she saw Dax next, he was dancing with Lady Arabella, and then with an unknown young beauty whom he appeared to be teasing and flirting with in his own inimitable way. A spurt of jealousy stung in Willa's throat. What she'd taken for affection, for the beginnings of love, even, could easily just have been Dax being Dax. She no longer had any faith in her own judgement.

She danced with a stranger whom Kate introduced to her, and then with the poet, Mr. Yoeville, whose blatant admiration was balm to her wounded soul. And since Dax had not come near her in all that time, she danced again with Lord Tamar. This was the waltz and the supper dance.

If Willa had harbored any real hope of Dax and Tamar making up their quarrel over a convivial supper, she was doomed to disappointment. For one thing, Dax went into supper with the unknown beauty and sat at a completely different table where there was, inevitably, much hilarity. Willa and Tamar sat with the Grants and the Lamonts, which would have been very pleasant if only Dax had been there, too. And if Mrs. Holt had not looked across at her and laughed quite so loudly.

The evening, in fact, was becoming a bit of a nightmare when, as she returned to the ballroom, fingers closed around her wrist and pulled her into a curtained alcove.

Willa didn't fight it. In fact, her first reaction was one of joy and relief, for only Dax would have dared treat her so.

Or so she thought until she found herself gazing up at Sir Jeremy Leigh, a smile of mischievous welcome frozen on her lips.

Leigh's breath caught. "God you're beautiful."

"How dare you?" she whispered. "Have you not done enough harm?"

She reached at once for the curtain, but again he caught her wrist. "Yes, I have, and that's why I need to apologize to you."

She stared at him. "Write me a letter," she said coldly, tugging her hand free just as the curtain was wrenched aside.

Dax stood in the opening, his eyes blazing. "Out," he uttered, and Leigh, after a moment's hesitation, perhaps wondering what Dax would do to her, obeyed.

Dax didn't take his gaze off her throughout, merely stepped inside and closed the curtain once more. His furious eyes scorched her, but she refused to apologize again for something she hadn't done and had no control over. If he asked, she'd tell him.

Please ask.

He didn't. Deliberately, he advanced upon her and raised his right hand. She lifted her chin in outraged defiance, but it seemed he had no intention of striking her. Instead, his hand closed around the back of her head, careless of her elaborately dressed hair, and pulled her hard against him.

Before she could speak, his mouth covered hers and ravished. Stunned, she could only weather the storm, her fingers clutching at his back for support. But this was Dax, and inevitably, she not only melted but kissed him back with everything she felt and wanted in her heart. And she never wanted it to end.

But it did. He lifted his head, still without speaking and turned, drawing her hand over his arm. "We're going home," he said with an odd edge of grimness she'd never heard in him before.

"Your mother—" she began, glancing toward where she'd last seen Lady Romford with some matrons of her acquaintance.

"I've said our goodnights," he replied shortly. Shielding her from the majority of the ballroom with his own large body, he strode from the room so quickly that she had to trot to keep up with him.

He waited impatiently while she changed her shoes and donned her cloak and then whisked her out of the Assembly Rooms and along the street to the hotel. It had begun to rain, which at least gave her an excuse to draw up the hood of her evening cloak while she all but ran to the hotel.

Still, he didn't speak, leaving her time to compose what she would say when they were finally alone, only words seemed to fly away, eluding her utterly as she wondered how angry he was going to be, how open to her innocent explanations. He'd never been a bully, but she was his wife now and entirely in his power. Of course, there was nothing she wanted to change in that, but it wasn't always comfortable to be Daxton's wife.

Her heart raced as he barged into the sitting room, dismissing Clara and Carson with one silent jerk of his head. Clara seemed inclined to merely go into her own little bedchamber to await Willa's summons, but Carson, with more experience of his master, seized her arm and pulled her out into the passage with him. This was even less comforting.

Impatiently, Dax threw his hat on the sofa while she took off her cloak, but before she'd even laid it down, he seized her hand once more and all but dragged her into her bedchamber.

"Dax—"

"Hush. No talking tonight," he said huskily. "It isn't words we need."

That was when she realized his intentions, even before he unlaced her gown with one tug, and with two consigned it and her undergown to the floor. Alarm, anticipation, sheer excitement, all clashed within her as her underwear joined the pile on the floor and he carried her in one arm to bed.

He made love to her, just as he was, still half dressed. Nothing like the first time, this was swift and hard and glorious, and she could do nothing but surrender utterly to his every demand until, utterly overwhelmed, she fell apart under the onslaught, writhing in uncontrollable bliss.

Only then did he let her help him out of his shirt and breeches.

After that, allowing neither of them much in the way of recovery time, he began it all again, this time with slow, languorous tenderness that made her want to weep. She had the leisure to concentrate on his body more than her own, to give as well as receive all the sensual pleasures of the journey before the slow, glorious climax broke over them both.

He fell asleep in her arms, a faint smile playing on his lips. And although he couldn't see it, she answered it with her own, because she knew now that everything was going to be well after all. Amazingly, he neither doubted nor was enraged with her. Somewhere in that hectic night without words, he had been asking for reassurance. And she had given as well as received it.

She didn't want to sleep. She wanted to savor these moments in wakefulness. But she'd been up since before the previous dawn. Inevitably, before this one, her eyes closed and she fell into a deep, untroubled sleep.

Chapter Sixteen

D AX WOKE THE INSTANT the outer door opened. Tucked around Willa's soft, sleeping body, he found it something of a wrench to ease back from her and slide out of bed. She slept on, her face quiet and contented. He allowed himself a moment to appreciate her like that, a peaceful contrast to the wild, passionate woman he'd aroused last night.

He'd have liked to stay, to wake up naturally with her and talk about all the things he couldn't say last night. He'd just needed Willa in his arms, and though he couldn't find the words, he'd known she needed him, too. First, though, he had to clear up this mess and keep her safe.

So, naked, he padded from her chamber and crossed the sitting room to his own bedchamber, where Carson awaited him.

"No wonder people call you insane," his valet said. "Look at you, dressing to fight two more duels while you're still injured from the last one."

"I could take the sling off," Dax said. "But I feel it makes me look more dashing. And less dangerous."

Carson cast him a sour glance.

"There's a letter under my pillow for her ladyship. You'll give it to her if anything goes wrong."

"'Course I will," Carson muttered, hooking the coat over his still injured shoulder. "Just pay attention to what you're doing and don't die on us. Where else would I get a job where I get to hit the master?"

Dax scowled at him. "When did you last have to hit me?" he demanded.

"Few weeks ago," Carson admitted. "Mind you, her ladyship might say I should be hitting you now."

Dax grunted and picked up his hat and his pistol case. He hoped she would understand.

LEIGH WAS ALREADY at the Cove with a lantern when Dax made his way down to the beach alone. Which was good. It meant the whole thing should be over quickly before Tamar made his appearance. Unless he was completely wrong about his old friend and the culprit had been Tamar all along. Dax couldn't believe that. For one thing, Tamar had no motive that he could think of—unless the impoverished marquis had set his sights on Willa. Who would, thanks to Daxton's efforts last night, be an independently wealthy woman if he died today.

Dax was aware that if he could choose a culprit trying to kill him, it would be Leigh. The man had dared to put Willa in danger, had intended worse, and Dax was eager for an excuse to kill him. There was also the less important and yet nagging knowledge that Leigh had shared no part of his childhood. For some reason, that made his guilt much more desirable than either of the other two alternatives.

And Leigh had, Dax realized, someone with him. Hairs prickled on the back of Daxton's neck. His fingers curled around the small pistol he'd hidden in his sling, and he kept walking steadily.

"We agreed no seconds," Dax pointed out.

The third man turned to face him with a glare of disapproval, and in spite of himself, Dax let out a crack of laughter.

"I brought the doctor," Leigh said abruptly. "Hope you don't mind. He is a gentleman after all, as well as possessing those professional skills we might need."

"Actually, he promised to shoot me himself," Dax said.

"Next time, my lord," Dr. Lampton promised.

"I hope not," Dax said fervently, since his next time was likely to be in about an hour. "Shall we?" he said, setting down his dueling pistol case and opening it. "One of these, Leigh, or do you prefer your own?"

"I brought my own, but yours are prettier. Are they well matched?"

"I've always found them so," Dax replied. "Help yourself. They're loaded already, though, so take care."

Dr. Lampton swore at this amiable interchange, but Leigh seemed to see nothing wrong with it, carefully lifting one of the pistols and turning his back on Dax. Dax took the other, straightened and turned to face the shore, scanning it as he had the morning of his duel with Shelby. Now, of course, he knew where to look, but he saw no sign of any movement at all.

"One," Dax began, pacing away from Leigh, his eyes constantly searching the shore for any sign of movement. But even the birds were still. "Twenty," he said finally, and with huge reluctance, turned to face his enemy, stretching out his pistol arm and taking aim.

Leigh stood opposite, pointing his pistol deliberately into the air. And then suddenly, Leigh's face changed. "Get down, Dax!" he yelled, hurling the pistol away and rushing at Dax in almost the same moment.

The crack of the gunshot exploded before Leigh had finished speaking, before his thrown pistol hit the ground. But Dax was already flat on the sand, hitting it on Leigh's first word. The *woosh* of his stomach came from excitement, from plain fear, not from injury...he hoped.

Leaping to his feet, just as Leigh got to him, he demanded, "Are you hit?" even as he swung around to see three men wrestling on the shore line, more or less where Dax had expected the trouble to be. One man went down under the other two. Dax could only pray, grimly, that it was the right way around, for he couldn't see who was who.

"I'm fine," Leigh said shakily. "What the devil is going on?"

"Let's go and see," Dax suggested, running up the sand.

The instantly recognizable figure of Carson stood up among the bushes, his thumb pointing upward.

"Got him," he said laconically as Dax scrambled up the rocks, Leigh and Dr. Lampton at his heels.

"Got who?" Leigh demanded.

Dax reached the top and gazed down at Daniel Doone, who sat with some satisfaction on the back of another man who, when he angrily wrenched his head up, looked vaguely familiar.

"This is Jem Brown," Dan said. "The bastard who abducted my Clara."

"And shot his lordship," Carson growled. "During his last duel."

"With Shelby," Lampton said slowly. "So that was you who shot him? What the devil for?"

"Money, I expect." Dax said, crouching down to search the culprit's pockets. "I'm pretty sure it was he tried to knife me the other week, too. Did you try to shoot me over by Haven Hall, as well?"

"You're a *lucky* bastard," Jem snarled bitterly.

"Either that or you're a shockingly poor assassin." Dax pulled a purse from Jem's coat pocket and held it up to the rising sunlight. It felt a little lighter than the last time he'd held it, but it was instantly recognizable. "Which I suspect is more likely. I wonder who would have hired someone as incompetent as you?"

"Shelby," Lord Tamar's voice said, causing Dax to swing around.

The marquis had appeared silently on the ridge of the cliff, carrying something large and wrapped in canvas over his shoulder. Beside him, her eyes wide with fear, stood Willa.

For an instant, Dax was completely thrown. She looked so sweet and vulnerable and cold, her cloak clutched around herself with trembling fingers as she stared at him. He wanted to take her in his arms and hold her tight forever. He wanted to send her back to the hotel immediately, only he knew she wouldn't go. She'd followed him.

If she'd been any earlier, she'd have been in acute danger and it would all have been Daxton's fault. If anything happened to her…ever… His throat closed up with sudden, rushing realization.

Which he couldn't reveal, not here.

"God damn it, Rags!" Dax exploded. "You brought my *wife* to a duel?"

"Of course I didn't bring her," Tamar retorted. "I've been chasing her along the road for the last ten minutes!"

"I woke up and you'd gone," Willa said unsteadily. "I *knew*—" She broke off to point at Jem, now pulled onto his front although Dan still sat on him. "That's him! The man I kept seeing. I'm sure he's been watching us."

"Jem Brown," Dan said again.

Willa frowned. "Clara's Jem? Then he's nothing to do with Dax? Where did Ralph's purse come from, then?"

"Because he's everything to do with me. Shelby hired him."

Willa regarded the fallen man without favor. "Is it sensible of him to repeat his failure of last time?"

"Not very," Tamar agreed. "But then again, he never knew we were onto him. We never revealed who really shot Dax, and Shelby's been telling everyone it was him."

"I think we need to go and see Shelby," Dax said grimly. "Right after our duel. What have you got there, Rags? A blunderbuss?"

"No." Tamar bent and deposited his bundle on the grass, unwrapping it to reveal two simply carved wooden swords.

Daxton's lips twitched as he raised his gaze from them to Tamar's face.

"My choice of weapons," Tamar reminded him.

"True. Are they blunt?"

"Of course they are. I don't want to kill you, Dax, and I've nothing to apologize for. Your wife is lovely, far lovelier than you deserve, but I'd never touch her. For one thing, she'd never let me. And for another, she's yours. And if you can't see that, you'll probably die of stupidity."

"Nice speech, Tamar," Leigh said admiringly.

"I thought so."

Dax picked up one of the swords. "So did I. Except the bit about stupidity. You shall answer for that right now. To the beach!" Pointing the wooden sword ahead of him, he began to charge along the ridge of the cliff to the path. He didn't bother to glance back. He knew that Tamar would grab the other sword and follow him, grinning, and that Leigh and Lampton and Willa would come to see the fun.

While Carson and Dan would guard the prisoner.

TO WILLA, IT was reminiscent of childhood, everyone trooping after Dax, gleeful for the next piece of fun. Perhaps it had something to do with relief at the capture of Jem, or the release of tension between Dax and Tamar, but the whole duel with wooden swords was hilarious.

Dax and Tamar leapt around, almost like ballet dancers, having at each other, spinning, bounding, rolling, and dodging, screaming with dramatic pain when a blunt blade touched them, and shouting with triumph when they scored a hit. Each of them died several times, according to Lampton's pronouncements, only to leap up and begin again. By the end, they were chasing each other over the rocks, and a small group of townspeople had gathered to watch.

Beside Willa, Leigh was in stitches. Somehow, she hadn't expected the morning's adventure to end quite like this, and the laughter seemed to be bubbling inside and out as she finally walked up the path to join Dax and Tamar who had declared a temporary truce, much to the disappointment of the towns people.

Carson and Dan joined them, dragging Jem between them.

"So, where now?" Tamar inquired. "The magistrate?"

Dax didn't even think about it. "Shelby." He glanced around Tamar, Leigh, Lampton, Willa, and the prisoner's escort. "But you don't all need to come."

"Yes, we do," Lampton said at once. "I want to know how this all ends, having patched you both up."

"Please yourself," Dax said, offering his arm to Willa. "Lady Daxton."

"Lord Daxton," she said gravely, although she still wanted to laugh.

They trooped back along the road and into the hotel.

"Oh dear," Dax said, spotting Lady Romford at almost exactly the same moment Willa did. But he didn't stop, merely pointed his wooden sword toward the stairs and kept walking.

"Daxton!" his mother called, hurrying after them all. "These stupid people have been denying you and Willa!"

"Well, we were out and now we're back. Clara will let you into our rooms, and we'll join you in a few minutes."

But of course, there was no way that would happen. Lady Romford followed them up the next flight of stairs, too, to the door Willa knew to be to be Ralph's. It was directly across the passage from Lady Shelby and Elvira.

Daxton's sharp knock was answered by his alarmed-looking valet who, on catching sight of Dax, merely pointed across the hall to Lady Shelby's rooms.

It was Haines, Lady Shelby's abigail who opened the door, her eyes widening in outrage and horror when she saw Willa, and then everyone else.

"Good morning, Haines," Willa said briskly. "Is my aunt receiving?"

"Mama! It's Willa!" Elvira squeaked. "And Lord Daxton! And, oh my goodness, Lady Romford and—"

"Oh good," Willa interrupted, catching sight of the back of a lady's head she recognized only too well. "I see that she has company already."

The lady didn't move, though Willa could have sworn her whole posture stiffened. Aunt Shelby, however, jumped to her feet as Willa walked into the room on her husband's arm. She blinked several times.

"Willa? What is the meaning of this…I do not wish to be rude, but the word invasion springs to mind! Lady Romford, how do you do?" she added incongruously.

Ralph sat by the fireplace, scowling. He looked as if he was considering being too wounded to rise for his guests, though in the end, he sprang to his feet quite spryly. It may have been the realization that he couldn't have properly won his duel if the other wounded protagonist—Dax—fared better than he. Or he might have just caught sight of Jem, still held between Dan and Carson, although he'd stopped struggling.

"Please sit, Aunt," Willa said. "And don't put yourself out, we aren't staying. We came only to set a few matters straight." She looked her aunt in the eye. "You've been accusing me of stealing."

Two bright spots of anger appeared on Lady Shelby's cheeks. "You took my purse and my money. Haines saw you."

"This purse?" Dax asked, dragging it from his pocket.

Aunt Shelby's eyes widened. "That's it!" she said triumphantly. "I knew you'd taken it!"

"I did," Willa agreed, "on Ralph's instructions, delivered to me by Haines. I took it to him in the back room of the hotel where some kind of low gaming party appears to take place every month."

Lady Shelby was gazing at her, perplexed. "Liar," she uttered at last, while behind her Ralph glared at Willa so fiercely she wanted to laugh.

"Oh no. There were many witnesses. Including Lord Wickenden. They saw Daxton win this purse from Ralph. Daxton elected to return it when I told him it was yours. It *was* returned to Haines—and then stolen by *this* man."

Jem was dragged forward by his captors.

"Then take him to the damned magistrate," Ralph growled. "Not my mother."

It was what Dax had been waiting for. "With pleasure." He reached out and tugged Jem back toward the door.

"Wait!" Ralph commanded, nervously. "What lies has he been telling you?"

"Not lies," Tamar put in. "Verifiable testimony that you—at Miss Pinkie's, no less—paid him to kill Dax, which he chose to try with or without your knowledge when Dax was fighting a duel with you."

"That's ridiculous!" Ralph scoffed.

"Well, the ball went in the back of his shoulder," Dr, Lampton put in. "When you, sir, were standing and shooting in front of him. Your pistol hadn't been fired and yet Lord Daxton was shot."

"You think I'm Daxton's only enemy?" Ralph demanded, his eyes lashing Mrs. Holt.

"No," Sir Jeremy said quietly. "But Mrs. Holt would not kill Dax."

She'd kill me, though, Willa thought, intercepting that lady's contemptuous glance.

"No but *you* might," Ralph retorted. It had been one of Willa's suspicions, until this morning.

"And then save my life from your man's next attempt?" Dax said mildly. "It doesn't make much sense. You paid Jem Brown, Shelby. Jem admits it and there are people who saw him with the purse and with you."

"Not people of repute," Ralph blustered.

Dax stared at him. "Ralph. We know. We all know."

Perhaps it was the use of his Christian name, the reminder of shared childhood experience, but Ralph subsided abruptly, dropping back into his chair with one hand across his eyes.

"You must stop this," Aunt Shelby whispered to Willa. "Do you really hate us so much?"

A sudden lump rose to Willa's throat. "I never hated you." Her lips twisted. "For one spark of affection from any of you I would probably even have taken the blame for the wretched purse."

Aunt Shelby clearly saw nothing in Willa's remarks that would help her, so appealed to Lady Romford instead. "Please, Lady Romford. You must stop your son saying such things about mine."

Lady Romford drew herself up to her full, regal height. "Lady Shelby. You must grasp that it is *your* son who will be stopped from *murdering* mine. The question is, do we let justice take its course and hang the scandal—which I own will be many times worse for you. Or is there some other way to deal with this?"

"How about a duel?" Tamar suggested, and Sir Jeremy laughed.

Willa glared at both of them. Dax only grinned but said nothing.

Lady Romford ignored them all. She spoke only to Lady Shelby. "Your son is an unpleasant man who steals, hurts women of all classes, and feels entitled to murder in return for any perceived slights. He should hang."

The room seemed to echo with silence. No one disputed Lady Romford's words. No one could.

"Or," Dax said unexpectedly. "He could find himself a purpose. Go home. Look after his estates as a way of reviving his fortunes rather than trying to win heiresses or fortunes at the gaming tables."

Everyone except Willa stared at Dax with varying degrees of astonishment.

Mrs. Holt actually laughed. "As *you* will, Dax?" she mocked.

He barely spared her a glance. "As I will. Hell, marry that little fortune hunter who is so devoted to you. She'll probably help. But this life, spilling out from London, can be poison. Something has certainly poisoned you, Shelby and it needs to stop, or I will lay everything before a magistrate. Even if the law won't move against you, the scandal will."

A faint frown formed between Ralph's brows as he gazed at Dax, as though trying to grasp this possible reprieve had come from his enemy himself.

"Well," Dax said. "I'm starving. Shall we go and have breakfast?"

"Excellent plan," Mrs. Holt drawled, rising from her chair. Perhaps she thought to place herself on the right side of the divide once more. Perhaps she really thought it would work and Willa would just sit and watch in silent misery.

"Oh, you're not invited," Willa said before she could help herself. "You are part of the poison as your presence here proves. And you'll stay out of my life and my husband's."

Mrs. Holt met her gaze with surprise, and then a tinkling, mocking laugh. "Really?"

"Really," Dax said. "For your benefit and everyone else's, let me say for once and for all, that whatever the beginnings of this marriage, Willa is my wife and will remain so."

His instant defense warmed her, but this was something she had to say for herself. "You might not have tried to kill Dax or even known about it, but your alliance with these people is clear. And known," she added warningly.

This could easily be one scandal too many, even for Helena Holt.

Helena's eyes spat venom, for she clearly recognized the truth and there was nothing she could do about it.

"Goodbye, Mrs. Holt," Willa said firmly. "Aunt Shelby. Elvira." And she turned on her husband's arm and walked out of the room, pausing only to give her mother-in-law precedence as they departed.

Chapter Seventeen

ORTUNATELY, THEY HAD the hotel dining room to themselves, for breakfast turned out to be a rather noisy and hilarious meal. Something of the fun spirit of Daxton's and Tamar's duel remained, together, perhaps, with relief that the Shelbys had been dealt with. Both Leigh and Dr. Lampton remained with them, and toward the end, the Grants appeared, since rumor had clearly been flying around the town.

"So, what did you do with Jem Brown?" Mr. Grant asked.

"Let him go, too," Dax said with a shrug. "Couldn't drag him before the law when I'd let his paymaster go."

"He seems to have a fancy for adventure," Tamar added. "So I sent him to see Alban."

"Well that should keep in order," Grant said, amused.

"Probably more constructive than breaking his legs," Dax agreed, "which was Carson's preferred alternative."

"Well, I'm glad it's all worked out," Kate said with a quick smile at Willa as she rose to go. "Welcome to Blackhaven."

"Is it always as hectic as this?" Willa asked, amused.

"Surprisingly so," Kate replied. "I used to think small towns were dull, but somehow Blackhaven never is."

Lampton left with the Grants, and Leigh and Tamar followed shortly afterward, just as Cousin Harriet arrived to collect Lady Romford.

With the dining room quiet at last, Willa glanced at her husband. "You wondered if it was Lord Tamar, didn't you? That's why you arranged the duel immediately after Sir Jeremy's."

Dax shifted uncomfortably. "It crossed my mind," he confessed. "And I acted on impulse. As usual. I hadn't seen him since we were fifteen years old. He could have changed, and I could see he liked you. Jealousy is a nasty trait. I never noticed it in myself before. Perhaps you're bad for me, Willie Blake."

"Willa," she said dangerously. "Willa Dacre."

He smiled, "Lady Dax," he teased. "Shall we go up?"

He seemed unusually thoughtful as they climbed the stairs and entered their rooms—where yet another surprise awaited them.

In the middle of the sitting room, stood Clara, wrapped in Carson's powerful embrace. They sprang apart immediately, both of them blushing a fiery red.

"Sorry, m'lady," Carson muttered. "But it's not what you think."

Willa, peering at Clara in vain for any signs of distress, said, "I don't know what I think."

"I want to marry Clara," Carson said firmly.

"Marry her?" Dax exclaimed. "Damn it, man, you've known her little more than a fortnight!"

Carson looked at him. "That right?" he said sardonically.

Willa couldn't help laughing. "Perhaps two weeks is a long court-ship by our standards, but Clara is only nineteen years old." A mere year younger than herself.

"But it seems right, m'lady," Clara said anxiously. "With Jem, and Dan, it was never right."

"You'll have to tell Dan," Willa said firmly. "And your father, Clara."

"I know. And we won't rush it, honest. We won't get married for a few months yet."

"Go and see your parents, then, and take Carson with you," Willa advised, going into her bedchamber to deposit her cloak and bonnet. "But speak to Dan first."

"No elopement for them, then," Dax said, wandering after Willa. Deliberately, he closed the door.

Excitement twisted through Willa. "Just as well," she said lightly.

"Oh, I don't know. I rather enjoyed ours."

"You were drunk or asleep through ours," she pointed out. "You barely remember it."

"I remember everything," he assured her, advancing. "Including a rather delightful and passionate interlude in the chaise. I kissed you here." He caressed her lips with one finger and then slid it downward over her chin and neck to the pulse that beat at the base of her throat. "And here, and here." Her breath caught. Teasingly, his hand slid lower to cup her breast. "And here. The only real mystery left to me is how I managed to fall asleep with you half naked and willing in my arms."

"A three-day spree and no sleep for twenty-four hours," she managed.

"What a waste of a life," he observed. "And certainly of those few hours in the carriage with you."

"Are you declaring your reformation?" she asked lightly.

"No, I wouldn't keep such a promise," he said frankly.

She reached up, slipping her arms around his neck to press her cheek to his. "I don't want to change you, Dax. I never did."

"It wasn't fun anymore," he said into her hair. "I woke up every morning knowing I would do the same thing. Drink and behave badly. Whenever I tried to do something different, something worthwhile, like at Daxton, I was thwarted, and instead of working at making it happen anyway, I just drank even more and behaved more badly yet. With you, I enjoy my fun again. There is more fun. I mean the convivial games and late-night sessions, all the old stuff, but also there is you. Every minute with you is fun."

She closed her eyes, smiling against his skin. "Thank you," she whispered.

"There's more. You never have to fear the humiliation of Helena or any other woman. Now there is only you. I will keep to that promise."

"Thank you," she said again, with more difficulty. "I only ask for discretion—."

"No, you misunderstand," he interrupted. "Don't thank me when it's what I want—I'm not granting you a favor here. I don't want anyone else." His fingers curled in her hair, drawing her head back to look into her face, his own unexpectedly fierce. "Willa, you're my rock, my life. I love you."

Her mouth opened in soundless shock. Sudden tears sprang into her eyes, her throat.

He stroked her hair, smiling. "Don't," he said. "Don't cry. I ask nothing more of you than what we already have. We are friends and lovers, and that is more than enough. God knows it's more than I ever deserved."

She took his face between her hands to make him listen. "Stop, Dax. Do you really not know that I love you? That I always have?"

His breath came quick and uneven. He said, "I know there was some childish hero-worship—"

"It's not childish now," she interrupted.

He stared down into her face. "You really love me," he whispered in wonder, touching the escaped tears trickling down her cheeks.

"You really love me," she said on a sob, and then he fell on her mouth with such overwhelming passion that she stumbled backward. Fortunately, the bed was there to catch them.

After that, there was really only one possible ending to the discussion. It was long and sweet and unbearably tender, an open and very sensual giving and receiving of love.

When the storm calmed, they lay in each other's arms. Willa had never believed such total happiness was possible.

Dax said, "Willa?"

"Yes?"

"Would you like to elope again?"

"We're already married."

"We can still run away together. Get up and just go."

She smiled. "Go where?"

"Daxton?"

Her new home. Her new life. With Dax—fun, flaws, and all.

"Yes," she replied, sitting up. "Let's just go."

And they did.

Mary Lancaster's Newsletter

If you enjoyed *The Wicked Husband*, and would like to keep up with Mary's new releases and other book news, please sign up to Mary's mailing list to receive her occasional Newsletter.

http://eepurl.com/b4Xoif

Other Books by Mary Lancaster

About Mary Lancaster

Mary Lancaster's first love was historical fiction. Her other passions include coffee, chocolate, red wine and black and white films – simultaneously where possible. She hates housework.

As a direct consequence of the first love, she studied history at St. Andrews University. She now writes full time at her seaside home in Scotland, which she shares with her husband, three children and a small, crazy dog.

Connect with Mary on-line:

Email Mary:
Mary@MaryLancaster.com

Website:
www.MaryLancaster.com

Newsletter sign-up:
http://ccpurl.com/b4Xoif

Facebook Author Page:
facebook.com/MaryLancasterNovelist

Facebook Timeline:
facebook.com/mary.lancaster.1656

Made in the USA
Middletown, DE
27 March 2019